brutalize me

·CORRUPTED ROYALS·

USA TODAY BESTSELLING AUTHOR

MICHELLE HEARD

Cover Designer: Cormar Covers

Cover Designer: Wander Photography

Cover Model: Andrew Biernat

Editor: Sheena Taylor

TABLE OF CONTENTS

Dedication

Jackie.

I hope all your dreams come true.

———————————

Songlist

Click here - *Spotify*

Make Me Believe – The EverLove

World on Fire – The Rigs

Hero (I Will Survive) – Supergirl, RAIGN

Witness the Masterpiece – Ganyos

When the Chaos Comes – PUBLIC NOISE, Ruelle

Madness – Tribal Blood

Before You Go – Lewis Capaldi

Someone You Loved – Lewis Capaldi

If I Could Fly – One Direction

You Are The Reason – Calum Scott

Beethoven's 5 Secrets – The Piano Guys

Synopsis

Home. It's the one thing I want more than anything. A husband I can love. Children I can give the world to. A house I can call my own. To many, it's a stupid wish, but to me, it's everything.

When my adoptive father demands that I marry one of his business partners, Karlin Makarova, my dream becomes nothing more than that – a dream. Karlin is a vile monster, a nightmare for any woman he crosses paths with.

I dread the time I have to spend alone with Karlin and hide the bruises that fill me with deep shame.

But then my beloved brother steps in and arranges a marriage with one of his best friends.

Armani De Santis is known to be coolheaded, aloof, and calculative. Sure, he's heartbreakingly attractive – emphasis on heartbreakingly – but it's clear he sees me as his friend's little sister that's become his problem.

Then again, I'd rather have my heart broken by Armani De Santis than be Karlin Makarova's punching bag.

And so, my dream of a happily ever after turns into a cold-blooded war between the two men, and I find myself praying that somehow I'll survive.

But life has taught me prayers are never answered.

Brutalize Me

Mafia / Organized Crime / Suspense Romance
STANDALONE in the CORRUPTED ROYALS
Book 3

Authors Note:
This book contains subject matter that may be sensitive for some readers.

There is triggering content related to:
Physical Abuse
Graphic violence

18+ only.
Please read responsibly.

"Stop making excuses for other people. For why they do certain things. For how they treat people or how they treat you.

Giving excuse and justification gives defense, which lets them act however they want. It allows them because you tolerated it.

Don't accept less than what you're worth because you're worth a lot."

— Dominic Riccitello

Chapter 1

Tiana

Armani De Santis; 24. Tiana Petrov; 21.

The world I live in is a cruel one. Nothing has ever been easy.

I don't remember my biological parents or what happened to them. My earliest memory is of Misha, my older brother, holding me tightly to his side while the harsh winter cold froze our bodies. A door creaked as it opened, and we finally got to escape the ice and wind. It was the day the orphanage took us in, but it never felt like home.

We spent five years amongst other abandoned children, but I had something they didn't have – Misha.

My brother was and is my everything.

Glancing out the window as the vehicle drives us toward St. Monarch's, where we'll meet the D'Angelos, I feel a sense of intense loss.

Misha is getting married to an Italian mafia princess.

After the wedding, Misha will no longer be mine. Aurora D'Angelo will become his wife and my sister-in-law. She'll be the most important person in his life.

Is she kind? Will she give Misha the love he deserves? Will she be home to him?

Will Misha be happy?

I always knew he'd get married at some point, but it's still a shock.

The car drives through massive iron gates, and my gaze locks on the old castle that's been converted into a resort and training center for the criminals of the world. It's the only neutral ground where no killing is allowed.

I've heard St. Monarch's also offers various services like tracking someone, assassination contracts, and things I'd rather not think about.

It's also where Misha and Alek have been training for the past three years.

The place terrifies me.

My stomach clenches, and a wave of emotion threatens to push tears to my eyes. It's all happening too fast for me to comprehend. In a matter of three months, Misha fell in love and a marriage was arranged between him and Aurora. I only learned about this a couple of weeks ago.

It's hard to share the only person who is truly mine.

Misha and I were adopted by the Aslanhovs, and even though they took care of us and never abused us in any way, I never quite felt like they were my family.

Blood is thicker than water.

But nothing is stronger than love.

It's hard to explain, and I don't want to sound selfish, but Misha is the only '*real*' family I have. I know he'd die for me in a heartbeat.

After the wedding, Aurora will become his priority.

After the wedding, I won't have anyone who'll put me first. It's a sobering thought.

And a frightening one.

Living in a world governed by the bratva and mafia, a woman is an easy target when she doesn't have someone to look out for her.

Ugh. I'm being overly dramatic. It's not like Misha will stop protecting me.

Be happy for your brother. You're gaining a sister, which is something you've always wanted.

The car comes to a stop, and Mrs. Aslanhov pats my hand. Even though I call Mrs. Aslanhov Mama, she's more like a favorite aunt to me. I call Mr. Aslanhov Papa, out of respect, but there's no real relationship between us.

Misha still calls them Mr. and Mrs. Aslanhov. He never felt comfortable referring to them as Mama and Papa. Misha bonded with Alek, their youngest son, and they've become best friends over the years, seeing as they're the same age.

Their oldest son, Vincent, didn't interact with us much because of the age gap. That was before he was killed, which is something we never talk about.

After Vincent died, everything changed. Mr. Aslanhov threw himself into work. Mrs. Aslanhov grew quiet, the loss of her son drowning her in sorrow.

And Alek…it broke him.

The past three years have been challenging, but somehow we all managed to get through it.

Taking a deep breath, I push the car door open and climb out.

When Alek and Misha come out of the castle to meet us, a rare smile forms on Mrs. Aslanhov's face. I swear she's aged twenty years since Vincent's death, and the sorrow only seems to lift in Alek's presence.

Maybe this wedding will do everyone good.

My eyes lock with my brother's, and the moment a smile curves his lips, I dart forward, slamming into the wall that's his solid chest. Misha's arms wrap around me, and I bask in the safety only he can make me feel.

Home.

"I missed you," I whisper, happy to be reunited with my brother.

"Not half as much as I missed you," he chuckles. "Let me take a look at you." He pushes me back, his hands resting on my shoulders as his eyes lock on mine.

I've never been able to hide anything from Misha, so I'm not surprised when he tilts his head. "What's wrong?"

Shaking my head, I brighten my smile. "I'm just nervous about meeting Aurora."

"Don't worry about it. You're going to love her," he assures me.

Misha lets go of me to greet Mr. and Mrs. Aslanhov while Alek comes to give me a hug. "Hey, T. Miss me?"

Pulling back, I smile as I tease, "A little."

"A little, my ass," he grumbles. His eyes sweep over me then he frowns. "What happened to the jeans and sneakers?"

I glance down at my black stiletto-heel ankle boots, the tight black pants, and the off-shoulder lace-up-front top I'm wearing.

Lifting an eyebrow at Alek, I smirk, "I'm not a teenager anymore and have to dress the part of a bratva princess."

He pulls a disgruntled face. "I liked the jeans and sneakers better."

"I agree," Misha says as he joins us. "Every asshole in this place is going to stare at you."

"Don't gang up on me," I pout playfully before linking my arm with Misha's. "When will I meet Aurora?"

"Now." His eyes, the same color blue as mine, tighten with a serious expression. "I love Aurora."

Reading between the lines, I say, "I'll do my best to welcome her to the family."

I can see he means it when he replies, "Thank you."

Misha leads me into the castle, and I glance around as we walk past a grand staircase. There are murals of old battles painted on the ceiling, and the air feels tense and ominous.

When we enter a dining hall, my eyes scan over the occupied tables.

I don't have anything to do with the bratva or mafia, so I have no idea who all the people are, but I'm sure Misha and the Aslanhovs know every single one of them.

I'm taken to a table where a man and woman are sitting. The man is the first to notice us and quickly rises to his feet.

Holy crap, he's heartbreakingly attractive.

The man's dressed in black combat clothes, the badass look making my abdomen clench. He has sharp cheekbones, a five o'clock shadow that's been groomed to perfection, and light brown eyes. He gives the impression of wealth and sophistication, making me think he's more comfortable in a tailored suit than a combat uniform. Not forgetting where I am, I know he's just as dangerous as the other people attending St. Monarch's.

Reluctantly, my eyes leave the attractive man to settle on the stunning woman who's looking at me.

I feel the pressure in my chest lift, and as I stop in front of her, my lips curve into a smile. "Hi, Aurora."

The most beautiful smile lights up her face right before she yanks me into a hug. "It's so good to finally meet you. Misha's told me so much about you it feels like I already know you."

A chuckle escapes me as we pull apart. "I hope it was all good." I send Misha a playful scowl. "Knowing my brother, he told you all the embarrassing stuff."

"Not at all," she assures me.

The attractive guy steps closer, and my eyes dart between him and Misha.

"This is Armani."

My lips part, and I feel a zap of shock. During our calls, Misha always talks about Armani with great respect. They met through work, and after training together, Misha, Armani, and Alek have become an inseparable trio. The only thing I know about Armani De Santis is that he's affiliated with the Italian mafia.

Because the head of the bratva, Viktor Vetrov, and the head of the Italian mafia, Luca Cotroni, are best friends, their soldiers sometimes work together to defeat a common enemy, so it's not weird that Misha is friends with Armani.

I'm just about to extend my hand to Armani when his strong fingers grip hold of my shoulders. An intense wave of tingles spreads over my skin, and as he leans down, I almost forget how to breathe.

Armani kisses my left cheek, the woodsy scent of his cologne filling the air between us.

Jesus, he smells divine.

His mouth brushes against my right cheek, then his deep voice hits me square in the chest as he murmurs, "It's a pleasure meeting you, Tiana."

Nope. I'm pretty sure the pleasure is all mine.

I manage to smile through the nervousness he makes me feel. "Likewise."

Armani pulls a chair out, then a devastating smile curves the corner of his mouth. "Please, sit."

Oh wow. It's not every day I cross paths with a gentleman.

"Thank you." I take the offered seat, and once everyone's comfortable around the table, I ask, "Where's Alek and his parents?"

"They'll join us later. I asked Alek to get them settled in their suite so we can have some privacy," Misha explains.

I nod and can't stop my eyes from flicking to Armani, that's sitting to my right. Our eyes lock for a second before I quickly glance away.

Geez, the man is too attractive.

"After the wedding, Aurora and I will leave for our honeymoon," Misha informs me of his plans.

A smile curves my mouth again. "Where are you going?"

"Bora Bora," Aurora answers, excitement sparkling in her eyes.

"I'm jealous," I tease them. "I hope you both enjoy it. Take lots of photos for me."

"We will," Aurora replies. "I was hoping we could spend some time together tomorrow. My best friend, Abbie, will join us. Think of it as an intimate bachelorette party."

"I'd love to spend time with you."

We pause our conversation when a server asks if we'd like anything to drink. I settle for lemon-infused water while Aurora asks for a soda. The men don't order anything, and after the server leaves, Misha pins me with a serious look.

"While I'm away on honeymoon, I want you to call Armani if you need anything," my brother drops a bomb I wasn't expecting.

A slight frown forms on my forehead. "Why? I have the Aslanhovs. I can call Alek."

Misha shakes his head. "We both know Alek's dealing with his own shit. There's no one I trust more with your life than Armani."

Misha has never trusted a man to be alone with me, so for him to say he trusts Armani with my life tells me how close they are. I'm still surprised, though.

"I just want you to know there's someone else you can call for help if you can't reach me," Misha explains.

I nod, and the second the server places the glass of water in front of me, I pick it up and take a huge sip.

My eyes dart to Armani's face, and I catch him staring at me with a sharp gaze.

He's trying to read my reaction.

It will take me a while before I'm comfortable with him. The time in the orphanage left me wary of people. Misha and I had to fight for every scrap of food we got, and we quickly learned that no one could be trusted.

Misha trusts Armani. Give the man a chance.

Forcing a carefree smile to my mouth, I say, "I promise I won't call you for every little thing."

"We're practically family," he murmurs. "Feel free to let me know if you need anything."

Family? Does he view me as his best friend's little sister?

Keeping the smile on my face, I reply, "Thank you, Armani."

Chapter 2

Armani

Misha was holding out on me. A while ago, we were in deep shit with the head of the bratva, and there was a good chance one or all of us could've died. Misha asked me to marry Tiana and to look after her. I said yes out of loyalty to my friend.

There were times I regretted the promise I made, but I was going to see it through because I'm a man of my word.

But fuck, Tiana is the most beautiful woman I've ever laid eyes on. I don't know what I expected her to be like, but it was definitely not the angel seated beside me.

She smells like vanilla cupcakes. Sweet and fucking edible.

Her eyes are the same light blue as Misha's, but there's something vulnerable hiding deep in her irises. Tendrils of dark brown hair frame her face before falling like silk over her shoulders and down her back.

Tiana's features are so damn petite, she gives the impression that she might break if you dared to hold her too tight.

Reluctantly my eyes leave the beauty beside me only to meet Misha's amused smirk.

The fucker knows I'm impressed by his sister.

Even though we've agreed on an arranged marriage between Tiana and myself, Misha will only tell her once we're done with our training here at St. Monarch's. He's taking two weeks for the honeymoon before returning to complete the last three months in this place.

Then we'll announce the engagement, and I'll be able to get to know Tiana on a personal level.

I feel her eyes on me and turn my full attention to her as I say, "Let me have your phone so we can exchange numbers."

"Right." A nervous chuckle escapes her, the sound making my heart squeeze.

I watch as her delicate hand pulls the device out of her purse, and when I take the phone from her, our fingers brush. The electric current passing between us is so fucking intense my eyes snap to hers.

Tiana's lips part, and for a moment, she looks startled before a smile wavers around her heart-shaped lips.

I felt it, too, piccola.

Calling her 'little one' feels as natural as breathing. Maybe it's because she barely reaches my shoulders. When I leaned down to kiss her cheeks, I noted the top of her head only made it to my chest.

I program my number into her device, then press dial so hers will show on my phone.

When I hand the device back to Tiana, she looks at the screen, then asks, "Is ICE your nickname?"

"No. It stands for in case of emergency. I've set my number as a favorite, so if anything happens to you, people will know to call that number."

Her eyebrows lift. "Oh." A nervous smile trembles around her perfect lips. "Hopefully, nothing will happen."

Do I make her nervous?

Between Misha, Alek, and me, I'm usually the one people get along with. Misha is quick to anger, and Alek is...let's just say he's a little unhinged. I'm the calculated one who tends to stay calm under pressure.

It's something my father taught me at a young age. If you remain calm when shit is going down, you already have the upper hand over your enemy.

But make no mistake, it doesn't make me any less dangerous than my friends.

As Aurora starts to tell Tiana about the wedding that's happening in two days, my thoughts turn to my father, who was gunned down when I was fourteen.

I wonder if he'd approve of Tiana.

I'm sure he would.

Will she get along with Mamma?

The real question I should ask myself is whether I'll get along with Tiana. I guess only time will tell.

I'm not going to lie, the attraction I feel toward her is instant and unlike anything I've felt before. Sure, I've been attracted to other women, but none of them instilled a protective feeling in me. Not the intense way Tiana does.

My eyes land on her exquisite face, and I watch as she smiles at Aurora when she admits, "I've always wanted an intimate wedding."

"Being from an Italian family, that's impossible. I have aunts, uncles, and cousins coming from every direction of the country," Aurora laughs.

There's a flash of something akin to loneliness on Tiana's face before she starts to fidget with her purse.

Knowing everything about her and Misha's past, I'm going to guess it's because they don't have family.

"I prefer an intimate wedding as well," I mention, hoping it will make Tiana feel better. "The focus should be on the bride and groom and not the guests."

Aurora lets out a sigh. "You try telling that to my mother."

Misha stands up from his chair. "Let me show you to your suite, Tiana."

"While you do that, I'm going to check if Abbie has arrived," Aurora mentions.

As Misha presses a kiss to Aurora's mouth, Tiana's eyes dart to me. It's only for a second before she rises to her feet. I get up as well, and when we walk toward the stairs, I notice all the men's eyes are on Tiana.

I make eye contact with every fucker who dares to look at her, not wasting any time showing them she's protected.

Reaching the suite, Misha swipes the keycard and steps inside. I wait for Tiana to enter the room before following after her.

My eyes rake down her back, settling on her ass that's nothing short of a masterpiece while Misha hands the keycard to her.

"It's beautiful," Tiana breathes as she glances around the suite where she'll stay for the next three days.

The wedding is being held at St. Monarch's because things are still volatile between D'Angelo and the bratva. The truce will be signed between Aurora's father and the head of the bratva after the marriage has been officiated. Then things should calm down.

From what I understand, my boss, Luca Cotroni, who's the head of the Italian mafia, won't be attending the wedding. But I'll be there, filling the role of best man and enforcer for the Italian mafia.

Even though Misha is one of my best friends, my loyalty lies with the mafia.

Which reminds me, I have to get Luca and Viktor's approval for the marriage between Tiana and myself. You don't just take a bratva princess without Viktor's blessing.

But I'm sure both heads will give their consent as it will strengthen the ties between the bratva and the mafia.

Misha glances between his sister and me, then asks, "Armani, will you mind showing Tiana around? I have to check on the wedding arrangements."

Liar. Everything has already been arranged. He's giving me time alone with Tiana.

The corner of my mouth lifts. "Sure. It would be my pleasure."

"Isn't there anything I can help with?" Tiana asks.

"No, you just traveled from Russia. Enjoy the afternoon." Misha lifts a hand and squeezes Tiana's shoulder. "I'll see you at dinner."

"Okay." Her eyes follow her brother out of the suite, then she cautiously looks at me. "Please don't feel obligated to show me around. I'm sure I'll be fine on my own."

I shake my head as my eyes lock with hers. "The only rule of St. Monarch's is that no killing is permitted. You're not safe walking around alone."

"Right." She glances toward her luggage that's been placed by the door of the bedroom. "If you have something else to do, I can unpack and get settled until it's time for dinner."

"I'd like to show you around," I say to reassure her.

I don't want her to feel uncomfortable around me, but I know it will take some time. Misha warned me that Tiana is as introverted as they come. Due to the time they spent in an orphanage and the shit they had to endure just to survive, it's made Tiana cautious of people, which is understandable.

She gives me an awkward smile that I find endearing.

I move closer to the door and wait for Tiana to step into the hallway before I shut it behind us. Placing my hand on her lower back, I nudge her in the direction of the staircase.

I notice how Tiana's fingers fidget with the keycard, her spine stiff.

Removing my hand, I clear my throat. "How was the flight from Russia?"

"It was good." Her eyes dart up to my face. "Thanks for asking."

As we descend the stairs, my mind races for anything we can talk about.

"You're twenty-one, right?"

"Yes. My birthday was in August."

We take a right by the stairs and walk toward the side entrance so I can show her the gardens where the wedding will take place.

Even though Misha's told me everything there's to know about Tiana, I still ask, "What do you do to keep busy?"

There's another nervous flick of her eyes to my face. "I help Mrs. Aslanhov around the house."

Jesus. It feels like I'm pulling teeth.

Just then, Tiana surprises me with a question. "Are you happy that you're almost done with training?"

"Christ," I chuckle, "you have no idea. I can't wait to return to my regular life."

"Misha said, after the wedding, he and Aurora will stay here in Switzerland," she mentions. Her teeth tug at her bottom lip as we step through the side doors. "Where's your home?"

"Italy."

As two cartel members walk toward us to get to the entrance, I place my hand on Tiana's lower back again. The moment their eyes land on her, I can't stop myself from wrapping my arm around her and tugging her against my side in a possessive move that catches me off guard.

Only when they enter the castle do I let go of Tiana and continue the conversation. "I have an apartment in Venice. I bought it with the inheritance I received when I turned eighteen."

Tiana tilts her head back, her eyes locking with mine. Compassion softens her gaze as she asks, "Inheritance? Your parents?"

"My father," I answer. "My mother is still alive. She lives with my aunt not far from my apartment."

"I'm sorry for your loss," Tiana whispers.

"Thank you." Glancing over the gardens, I say, "This is where the wedding will take place."

Tiana stops walking and takes in the beauty of the flowers, hedges, and manicured lawn, then she admits, "It's hard to believe Misha's getting married."

"Yeah," I agree. "But I suppose it's something we all must do at some point."

Tiana inhales deeply, worry flashing across her stunning features. "Yes. At least Misha loves Aurora, and she seems like a nice person."

"But you're worried?" My eyes sharpen on her face. "About getting married?"

Tiana shakes her head. "Like you said. It's bound to happen." She starts to walk again, and I let the subject go.

Showing Tiana the rest of the grounds, I focus on keeping the conversation flowing and comfortable.

When she seems to relax, I take it as a win and decide to just enjoy her company.

Soon enough, she'll learn about the arranged marriage, and God only knows how she'll feel about it.

Chapter 3

Tiana

I find myself wearing a sage green dress because it's the color for the bridal party. My hair is pinned up with curls framing my face.

I don't care what I look like as I slip my feet into the high heels. Today is Misha and Aurora's day, and I feel nervous for my brother.

I also feel overemotional.

Aurora really seems to be a good person, and I can see she loves Misha.

I'm happy for them.

But still, it's hard to let go of the one person who was mine.

The past years he's been at St. Monarch's for training were hard, and I always thought he'd come home to me.

Home. That's not something I've ever truly had. The Aslanhovs provide a roof over my head and food to eat, but their house has never felt like home. At the end of the day, they'll choose their own children over Misha and me. I understand it, though.

You're gaining a sister-in-law. Don't think of it as losing Misha.

Just as I walk into the living room, there's a knock at my door. When I open it, I'm surprised to see Armani standing in front of me, looking like a god in a dark green three-piece suit.

Slowly his eyes sweep over my body, then he murmurs, "You look breathtaking, Tiana."

The compliment makes me blush, and awkwardly, I reply, "You look breath…ahh..good…too."

God, that sounded awful.

I resist the urge to slap my forehead as my face flames up with embarrassment. Being painfully shy makes it hard to communicate with someone I've just met.

"Sorry," I mumble.

A devastating grin tugs at his lips. "Don't apologize." He holds his arm out to me. "Ready?"

Nodding, I slip my arm through his while I pull the door shut with my other hand. I feel the spark again, making my heartbeat speed up and a tremor shudder through my body.

I've never been in love, because I'm too awkward to talk to boys. Besides, Misha would kill any boy I tried to date.

But the effect Armani has on me is too intense to ignore, only adding to my already overwhelmed state of mind.

When we walk down the corridor, the silence feels heavy, and I struggle not to fidget.

It doesn't help that Armani is so damn attractive. It makes me more awkward than I usually am.

"Have you seen Misha?" I ask to break the silence.

"Yeah. He's excited and can't wait for the ceremony to be over so he can take Aurora on their honeymoon."

I nod again, not paying much attention to our surroundings as Armani leads me to the garden that's decorated in greens and whites.

Chairs are separated by an aisle, and people are standing around talking with each other. I see Mr. and Mrs. Aslanhov where they're talking to a younger couple. Mr. Aslanhov seems to be all business, while Mrs. Aslanhov smiles politely.

Out of all the guests, I only know the Aslanhovs, Armani, Aurora, and Abbie whom I met yesterday.

Still, there are easily more than a hundred people here.

Subconsciously, I tighten my hold on Armani's arm.

"This is why I prefer an intimate wedding. It's too crowded."

"Yeah," I agree. "I'm not a people person."

"Misha mentioned it to me." Armani leads me to the front row and gestures at a chair. "Take a seat here. That way, you'll sit right across from where I'm standing."

I can't stop a smile from curving my lips as I sit down, then think to ask, "Shouldn't I greet some of the guests?" After all, I'm Misha's only family. It would look bad if I don't, right?

"No, you don't have to. They're mainly affiliated with the mafia or bratva. Misha said to bring you to your seat."

I let out a relieved breath and steal a long look at Armani while his eyes scan over the guests.

Not only is he handsome, but he seems to be a good person.

Well, as good as they come in the mafia and bratva.

My eyes get stuck on his lips which look like they're frozen in a permanent, hot smirk.

What would it feel like to kiss him?

My stomach erupts with unexpected butterflies. I slap a hand over my stomach, and lifting my eyes higher, it's to see Armani staring at me.

Intense heat flushes my face, and I quickly look away.

Dammit. Does he know what I was thinking?

Luckily, Misha comes walking up the aisle, and I quickly rise to my feet to hug him. The safety of my brother's arms calms my overwhelmed emotions.

When we pull apart, I force a smile to my face and try to forget that Armani just caught me gawking at him. "How're your nerves?"

Misha lets out a chuckle. "I just want to say my vows and get out of here."

My smile turns real as I tease him, "You've always been impatient."

A man in his thirties walks toward us, and Misha instantly tenses. "Mr. Vetrov, thank you for coming."

Vetrov.

Hearing the name pours ice through my veins. I instinctively step closer to Misha, which has the man's sharp gaze landing on me.

"I wouldn't miss this important wedding for the world. He keeps staring at me, then asks, "Is this Tiana?"

A proud smile forms on Misha's face as he wraps a protective arm around me. "Yes. Tiana, this is Viktor Vetrov, the head of the bratva."

Oh, Jesus.

I start to tremble as intense fear engulfs me. My mouth grows dry, and I struggle to take a deep breath.

Surprisingly, Mr. Vetrov's features soften as he smiles at me.

It takes more strength than I have to shake his hand, then he says, "It's a pleasure meeting you, Tiana. Your brother is turning out to be one of my best men. If you ever need anything, don't hesitate to ask."

There's no way I'll ever ask Viktor Vetrov for a favor. The last thing I need in my life is to be indebted to the head of the bratva.

I don't dare to voice my thoughts and instead reply, "Thank you, Mr. Vetrov. It's an honor meeting you."

We're joined by Mr. and Mrs. Aslanhov, and I can finally breathe as Mr. Vetrov's attention is pulled away from me.

I don't know much about the bratva, but I do know Mr. Aslanhov used to work with Mr. Vetrov's godfather before he handed the reins over to Mr. Vetrov.

Mrs. Aslanhov comes to stand next to me, and I quickly whisper, "You look beautiful, Mama."

"Thank you." She gives me a smile that doesn't reach her eyes. "I haven't seen you since we arrived. Are you at least having some fun?"

I nod. "I spent yesterday with Aurora and her friend Abbie."

"It's good that you're trying to be friends with Misha's wife. Family is important."

I nod again, then take a seat. Alek takes his place next to Armani, where they're standing up front.

"We're leaving first thing tomorrow," Mrs. Aslanhov informs me.

"Okay."

All the guests take a seat, and I almost have a panic attack when Mr. Vetrov comes to sit on my right. I know it's because he's representing the head of the bratva family, but damn, I won't be able to focus on the ceremony at all.

My eyes remain glued to my brother while my hands clutch the purse containing my phone and all the tissues I could fit into it.

Needing something to do, I check that my phone is turned on silent even though everyone I know is here.

"Are you happy for your brother?" Mr. Vetrov suddenly asks.

Having no choice, I force a trembling smile to my lips and turn my head so I can look at the most dangerous man in our world. "Yes, sir."

"Call me Viktor. After all, we're family."

The bratva family.

I grip my purse tighter as I nod.

His eyes narrow slightly as he says, "Soon, it will be your turn to get married."

Dear God.

It feels like I swallowed sand as I nod again.

"Don't worry." Viktor gives my trembling hand a reassuring squeeze. "I'll make sure whoever you marry is a good man."

Are there any good men in the bratva?

"Thank you," I whisper.

The background music stops, and a second later, the piano notes of Pachelbel's Canon in D start to fill the air.

Instead of looking at Aurora, I watch Misha struggle to control his emotions. When his features tighten and his eyes mist with tears, I fail to keep my own from falling.

I really hope she'll make you happy, Misha. You'll finally have the home we've always wanted. Even though I'm sad to share you with Aurora, I'm very happy for you, my brother.

When Aurora reaches Misha, and I watch my brother stare at his bride with all the love in the world, I say a little prayer that whoever Viktor chooses as my husband will look at me the same way.

But deep down, I know the odds of that happening are slim to none.

Misha and Aurora turn to face the priest, and as they say their vows, I'm truly happy that my brother has found love.

After Misha and Aurora are pronounced husband and wife, they make their way down the aisle, and Armani moves toward me. Needing to get away from the head of the bratva, I quickly stand up and hook my arm through Armani's.

Walking to where the photos will be taken, I let out a sigh of relief.

Armani leans slightly down, then asks, "Are you okay?"

"Yeah. It was just scary sitting next to Viktor Vetrov. I'll have a panic attack if I have to sit with him at the reception."

He lets out a chuckle. "Don't worry, you're seated next to me at the table."

Thank God.

Reaching the bride and groom, I wait for Abbie and Alek to finish congratulating them before I hug Misha. "I hope you'll only know happiness and have a big family."

"Thanks, Tiana."

He pulls away and I step closer to Aurora. "Now you're a Petrov," I say with a wide smile. "Welcome to the family."

We share an emotional hug before she replies, "Thank you for sharing your brother with me."

Tears flood my eyes, and we hold each other for a minute longer before the photographer starts giving orders.

Chapter 4

Armani

I've been glued to Tiana's side, and as we listen to the last toast being given, I lean into her and whisper, "Once Misha and Aurora have opened the dance floor, we'll join them."

Tiana's hair brushes against my cheek as she replies, "I can't dance."

I let out a chuckle. "We'll just stand in one spot and sway."

Christ, she smells so fucking good.

She reaches for her glass of water but accidentally bumps it over. "*Pizdets,*" she snaps, quickly grabbing the napkin to wipe up the spilled water.

Picking up my own napkin, I help her clean the mess. A grin plays around my mouth from hearing her curse in Russian. I've heard Misha use the word several times and picked up that it means 'dammit.'

"I'm sorry," Tiana mutters. "I'm clumsy."

"It's just water." I gesture for a server to come to us and order, "Bring us more napkins and another glass of water with ice and lemon."

When the server rushes off to carry out the order, Tiana gives me a sheepish smile that tugs at my heartstrings. "At least I didn't spill the water on us."

Not thinking, I rest my arm on the back of her chair. My fingers gently caress her shoulder, the touch increasing the attraction I feel for her tenfold.

"A little water never killed anyone," I murmur.

A light blush forms on her cheeks, and I take it as a win when she doesn't look uncomfortable or try to pull away from me.

Misha and Aurora get up and walk to the middle of the dance floor. When the opening notes to *A Thousand Years* by *Christina Perri* start to play, I move my arm from behind Tiana and take hold of her hand. Her fingers feel so fucking delicate in my hand, it makes a wave of protectiveness crash through my chest.

I wait until the first chorus starts, then rise to my feet. Alek leads Abbie to the dance floor, and I smile when I think of the weird friendship that's formed between them. A while back, I thought there was a possibility they'd try to kill each other.

Reaching the dance floor, I pull Tiana into my arms, and I'm not surprised at all when she fits perfectly against my chest.

I smile down at the nervous expression on her beautiful face, and holding her tighter, so I have control over her body, I take the first step.

As I lead her across the floor, and she doesn't stumble over her feet, a smile starts to spread on her face until it looks like the sun just rose in her eyes.

I'm so lost in the girl in my arms that I don't notice the song ending and the next beginning.

Tiana's eyes lock with mine, and for a moment, there's no nervousness to be seen on her face.

So this is what she looks like when she's happy.

As the song ends, I slow my steps until we're standing still. "See, you can dance."

She lets out a chuckle. "No, you're just good at leading."

Someone clears their throat behind me, and when I look over my shoulder, I see Viktor.

"May I cut in?" he asks.

Reluctantly I let go of Tiana and step back. "Of course, sir."

Viktor might not be my boss, but he's best friends with Luca, so I have to obey him. Luca also married Mariya Koslov, who's like a sister to Viktor. The ties between the bratva and the mafia run deep, and none of the soldiers would dare do anything to risk it.

I hate the fear tightening Tiana's features, but knowing Viktor won't hurt her, I force myself to walk away.

I head for the bar and order a tumbler of whiskey. While sipping on the drink, I watch as Tiana stumbles over her feet.

Christ, she looks uncomfortable.

"You look good together," Misha suddenly says.

The corner of my mouth lifts. "Let's hope Luca and Viktor feel the same way. If we don't get our bosses' approvals, there's nothing we can do short of me kidnapping your sister."

Misha lets out a chuckle. "I'm sure they'll give their blessings. It will solidify the ties between the bratva and the mafia."

"How do you think Tiana will handle the news of the arranged marriage with me?"

Misha's eyes meet mine. "It will take her time to adjust, but I think she'll be happy with my choice of husband for her."

I hope he's right.

Misha's expression grows serious as he leans closer so our conversation will be private. "Just take it slow with Tiana. Once she's comfortable with you, your patience will be rewarded."

Wanting to set Misha at ease, I reply, "It's a reward just looking at her, brother. Tiana will be safe with me."

"I know." A grin tugs at the corner of his mouth. "That's why I chose you." His eyes settle on his sister, and emotion washes over his features. "All she's ever wanted was a home to call her own. She never felt like she fit in anywhere, and our time in the orphanage left her scarred." His eyes swing back to meet mine. "I just want my sister to be happy."

Lifting my arm, I squeeze Misha's shoulder. "I'll do everything in my power to make that happen."

The song ends, and the second Viktor lets go of Tiana, she makes a beeline for us. Her face is ghostly pale, as if she's a second away from passing out.

I glance at the bartender. "A glass of rosé, please."

She's visibly trembling when she comes to stand between us. "Your boss is going to give me an anxiety attack," she complains to Misha.

"Relax. Viktor won't hurt you. The Vetrovs don't prey on women," Misha assures her.

"He still terrifies me."

When the bartender sets the glass of wine down, I take hold of it and hand it to Tiana. "It will calm your nerves."

"Thank you," she breathes before taking a couple of sips.

"I'm heading back to Aurora," Misha announces.

Wanting to make Tiana feel safe, I rub my hand up and down her back. "Do you want to take a walk?"

She gives me a pleading look. "Please."

My hand stills on her lower back, and I nudge her to the side of the dining area. Lights hang from all the trees, lending a mystical feel to the grounds of St. Monach's.

"I tripped fourteen times," Tiana mutters before she takes another sip of her wine.

"It's because you were nervous." I move my arm around her shoulders and smile inwardly when Tiana leans into my side.

I think it's safe to say she's okay with me touching her.

I steer Tiana down a path that leads to a waterfall. The soft glow of the lamposts gives enough light for us to see where we're walking, and soon the rushing sound of water fills the air.

"It's so pretty here," Tiana whispers as if she doesn't want to disturb the night.

Taking the glass of wine from her hand, I set our drinks down on a bench.

The music is faint in the background as I step closer to her. A nervous expression tightens her features, her eyes growing wide.

Christ, nothing in this life could've prepared me for this woman. Everything about her draws me in like a moth to a flame.

Honestly, I expected to marry an Italian woman. A mafia princess like Aurora or Abbie. Not once did I think someone like Tiana existed in our world.

Misha did well to protect his sister. At twenty-one, she's still innocent, which is rare if you're raised in the bratva.

Slowly I pull her into my arms, and when she realizes I'm going to dance with her, a smile breaks through her nervousness.

I wonder if she's ever been kissed. I wouldn't be surprised if she hasn't. Misha said she's never dated because he wouldn't allow a man near her.

The thought that this woman might be untouched has a possessive feeling, unlike anything I've ever experienced, roar in my chest.

Tiana's tongue peeks out to wet her lips, then she asks, "Do you like working for the mafia?"

"My grandfather and father worked for the Cotronis, so it was always a given I'd follow in their footsteps."

Tiana tilts her head, her eyes searching mine. "You didn't answer my question."

With my hand pressing against her lower back, I pull her closer until she's forced to rest her cheek against my chest.

"I'm loyal to the mafia. I can't tell you whether I like or hate working for *la famiglia* as emotions don't play a role in my work."

I'm lying to her, but she asked a question I don't dare answer. You don't work for the mafia because you like it – you do it because you're bound to them until death.

My grandfather died in a bombing, and my father was gunned down by an enemy. One day my time will come, and I can only hope my death will be quick.

Letting go of Tiana, I say, "Let's head back."

I pick up our glasses and down the rest of my whiskey while handing Tiana her wine.

Walking toward the area where the celebration is in full swing as the guests enjoy themselves, I look at the castle that's been my home for over three years.

Christ, I'm ready to be done with my training. I want to get back to my own life in Venice – with Tiana as my wife.

Chapter 5

Tiana

On the flight back to Russia, I kept replaying the weekend over in my mind.

I really enjoyed the two days. I got to meet Aurora, and I think with time, we'll become friends.

I'm glad Misha's happy.

But the person occupying my thoughts is Armani. He was nothing but polite and protective toward me.

Is it possible to form a crush on someone so quickly?

There's a fluttering in my stomach when I relive dancing with him. Feeling his strong arms and solid body guiding me across the dance floor was something from a movie or dream.

Whenever his intense brown eyes met mine, there was a tightening sensation in my chest as if the space was too small to contain my heart.

God, I can spend hours going over every detail of him. His piercing gaze that felt like it could look into my soul.

His sculpted face. His five o'clock shadow. The way his muscled body fills a suit. The strength I felt in his arms.

What caught my attention the most was the way he carried himself. It's hard to put into words. Armani came across as coolheaded, aloof, and calculative, as if every step he took was planned and every word he said had purpose.

It gave me the impression that nothing can catch him by surprise, and he's always in total control of his surroundings.

It's hard to explain.

In a nutshell, Armani De Santis impressed me like no man has before. He's a perfect mixture of a gentleman and a dangerous mafia enforcer.

"I think the cupcake batter is ready," Mrs. Aslanhov says, startling me out of my thoughts.

"Sorry," I say as I set the bowl on the table. I prepare the tray with baking cups and pour some batter into each one.

When I place the tray in the oven, Mrs. Aslanhov asks, "What had you so deep in your thoughts?"

If I'm honest and tell her about Armani, it will get me in trouble because, as a woman, I'm not allowed to choose my own husband, and it's expected of me to marry to strengthen business ties for the bratva.

Deciding to play it safe, I answer, "I was thinking about Misha and Aurora. I hope they'll be happy together."

Mrs. Aslanhov lets out a deep sigh. "They have no choice but to make it work."

It's risky asking the question, but I can't keep it from falling over my lips. "Were you happy when you married Mr. Aslanhov?"

She prepares herself a cup of tea, and only when she's sitting at the kitchen table does she answer, "No. I was terrified of him." She shrugs before taking a sip of her tea. "But I grew accustomed to the way things are. Once a marriage is arranged for you, you'll do the same. Just be a perfect wife, and there won't be any problems."

Mrs. Aslanhov has gone to great lengths to teach me how to cook and bake. It's one of the ways we bonded. I know everything that's needed to be a good wife.

Her eyes soften on me with something like pity in them. "And if he sleeps with other women, take it as a win. At least it will keep him out of your bed."

Jesus.

My mouth drops open, but knowing better, I say nothing in response and start to clean the countertops.

My hands freeze when she adds, "And try not to anger him. The men in the bratva live stressful lives. When they come home, they want peace and quiet."

In other words, a wife should be seen and not heard, just do her tasks and not cause any trouble.

"Tiana, bring tea for two to my office," Mr. Aslanhov suddenly says from the doorway. "And add some of the *medovik* you baked."

"Yes, Papa," I answer obediently.

I didn't even know he was home and hope he didn't overhear any part of the conversation I had with Mrs. Aslanhov.

Feeling nervous, I quickly prepare a tray with the tea and slices of honey cake I baked this afternoon.

Mrs. Aslanhov gives me an encouraging smile as I carry the tray out of the kitchen, and with every step I take toward the other side of the house, the tension in my stomach grows.

I don't interact much with Mr. Aslanhov, because he's always busy with work. The rare instances we talk, it always feels formal and awkward.

When I reach the study, I let myself into the room. I hardly glance at the man sitting across from Mr. Aslanhov and quickly set the tray down on the coffee table.

"Take a seat, Tiana," Mr. Aslanhov orders.

What?

The shock of being asked to stay for their meeting takes a moment to hit. Cautiously, I sit down on the edge of an armchair, my spine stiff and my muscles tense.

My heartbeat speeds up until it's pounding against my ribs.

Slowly my gaze travels from Mr. Aslanhov's serious face to the other man who's looking at me as if he's considering a purchase. He's easily in his late thirties.

No.

Mr. Aslanhov waves a nonchalant hand over me. "As you can see, she's beautiful and healthy."

Oh, God. No.

"Hmm," the man grumbles, his eyes raking over me again.

Even though I'd classify him as attractive, there's something cruel in his eyes that makes my skin crawl.

"I feel you're getting the better end of the deal," Mr. Aslanhov says. "Tiana is fully trained to perform all wifely duties expected of her."

The way they're talking about me, as if I'm a horse that's for sale, makes my heart shrink into a tiny ball.

"And her innocence is intact," Mr. Aslanhov mentions.

Intense embarrassment washes over me, setting my face on fire.

"Good." The man lifts an eyebrow at Mr. Aslanhov. "Do you have medical proof of her virginity?"

A dark expression tightens Mr. Aslanhov's features until he looks like a thundercloud. "You'll take my word as proof."

The air is so tense it turns my breaths to shallow puffs.

"I accept the deal," the man mutters with a tone that makes me feel like we're wasting his time.

Mr. Aslanhov turns his stern gaze to me. "This is Karlin Makarova, Tiana. I've arranged a marriage for you."

It feels as if a ton of lead fills my veins, and my stomach sinks. I have no idea where the bravery comes from as I ask, "Does Misha know?"

Mr. Aslanhov gives me a look filled with warning. "Misha will find out when he returns from his honeymoon. With your brother married, it's your turn. You will not argue and accept the arranged marriage like any other bratva princess. Do you understand?"

My mouth is bone dry as I whisper, "Yes, Papa."

"Good." Mr. Aslanhov gestures at the tray. "Have some of the *medovik*, Karlin. Tiana baked it this afternoon."

I watch as Karlin helps himself to a cup of tea and a slice of honey cake. Staring at the man, I try to find any glimmer of hope that he'll be a good husband. I know it's too soon, but I can't help it.

"During the next two weeks, you'll join Karlin for dinner every other night. As soon as Misha returns from his honeymoon, we'll have the wedding." Mr. Aslanhov instructs.

Two weeks? How will I get to know the man in such a short time? It's only six or seven dinners.

Knowing I can't argue and I have to find a way to accept my fate, I nod.

Maybe I'll be lucky, and Karlin will be a good husband.

I look at him again and find his cold eyes locked on me with an expression that says he hopes I taste as good as the honey cake.

My body tenses even more, and my hands are clenched tightly on my lap.

Mr. Aslanhov waves a hand toward the door, dismissing me.

Remembering my manners, I stand up and try to smile at Karlin. "It was a pleasure meeting you."

It was anything but a pleasure.

He nods. "Be ready at seven tomorrow night. Don't keep me waiting."

"Yes, sir," I answer automatically. I didn't mean to call him sir, but the fear coiling in my body makes it impossible to be informal with the man.

Laughter erupts from Karlin as he glances at Mr. Aslanhov. "At least the mouse will be entertaining."

Mr. Aslanhov doesn't find the comment amusing and pins Karlin with a harsh look. "Men would kill for a woman like Tiana. Show some respect."

Hope trickles into my chest. Maybe Mr. Aslanhov will change his mind.

"You can go, Tiana!" Mr. Aslanhov snaps.

As I hurry out of the office, I don't miss the wrathful look Karlin shoots my way.

My heart hammers in my chest as I rush toward the kitchen, where Mrs. Aslanhov waits for me with a questioning gaze.

"How did it go?" she asks.

She knew?

Why didn't she warn me?

When I don't answer her, she pats the table. "Sit, Tiana."

Shocked, I drop down in a chair.

"The business Mr. Makarova will give the bratva is important. Just do everything I taught you, and you'll be okay."

I nod, then get up again to check on the cupcakes.

"Don't bother Misha on his honeymoon. It's not your place to tell him of the arrangement. Leave the business to the men," she warns me.

I nod again.

I'll wait for Misha to return, not because I'm ordered to do so, but because I don't want to ruin his honeymoon with Aurora.

At least they won't marry me off while he's gone. I'll go along with everything for the next two weeks, and hopefully, Misha will stop the arranged marriage once he finds out about it.

I know I'm not allowed to interfere with bratva business, but Misha won't let me marry a cruel man.

I calm my emotions and racing heart and focus on cleaning the kitchen while I wait for the cupcakes to be done.

"Karlin is a wealthy man," Mrs. Aslanhov informs me.

I don't care about money. I only want a loving home I can call my own.

"You'll get used to the idea."

I doubt that.

"Yes, Mama," I say obediently, hoping it will set her at ease so she'll stop talking about it.

"I'll help you with your hair tomorrow. You want to look pretty for your first date."

"Thank you." I open the oven and remove the cupcakes. Setting them down on a cooling rack, I force a smile onto my face. "I'm going to do my laundry."

She nods, and her eyes follow me out of the kitchen.

Once I reach the safety of my bedroom, I check my phone to see if there are any messages from Misha. My smile turns real when I see two, and quickly opening them, I look at the photos of him and Aurora smiling where they're standing on a beach.

Misha: The wifi is spotty where we are. If you can't reach me, call Armani.

I quickly type out a reply.

Okay. Don't worry about me, and enjoy your honeymoon.

Just then, a message pops up on my screen, and when I see it's from Armani, my smile widens for a moment.

Armani: Did you get home safely?

Tiana: Yes. Thank you.

Armani: Do you need anything?

He holds no power in the bratva, so I don't bother telling him about the arranged marriage. Besides, I don't know him that well to share something so personal with him.

Tiana: No, but thanks for asking.

Armani: Have a good night.

Tiana: You too.

I stare at our exchanged messages, wishing the arranged marriage was with Armani instead of Karlin.

Chapter 6

Armani

Needless to say, I can't focus on training for the life of me.

The remaining three months at St. Monarch's are going to feel like a lifetime.

When Misha returns, I'm going to talk to him. I think it would be better if we announce the engagement as soon as he's back. It will give Tiana three months to get used to the idea of an arranged marriage with me.

Standing in the combat training studio, I give Pedro, a cartel member, a bored look.

I'm so over this training. I feel I've learned everything there is to learn and would rather return to work.

Pedro rolls his shoulders as he sneers at me. We've been instructed to fight until there's a knockout. Normally I'd wait for my opponent to attack, but needing to blow off some steam from the sexual attraction I feel toward Tiana, I dart forward. Spinning my body, I bring my right leg up and slam the heel of my boot into the man's jaw.

While Pedro shakes his head, I lunge at him, delivering an uppercut to his chin. He staggers back, and I follow, slamming blow after blow into his face, ensuring he has no time to recover.

The attack is aggressive, and I end it with a knee to Pedro's dick. The man crumbles to the floor, and an easy kick to his head renders him unconscious.

"Who pissed in your lunch?" Alek mutters, giving me a worried look.

I shake my head as I catch my breath, then reply, "No one. Just felt like kicking ass."

My friend lifts an eyebrow at me. "Right."

"That's it for today," Instructor Inna calls out. "Good fight, Mr. De Santis."

I nod in her direction before walking out of the room.

"So you're not going to tell me?" Alek asks as he falls into step next to me.

I let out a chuckle. "You're dying to know what I think about Tiana, aren't you?"

"Yes," he admits. "Out with it."

Knowing Tiana is like a little sister to Alek, I don't admit anything sexual and keep it respectful. "I like Tiana. She's beautiful and well-mannered."

He shoots me a scowl. "You can do better than that. Tiana's a fucking goddess."

"That she is," I agree as we head up the stairs toward our suites. Shooting Alek a glare, I mutter, "You could've warned me, though. When I met her, my jaw was practically lying on the floor."

He lets out an amused chuckle. "I would've paid good money to see your reaction."

"Misha fucking enjoyed it," I say. When I reach my door, I add, "I'll do everything in my power to make Tiana happy."

"I know." Alek's eyes lock with mine. "That's why you haven't heard an argument from me when Misha brought up the arranged marriage."

"How do you think your parents are going to react?" I ask.

Alek shrugs. "If Viktor gives his blessing, there's nothing they can say. They'll accept the arrangement."

Nodding, I open my door. "That's good to hear. I'll see you at dinner."

I step inside and shut the door behind me. Walking toward the bathroom so I can shower, I pull my phone out of my pocket.

There are no messages from Tiana, not that I expected any. I get the feeling she won't ask for help if she needs any, so it's up to me to keep tabs on her.

I quickly type out a text to her, asking how her day was, then drop the device on the counter. Opening the faucets, I strip out of my combat uniform and step beneath the warm spray.

My thoughts turn to the training and the work I'll do once I leave here. Before I started my training at St. Monarch's I worked as an enforcer for three years. I have twenty-two kills under my belt and know over a hundred ways to torture someone.

A woman like Tiana will make the brutality of my work bearable. Coming home to an angel after spending the day in the pits of hell will make a huge difference.

The mafia's not all bad, and it pays fucking well. I've invested part of my inheritance and income. Turns out I'm good at reading the stock market, and I've managed to increase my investments dramatically. I'll be able to give my wife and children a good life, and if I'm killed on a job, there'll be enough to take care of them in my absence.

Just like my father did for us. He might have fucked around with other women, but he was a good father, and he made sure my mother would never suffer financially.

I'll never cheat on my wife. I saw what my father's infidelity did to my mother. It's also not something I'll tolerate. If I catch my wife fucking around, I'll end her and the bastard.

But I can't see Tiana being disloyal. If she's anything like Misha, she'd rather die than betray a loved one.

After I'm done showering, I get dressed in a clean combat uniform. Picking up my phone, I see a reply from Tiana and open the message.

It was good. How was your day?

Christ, I hate unnecessary pleasantries. I'd much rather ask her personal questions so I can get to know her.

Training is boring. I can't wait to go home.

I'm hoping the honest answer will encourage her to open up to me.

While I wait for Tiana's reply, I dial my mother's number.

"*Amore mio,*" Mamma answers, "I was just about to call you. How are you? Are you eating enough? How's the training? When are you coming home for a weekend? I miss you," she rambles one question after the other.

I let out a chuckle. "I'm good. I'll make arrangements to come home next month."

"*Mammamia*! That's too far from now. Your mamma misses her baby."

Yeah, at twenty-five, I'm still my mother's baby. Nothing in the world will change that.

"I'll be home for good in three months," I remind her. "Listen, I have something to tell you."

"What?" The word is sharp, telling me my mother is probably busy going into worrying mode.

"Nothing bad," I say to set her at ease, then I drop the bomb, "I'm going to get married."

There's a moment's silence, and I can picture my mother blinking as if she's short-circuiting, then the words flow from her. "Who? Is she Italian? When did you decide this? Why haven't you brought her to meet me?"

"She's Russian, and you'll only meet her once I'm done with my training. She's a beautiful, respectful woman."

"Who is she?" Mamma demands.

"Misha's sister."

"Oh." Mamma lets out a relieved sigh. "Oh, good. I like the boy. You say she's pretty?"

Chuckling, I shake my head. "She's the most beautiful woman I've ever seen." Knowing the information will soften Mamma's heart toward Tiana, I say, "She's introverted and vulnerable. We'll have to take good care of her."

"Of course," Mamma mutters. "Can she cook?"

"Yes. Misha says Tiana loves cooking and baking. She even smells like vanilla cupcakes."

"Aww, bless the girl. I want to see her with my own eyes before I give my blessing."

"Of course." I chuckle, then tell her, "I'm heading to dinner now. I'll call you again next week."

"Make sure you eat enough," Mamma warns before we end the call.

I smile as I leave my suite, and finding a message from Tiana waiting for me, I read it quickly.

Hopefully, the three months will go by in a blink of an eye. Thank you for checking in on me. Have a good night's rest.

Unable to resist the urge to make things less formal and more personal between us, I reply, **Sweet dreams,** *piccola.*

Chapter 7

Tiana

Piccola?

I type the word into Google then stare at what the search throws back at me.

Piccola means small or little. It's a term of endearment for a young child.

Armani thinks of me as a young child. That sucks.

With a sigh, I drop my phone on my bed, and not at all in the mood to go out for dinner with Karlin, I drag myself over to my closet so I can change out of my cozy sweater and leggings.

It stings a little that Armani sees me as a child. It means there's no hope of Misha arranging a marriage for me with him.

But that's the least of my problems. Right now, I have to worry about the date with Karlin.

The thought makes panic whirl in my stomach.

Misha will stop the marriage between Karlin and me.

I almost sent Misha a message this afternoon, but not wanting to ruin his special time with Aurora, I decided against it.

He has other priorities now that he's a married man, and the sooner I learn to stand on my own two feet, the better.

It's easier said than done, though.

Reluctantly, I change into black pants and a warm turtleneck long-sleeve shirt. I pair the outfit with knee-high boots and grab my fur coat. With winter just around the corner, the nights are quite cold.

Making sure I'm ready with ten minutes to spare, I head downstairs to wait for Karlin. As I reach the foyer, I hear voices coming from the living room, and my stomach sinks.

He's early.

The instant I step into the room, Karlin's eyes flick to me.

"Finally!" The single word sounds like a lash of a whip.

"You look beautiful, Tiana," Mrs. Aslanhov compliments me.

"Let's go." Karlin glances at Mr. Aslanhov. "We'll talk after dinner."

"Enjoy the date," Mrs. Aslanhov calls out.

Karlin grabs hold of my bicep, and I'm practically hauled out of the house before I can think to reply to Mrs. Aslanhov. I have to jog to keep up with his long strides, and I'm shoved toward a black G-Wagon.

Jesus, he doesn't have to be such a brute!

I notice two guards who climb into the front of the car while I get into the back seat. The moment Karlin slides in beside me, his arm darts out, his fingers clamp around my throat, and I'm yanked closer to him. A startled squeak escapes me.

"The next time you keep me waiting, you'll crawl out of the house," he threatens.

Paralyzing fear pours through my veins. It's more potent than the fear I feel when I'm in Viktor Vetrov's presence.

I stare at his cruel face, and not seeing an ounce of humanity in his eyes, the fear multiplies.

"Do you fucking understand me?" he hisses.

My lips are dry, and my throat aches as I struggle to get the words out. "Y-yes, sir."

I'm shoved away from him and fall against the door as the vehicle turns right onto the main road. My eyes dart to the front seats, but the guards are unbothered by what just happened.

Wrapping my arms around my middle, I hunch my shoulders and keep as still as possible. Karlin pulls his phone out and ignores me for the rest of the ride.

In the silence filling the car, my heart shrivels as I realize I might have to marry this man if Misha can't stop the arrangement made between Mr. Aslanhov and Karlin.

I should feel some kind of disappointment, but all I feel is the usual empty acceptance.

I just accepted it when the orphanage made us work like slaves for the meager food they provided.

I just accepted it when we had to fight the other kids like savage animals so they wouldn't take the few possessions we had.

I just accepted it that as a woman in the bratva, I'd never have a voice of my own.

And now I'll accept I don't have a say in who I marry.

This is my life, and there's nothing I can do to change it.

When the G-Wagon stops in front of a restaurant in a rundown part of town, I quickly get out of the vehicle.

I lay my hand against my throat, the feel of his painful hold still there.

I've been beaten many times in my life, so physical abuse is nothing new to me, but still, it chips away at my soul.

If Misha were here, he'd beat the shit out of Karlin.

Karlin grabs hold of my bicep again and yanks me toward the restaurant. From the outside, it looks like a place where criminals like to hang out and not an establishment where I'll be safe.

Stepping inside, the lights are dimmed, and many tables are occupied by men who've been hardened by the bratva life.

An uneasy feeling curls around my spine, and I keep my eyes lowered, so I don't accidentally make eye contact with a man.

I'm shoved toward a chair with an impatient order. "Sit."

It's on the tip of my tongue to tell Karlin to stop manhandling me, but not knowing how he'll react, I suppress the urge to stand up for myself.

A woman who looks more like a stripper than a waitress comes to our table.

"Hi, Mr. Makarova," she purrs. "Will it be your usual order?"

I watch as she practically eye-fucks him. Karlin gives her a raunchy smile and slaps her ass. "Please, Nina. Get the same for the girl."

The waitress doesn't even look at me and walks off to order whatever Karlin's usual is.

No. There's no way I'll settle for becoming this bastard's wife. I'll call Viktor Vetrov myself if I have to and beg him to arrange a marriage for me with someone else. Screw owing the head of the bratva a favor. Anything is better than a life sentence with this vulgar man.

Karlin's harsh gaze settles on me as if I'm nothing but a piece of shit stinking up his air.

"This marriage will only be on paper. You'll cook and clean to earn your keep and stay out of my way."

Surprise ripples through me. "On paper?"

"A bag of bones that's nothing but a spineless mouse doesn't do it for me. I'll find my pleasure elsewhere. This marriage is only happening so the bratva will allow me to trade in Russia without breathing down my neck."

So the marriage won't be consummated? I'm not misunderstanding what he's saying, right?

It offers me a glimmer of hope. At least I won't have to sleep with the man.

Wow. I never thought I'd be happy to have an unfaithful husband.

But then I realize what it means, and I ask, "Won't we have children?"

Karlin makes a scoffing sound. "I don't want children with a weak and pathetic little girl like you."

His words hit hard, and the prospect of a future without children fills me with hopelessness. I've always wanted to be a mother, so I could give my children the life I never had.

Suddenly a plate with a massive steak and huge wallop of mashed potatoes is placed in front of me. My stomach lurches at the sight of the oil and blood pooling around the barely cooked meat.

God, it looks disgusting.

Karlin picks up his cutlery, and pointing his knife at me, he mutters, "Eat."

I take hold of my fork and scoop up a bite of the mashed potatoes.

Just keep up the act of a good little bratva princess until Misha returns.

I take the bite and swallow hard.

You can always call Armani.

I shake my head at the thought. Armani has no power in the bratva.

Karlin shoves a big bite of the rare cooked steak into his mouth, and I almost gag at the sight. Grabbing my glass of water, I take a couple of sips, hoping it will settle my stomach.

Now that I know Karlin a little better, I wonder how I ever thought he was attractive. He has a crooked nose like it's been broken one too many times. His lips are thin and always turned down.

Just as I'm about to force another bite of mashed potatoes down my throat, Karlin says, "During our dinners, you better pay attention to how I like my food. If you fuck up, I'll beat you."

So much for all the cooking lessons Mrs. Aslanhov gave me. Apparently, this man only eats shit.

"You won't move a thing in my house, and I don't want any of your belongings lying around. If you fuck up, I'll beat you."

This time he looks me dead in the eyes as he repeats the threat.

"I will give you an allowance, and you'll only use it to buy food. If you spend anything on yourself–"

"You'll beat me," I mutter. "I get the message."

The cutlery drops from his hands, and in a heartbeat, he's towering over the table, and the back of his hand connects with the side of my head. The blow is so hard it throws me off the chair, and I sprawl across the floor.

For a dazed moment my ear rings and my vision blurs, then everything comes back into focus.

My ear is on fire from the slap as I push myself up off the floor. I climb to my feet and suck in a shaky breath as I turn to look at Karlin.

He throws money onto the table then pins me with a look that spells nothing good for me. "Now that we've discussed the terms of our marriage, you'll behave or bear the consequences."

My bottom lip trembles, and I bite down on it to keep the tears back.

Yes, I've been slapped before, but it doesn't lessen the shock.

For a moment, I fantasize about grabbing the steak knife and plunging it into his neck. But it's only for a moment.

I nod to show that I heard him, and when he grabs my arm again, I feel like a rag doll being yanked from one place to the next.

I feel like a mouse without a spine.

I've always felt like that because everyone is bigger than me.

I've gone from being a bag of bones in the orphanage to being a vile monster's punching bag.

It's funny how once your life has taken a particular path, you can't change things.

Misha will forgive me if I call him.

You can't ruin your brother's honeymoon. You knew what would happen, and you still mouthed off to Karlin. Just behave for the next two weeks.

Chapter 8

Tiana

When I got home from the first dinner, I told Mr. and Mrs. Aslanhov what had happened. Mr. Aslanhov warned me not to screw up the deal for him, and Mrs. Aslanhov looked at the marks on my neck and told me it could've been worse. It was my fault for provoking Karlin.

Staring at my contact list for the hundredth time, I'm actually thinking about calling Alek.

Alek's dealing with his own shit. I can't force my problem on him.

Opening my chat with Misha, I start to type.

I need you to come home. Mr. Aslanhov has arranged a marriage with Karlin Makarova. He's a monster, Misha. He manhandles me and slapped me. Come home and stop the arrangement. I want to be in a happy marriage like you are. Please come home. I need you.

I stare at the words and once again end up deleting the message.

Letting out a sigh, I close my eyes.

I've never felt so alone in my life.

It's been five days since Misha's wedding. I've been on two dates with Karlin. On the second one, he ignored my existence while he got a lap dance from a gorgeous blonde. I'm not complaining, rather her than me.

Still, I can't help but worry that Karlin can lose his temper at any second and beat me to a pulp.

My phone starts to vibrate, making my eyes snap open. Seeing Armani's name flashing on the screen, my heart starts to race in my chest.

I quickly answer the call and press the device to my ear. "Hello?"

"Hey, *piccola*. How are you?"

Hearing his deep and calm voice sends a shiver through my body.

"Ah...I'm...okay."

"What are you doing?" he asks.

"I'm sitting on my bed." I roll my eyes at myself because I feel so ridiculously awkward whenever I interact with Armani.

No wonder he thinks I'm a child.

"I'm going to hang up and video call you."

The line goes dead, and a moment later my phone vibrates again.

"Crap!" I dart off the bed and quickly look at my reflection in the mirror.

Ugh, my hair looks like something died in it.

I quickly tie the strands in a ponytail, then answer the call. Armani appears on my screen in all his handsomeness.

A smile spreads over his face. "That's better."

I walk back to my bed and sit down while I give him an awkward smile. "How are you?"

"Good, now that I get to see you."

I know I'm inexperienced, but that sounds a lot like flirting.

Unable to think of a single thing to say, I just stare at him.

"Are you always this quiet?" he asks.

"I'm sorry. Communicating isn't one of my strong points."

He lets out a chuckle, and I watch as he gets comfortable on his bed. "You don't have to apologize."

Dear God. He looks hot.

"So, what have you been up to this week?" he asks.

As much as I want to stare at his handsome face and listen to his voice, I can't forget that he sees me as a child.

I also have to get ready for another date with Karlin.

"You don't have to do this, Armani."

"What? Call you?" He tilts his head, and it feels like his eyes are trying to pierce into my soul. "Is something wrong?"

Everything.

Not wanting a war because I couldn't deal with my own shit, I shake my head. "No. I just don't want you to feel like you have to babysit your best friend's little sister."

A frown forms on Armani's forehead. "Turn your head to the right," he orders, his tone no longer polite but biting.

My eyebrows draw together as I carry out his instruction.

"What's the mark on your jaw near your ear?"

Shit.

I quickly untie my hair and let it fall over my ears. "It's nothing. I…ahh…bumped the side of my head against a cupboard door in the kitchen the other day." My heart is pounding in my chest. "I told you I'm clumsy."

Armani stares at me for an intense moment before his features soften again.

Jesus, what was that? He went from polite gentleman to death incarnated in a split second.

Tell him the truth.

No. The last thing I want is to start a war between the bratva and the mafia.

"I'm sorry you got hurt."

The words, along with the genuine compassion on his face, take a swing at my heart. Suddenly I don't feel as alone anymore, and it makes emotion flood my chest.

So what if he thinks I'm a child? Having someone who cares about my well-being is rare, and I'm going to appreciate it for what it is.

"Thank you, Armani. It means a lot to hear that from you."

A gentle smile tugs at his lips, making me wish I could crawl through the screen to be with him.

"You look sad."

Damn, he's perceptive.

"I'm just tired," I lie. "I baked a ton of cupcakes for the local orphanage."

And I have a date with a monster later tonight.

A stunning smile spreads over Armani's face. "So that's why you smell like vanilla cupcakes. I hope I'll get to taste one soon."

"If I ever see you in person again, I'll bake you a dozen."

"You make it sound like ever means never."

I shrug. "We live in different countries. The odds of us crossing paths on the street is slim to none."

"I'll have to see what I can do about those odds," he jokes.

I stare at Armani for a moment wishing with all my heart he was the one I was marrying.

"Thanks for the call," I say, the loneliness settling heavy around me again. "I appreciate it."

"I'm only a call away, *piccola*," he murmurs. "Get some rest and watch out for the kitchen cupboards."

"I will."

When the call ends, I keep staring at the phone, wishing with all my heart it could magically transport me to St. Monarchs.

Or Bora Bora.

Anywhere but here.

Expecting Karlin to take me to another grimy restaurant or strip show, I wear a pair of jeans, a sweater, and comfortable boots.

The man isn't interested in me as a woman, so there's no use in me dressing up for him.

Thank God he isn't interested in me. I guess I have to be thankful for every miracle coming my way. I can't even bring myself to be offended.

Letting out a sigh, I leave the bedroom with thirty minutes to spare. There's no way I'm giving the man the opportunity to abuse me because he decided to come early.

When I walk into the foyer, Mr. Aslanhov comes out of the kitchen with a cup of tea.

His eyes sweep over me then he frowns. "You could've made more effort with your clothes."

"I'm sure Karlin doesn't care what I wear. I told you he said the marriage will only be on paper."

Mr. Aslanhov's frown deepens. "That's unacceptable. If a marriage isn't consummated, it isn't a marriage in my eyes. Go back to your room and change your clothes."

I shake my head. "I'll be late. Karlin will lose his temper."

"You should've thought about that when you decided to dress like a teenager," he barks.

God, I hate my life.

Rushing up the stairs, I change into tight-fitting leather pants, a cream long-sleeve blouse, and high heels. I grab the same fur coat I wore for the past two dates and run out of my room.

When I hear Karlin's voice downstairs, I almost trip but catch my balance.

No use in breaking your neck on the stairs.

Darting into the living room, I'm breathless and probably look a mess.

Mr. Aslanhov's eyes flick to me before they settle on Karlin. "You're not married to Tiana yet. I don't appreciate you damaging her. Keep your fists to yourself."

Oh, Jesus.

A calculating expression forms on Karlin's face as he looks from Mr. Aslanhov to me. "I think we should discuss the deal again. Taking a child for a bride doesn't look favorable for me."

Mr. Aslanhov takes a threatening step toward Karlin. "We signed a contract. Are you willing to go back on it and to lose your foothold in Russia? It's only a matter of time before Viktor Vetrov orders your death. This deal is your last chance to make peace with the bratva."

The men are caught in a stare-off that makes tension build in the air.

I should've kept quiet. God, I don't want to be responsible for starting a war.

"I'm sorry," the words burst from me. "I overreacted. Karlin has been nothing but polite. I'll do better to be the wife he needs."

Nothing on this planet compares to when you betray yourself. The sick feeling in my gut is crippling, and my conscience revolts, demanding that I stand up for myself.

A triumphant smile spreads over Karlin's face as he gestures to me with a wave of a hand. "I think I'm owed an apology."

Mr. Aslanhov looks like he's a second away from killing Karlin, but instead, he mutters, "I apologize for the misunderstanding. You know how dramatic a woman can be."

How much power does Karlin Makarova hold that Mr. Aslanhov is going to such great lengths to secure this deal?

A ball of ice settles in my stomach as I realize Misha might not be able to stop this wedding from happening. He's just an enforcer for the bratva, where Mr. Aslanhov is one of the higher-up bosses.

I'm grabbed by my bicep again and hauled out of the house. Dread pours into my heart because I have no idea what Karlin is going to do after the fiasco in the living room.

He can't kill you.

You've survived the hell in the orphanage, you can survive a couple of slaps. It's just nine more days.

I climb into the car, my body tense as I brace myself for whatever's going to happen.

Karlin slides in beside me, and I cringe closer to the door. Instead of beating me, he orders the driver, "Take us home."

No restaurant?

No people to witness as he beats the shit out of me.

Crap.

My hands grip my purse, and for a moment, I think about yanking my phone out and calling Misha.

It will only make things worse. Karlin is more powerful than my brother.

I could try to run away, but I don't have any money, and facing the harsh winter on the streets isn't an option.

Call Armani. He seems to be a reasonable man. Maybe he can think of a way to help you.

Shit. Somehow I'll just have to get through tonight in one piece, then I'll call Armani and ask him what he thinks I should do.

Chapter 9

Tiana

We pull up to a mansion that looks like something Count Dracula would live in. It's dark and somber, and somehow the approaching winter chill feels even colder as I step out of the vehicle.

It doesn't look like a home but a prison.

I follow Karlin into the house. The guards leave us, heading in the opposite direction of the living room. Karlin pours himself a tumbler of vodka, and as I watch him sip on the drink, my stomach turns into a burning ball of nerves.

The tension of waiting for him to beat me for complaining to Mr. Aslanhov is unbearable.

I glance around at the brown leather couches and heavy wooden coffee table. There's a furry mat made of bear skin, the head still attached, and the mouth open to display its teeth.

"You have a lovely home," I whisper the lie, hoping if I come across as pleasant and submissive, he won't hurt me for the crap that went down with Mr. Aslanhov earlier tonight.

Suddenly the tumbler is thrown at me, the glass hitting my head. The sting is sharp, making me gasp in shock. The cold vodka soaks my hair, but it's fear that drenches my body.

I stumble a step back, my hand flying up to where the glass hit me. My fingers tremble as they probe the tender spot.

Karlin pins me with an enraged glare, making me tremble harder, my eyes huge and every muscle in my body on high alert.

"Fucking little cunt," he spits out. "You almost cost me the deal with Aslanhov by complaining to him like a sniveling child. Beg for forgiveness."

"I'm sorry," I whimper, the same old feeling of helplessness I endured in the orphanage rearing its ugly head.

Karlin's cruel stare rests on me for a tense while, then he stalks toward me. His arm darts out, and before I can flinch, his fingers wrap around my throat in a chokehold.

His fingers dig into my flesh, ripping a gagging sound from me.

"Take off your fucking coat and bend over," he orders in a tone that leaves no room for argument.

Trembles rack my body as if I'm caught in a blizzard. I struggle out of my coat and let it fall to the floor while desperately trying to get air past the merciless hold he has on my neck.

He shoves me backward, then undoes his belt, his movements angry and cruel.

Jesus. No.

"I'm sorry," I whimper again. "I'll behave. I promise."

The belt lashes through the air and whips across my right shoulder.

"Bend over!" he shouts.

Feeling utterly humiliated, my movements are jerky as I turn. I can't bring myself to bend over.

The belt lashes across my lower back, the pain so intense I stumble forward.

You call that scrubbing a toilet? I want every yellow stain gone.

Another blow hits the same spot on my lower back, forcing me forward. I fall onto my hands and knees.

My stomach rumbles loudly as I cling to the piece of moldy bread Misha stole for me. Aunt Nadia keeps hitting Misha with the whip while screaming at me to eat every crumb.

The longer I take to eat the bread, the more she'll hurt Misha.

I shove the piece that's covered in blue and green patches of mold into my mouth and chew as fast as I can while tears streak down my face.

I don't know how many times Karlin hits me with the belt or when he stops. With my mind stuck in the past, the present doesn't exist.

I wring out the stained cloth I managed to find and try to be as careful as possible while wiping the blood off Misha's back.

'I'm sorry,' I whisper.

'It doesn't hurt that much,' Misha mumbles. 'I'll be okay.' He glances at me as I rinse the cloth out again. 'Did the bread help? Do you still feel dizzy?'

I shake my head, my bottom lip trembling. 'It wasn't worth you getting a beating.'

'Shut up!' One of the aunts hisses from the open door. 'Get in bed and sleep!'

I quickly lie down beside Misha, and we both close our eyes. Only when I hear the aunt's footsteps die away do I sit up again to clean the rest of Misha's back.

I suppress the groan, and shaking my head, I push myself up to my feet.

"Next time, you won't be able to stand up," Karlin threatens.

My lower back is on fire, my body shaking so badly that I hardly manage to stumble to the nearest couch. As gingerly as possible, I sit down. I keep my head lowered and wrap my arms around my middle.

I hear Karlin leave the living room, and closing my eyes, I fight the humiliating tears while trying to process what just happened.

Degraded and frightened, I'm angry with myself for allowing things to go this far.

And they won't get any better. If I don't do something, I'll end up in a marriage with a monster who will probably beat me daily.

That's no life.

Everything stills in me as I lift my head. Not thinking about the consequences, I stand up and grab my coat off the floor. I shrug it on as I walk to the front door, not even bothering to look around to make sure no one sees me leave.

I don't shut the door behind me but just walk down the steps. I follow the driveway until I reach the gates. Grabbing hold of the iron bars, I climb over and drop to the ground with a thud.

I regret wearing high heels. My boots would've been a hundred times warmer and more comfortable.

Seeing the city lights shining in the distance to my right, I head in their direction.

Only when I turn up a different street do I allow my emotions to surface.

I should've grabbed the belt from him and hit him until he was dead.

I should've fought back.

I should've refused the arranged marriage and dinners.

I should've called Misha and told him what was happening.

I should've asked Armani for help. Or even Mr. Vetrov.

I'm still trembling, but now it's from a mixture of cold and shock. And overwhelming humiliation.

Digging my phone out of my purse, I let out a groan when I see there's no signal. I hear the rumbling of a car's engine, and wildly glancing around me, I look for a place to hide.

Until now, I haven't even taken in my surroundings.

Seeing that I'm in a quiet street, lights shining from the houses and smoke billowing from the chimneys, I hurry toward the nearest tree and crouch behind it.

A couple of seconds later, an old sedan drives by. I let out the breath I was holding and check my phone to see if I have a signal.

My heart is beating frantically, and desperation fills every inch of me.

Rising to my feet, I walk as quickly as I can up the street. I keep glancing over my shoulder and pick out hiding spots so I'm prepared should another car drive by.

God, I can't believe I've gotten myself into such a mess. What was I thinking?

I start to doubt my decision to walk away, making my anxiety spike dangerously high.

I should've stayed. If Karlin finds me next to the road, God only knows what he'll do to me.

Shit, I can't go home. Mr. Aslanhov will be so angry, and I'll have to face Karlin.

God, what have I done?

Suddenly my phone vibrates in my hand, and seeing I have a signal, elation makes me dizzy.

My cold fingers fumble as I go into my list of contacts and press dial on Armani's number.

As the call connects and ringing sounds in my ear, a raindrop splats on my cheek.

I glance up as the heavens open, an icy sheet of rain coming down in full force.

Just my freaking luck.

"Hey," Armani's voice comes over the line, "I just sent you a message."

"I need help." The words rush from me, my voice tight with panic. "God, I don't know what to do. I think I screwed up badly." My voice strains as tears push to my eyes, and my emotions spiral out of control. "I don't know what to do," I gasp as I start to run.

"Tiana, where are you?" His voice is filled with a world of danger, and there's no sign of the gentleman I got to know last weekend.

"I'm running toward the city," I say breathlessly.

"What are you running from?" I hear movement on Armani's end. "I'm coming to you."

"Karlin Makarova. Mr. Aslanhov arranged a marriage between us. I tried to hold out until Misha got back from his honeymoon, but I can't."

"Send me your location so I can keep track of where you are," Armani demands. "Go to the nearest hotel and call me from there. I'm on my way."

Unable to run any longer, I slow my pace to a brisk walk as I frantically glance around me. "I made a mess of things, right? God, they're going to be so angry. I shouldn't have run away."

"You did the right thing, Tiana. Send me your location, find a hotel, and call me. That's all you have to do right now."

I nod like a lunatic and quickly go into my map app to send Armani my location. When I put the phone back to my ear, I ask, "Are you still there?"

"Yes, *piccola*. I'm here. I'll be in Russia in three and a half hours," he assures me.

Feeling horrible, a sob escapes me. My voice is thick with tears as I say, "I'm sorry for dragging you into this. I didn't know what else to do."

"You did the right thing."

I hear another car and quickly glance over my shoulder. Seeing headlights beaming through the rain, I break out into a run and duck behind a car that's parked in a driveway.

"What's happening?"

"There's a car coming up the road," I whisper. "I'm hiding."

"You're doing good, *piccola*. Stay hidden until it's safe to move again."

Huddled against the tire, I'm shaking so badly my breaths are audible. The rain is soaking through my coat, making me feel like a frozen block of ice.

"Tiana?" Armani asks. "How are you holding up?"

"I'm scared." I gasp, and with my free hand, I wipe the rain from my face. "It's raining, and I'm cold."

"*Cazzo!*"

It sounds like a curse, and my wild guess is it means fuck.

When the car has passed and I'm sure it's safe to move again, I get up and run.

"I'm at the airfield. I have to end the call. If anything happens while you can't reach me, call Alek."

"I don't want to drag him into this mess. It will only create more trouble between him and his father."

"Tiana," Armani's voice is harsh and commanding, "call Alek if you can't reach me. It's an order."

Chills rush down my spine, and I nod even though he can't see me. "Okay."

"You can do this, *piccola*. Just stay safe until I get to you," he says, the urgent tone making my blood pump faster through my veins.

"I'll do my best."

The call ends, and I quickly shove my phone into my purse. I start to run again, and even though my lungs are burning from all the exercise, I keep pushing myself while constantly checking my surroundings.

My nerves are worn thin by the time I reach the city. Even though there are more people out and about, I'm still on guard as I search one street after the other for a hotel.

I have no idea how long I've been walking in the rain when I finally find a hotel. I hurry into the lobby and rush to the reception counter.

"I need a room, please."

The receptionist smiles compassionately at me. "Poor thing. You got caught in the rain." She types on the keyboard, then says, "Can I have your ID?"

I pull the document out of my purse and hand it to the lady.

"How long will your visit be?"

I have no idea how long I'll be here, so I give her a random number. "Three days."

"The account needs to be settled in full before you check out," she warns me.

"Okay."

I'm given a key and room number, then she smiles brightly, "Enjoy your stay."

"Thank you."

Walking to the old elevator, I glance around the lobby, and only when the doors close behind me and I'm taken to the second floor, do I release a breath of relief.

I dig my phone out of my purse and quickly send Armani a text.

I'm at the S7 hotel. Room 203.

The elevator doors slide open, and rushing to the room, I let myself in and make sure to lock the door behind me.

I only spare a second to look at the plain furniture before going to the bed. Stripping out of the wet coat, I pull the cover from the mattress and wrap it tightly around my feezing body.

I glance around me again, feeling terrified of what's going to happen once Mr. Aslanhov finds out I ran away.

Oh my God! I should've stayed and held out until Misha came back. What have I done?

I sink down to the floor, and bringing my knees to my chest, I wrap my arms around my shins and bury my face in the covers.

What have I done?

Overwhelmed by everything that's happened, my tears start to fall.

Chapter 10

Armani

Karlin Makarova is an arms dealer and enemy of the bratva because he trades in Moscow without Viktor's permission.

I don't understand why Alek's father would arrange a marriage between the man and Tiana.

And I'm fucking pissed off. She's promised to me.

Stalking into the hotel, I head up to the second floor and knock on the door.

When Tiana doesn't open, I knock again, calling, "It's Armani."

Not even a second later, the door swings open. My eyes lock on Tiana's pale face and damp hair. I step into the room and shut the door behind me, then take a good look at her.

She looks fucking terrified, the fear trembling in her eyes.

My heart stutters in my chest from the sight. I take hold of Tiana's shoulders and pull her to my chest. Pressing a kiss to the damp strands, I say, "I'm here. I'll take care of everything."

She lets go of the blanket she's been clinging to and wraps her arms around me. "I'm in so much trouble. I shouldn't have called you, but I didn't know what else to do."

"When did you find out about the arranged marriage?" I ask as I push her back so I can see her face.

"On Monday. I've been on three dates with Karlin. I was going to wait for Misha to get back, but then…" Her words trail away.

"Why didn't you tell me on Monday?"

Tiana takes a couple of steps back while wrapping her arms around her middle. Her fear-filled eyes dart from my face to the floor. "You're mafia, and this is a bratva matter. I didn't want to get you in trouble." She gives me a pleading look. "I didn't want to be the cause of a war between the mafia and the bratva."

I shake my head. "That won't happen easily." I glance around the room, and seeing the wet coat on the floor, I shrug out of my jacket and wrap it around Tiana's shoulders. "Tell me what happened. Don't leave anything out."

She pushes her arms into the sleeves and sits down on the edge of the bed. Looking defeated, her eyes drift closed.

"Mr. Aslanhov called me to his office and said I'm to marry Karlin. We went on three dates." Her eyes open, and she looks self-conscious as she adds, "He's not a nice person, and I tried to handle it on my own." Her shoulders fall in defeat, and she shakes her head. "I shouldn't have run."

Walking closer, I crouch in front of her and place my hand on her knee. When her eyes meet mine, I say, "You did the right thing, *piccola*, but you should've told me what was happening on Monday. Don't keep things like this from me."

Worry forms a frown on her forehead. "But you're mafia, Armani. What good will that do? You have no power in Russia."

Taking a deep breath, I rise to my full height. Locking eyes with Tiana, I say, "We need to get back to St. Monarch's. You'll be safe on neutral ground."

"I don't have my passport. It's at the house."

"You don't need one." I hold my hand out and wait for her to place her palm in mine, then pulling her to her feet, I lace our fingers as we walk to the door.

"I need to settle the hotel fee, but I don't have money," she informs me as we leave the room. "I'm so sorry."

"I'll take care of it." My eyes flick to her face. "Stop apologizing, Tiana. It's my duty to take care of you."

Because that's what a fucking fiancé does. He doesn't terrify the ever-living shit out of the woman he's going to marry.

I'm on guard for an attack as we head down to the lobby. I only have one gun, which won't get us far if Makarova's men find us.

I quickly settle the bill and hurry out of the hotel with Tiana's hand firmly in mine. Glancing around us, I walk to the old sedan I borrowed from the airfield where the private jet is waiting.

This little trip is costing me fifty thousand euros. Carson, the director of St. Monarch's, made the travel arrangements. He's related to Viktor, so it's only a matter of time before the head of the bratva hears of this.

Knowing how valuable every second is, I pull out my phone as we climb into the car. I start the engine, and as I pull away from the curb, I dial the only number that can help us.

"Cotroni," my boss answers.

"It's Armani De Santis." Not wasting time, I inform him of everything. "I'm in Moscow. I have Tiana Petrov with me, and I'm taking her to St. Monarch's."

Christ, Tiana's going to learn the truth. I can't wait for Misha to tell her.

"Mr. Aslanhov agreed to an arranged marriage between her and Karlin Makarova, but her brother, Misha, already promised her to me."

My eyes leave the road, and I see the shock flutter over Tiana's beautiful features. Her lips part, the gasp leaving her filled with surprise.

With wide eyes, she stares at me as if I've lost my mind and I'm spouting the biggest load of bullshit.

She quickly turns her head to look at the road again, blinking as if she's struggling to comprehend the idea of us getting married.

Christ. It doesn't look as if she's taking the news well.

"When was the agreement made between you and Misha?" Luca asks, drawing my attention back to the conversation.

"When the shit went down with D'Angelo and Sartori. Misha asked me to marry his sister. I made a promise to him which I won't go back on."

"Why am I only being told now?"

"We were waiting to complete our training. I apologize for not telling you sooner, sir."

Luca lets out a heavy sigh. "Let me talk to Viktor. I'll get back to you."

The call ends, and leaving the phone on my lap, I glance at Tiana, who's a frozen pillar next to me, her eyes locked on the road ahead.

"I'm sorry you had to find out like this," I murmur. "Misha and I wanted to tell you once he returned from his honeymoon."

Tiana shakes her head. "The news is sudden, but I'd rather marry you than Karlin."

Thank God.

"So you're okay with the arrangement?"

Not looking at me, she nods. "Misha knows what's best for me. I'll marry whoever he chooses for me."

Misha's going to lose his fucking mind when he hears the message I left on his voicemail.

An uncomfortable silence falls between us, and I let out a breath of relief when we make it to the airfield without being attacked.

I'm taking it as a win. Maybe Makarova doesn't give a fuck that Tiana ran away.

After we climb out of the sedan and I return the keys to the office, we head to the aircraft.

Boarding the private jet, I instruct the pilot to take us back to St. Monarch's. Tiana sits down across from me and fastens her seat belt. Her eyes dart all over the plane, refusing to look at me.

Christ, she looks so fucking uncomfortable, but it's expected with the bomb I dropped on her a couple of minutes ago.

I take in her pale face, and as my gaze lowers, I see the red marks on her neck, which I haven't noticed before.

There's an instant flare of anger in my gut as I see the unmistakable imprints of fingers on her pale skin.

"What happened to your neck?"

Unable to avoid eye contact any longer, Tiana finally looks at me. "Karlin grabbed me."

Slowly, I nod, rage filling my chest.

"Is he responsible for the mark I saw on your jaw?"

She nods, and clearly embarrassed, she lowers her eyes from mine.

The fucking bastard hurt her.

"What else did he do?" The words rumble from my chest as my control starts to slip.

She shakes her head. "Nothing that will leave a permanent mark."

My anger increases tenfold, but outwardly I look calm.

"What else?" I demand.

Her hands are clutched together on her lap, her shoulders hunched.

I want to hold and comfort her, but as the plane takes off, I remain seated.

"He hit me with his belt," she whispers. "Like I was a disobedient child."

He fucking shamed her.

I look at the woman who's only evoked protectiveness and possessiveness in me, and I find it hard to comprehend how anyone can hurt her. It's like kicking a kitten.

I never interfere with bratva business unless ordered to, but Makarova made it personal by assaulting the woman that's promised to me.

When he least expects it, I'll retaliate.

"I'm sorry you got hurt."

She shakes her head again, and I notice a tear falling on her fingers. She quickly wipes the evidence away.

I watch as Tiana cries without making a single sound, and it's the most heartbreaking thing I've ever witnessed.

The moment the seat belt sign is off, I get up and unbuckle her belt. Pulling her up, I wrap her tightly against my chest. Her body trembles against mine, her shoulders shuddering with the silent sobs.

For this, Makarova will die.

I brush my hand up and down Tiana's back, but suddenly she flinches and pulls away from me. The flash of pain on her face is so fucking fleeting I almost miss it.

I'm going to fucking rip that piece of shit limb from limb.

"Show me your back," I growl, my tone too harsh as the last of my control slips through my fingers.

She shakes her head, and wrapping her arms around her middle, she takes another step away from me.

Softening my voice, I say, "Show me your back, *piccola*."

"Stop calling me a child," she mutters, her eyes flicking to me with a bruised expression in them.

"*Piccola* means little one." I take a step closer to her. "It's a term of endearment."

Her gaze flicks to mine, then slowly, she turns around. When she doesn't lift her top, I close the distance between us and pull the fabric up.

Red and blue welts cover her entire lower back. The sight has me clenching my jaw as uncontrollable rage floods me.

Jesus, that had to hurt.

As gently as possible, I lower the fabric and take a couple of steps away from her as I try to regain control over the rage threatening to make me destroy the cabin. Me losing my shit in the confined space of a plane is the last thing Tiana needs to witness.

"It's not as bad as it looks," she whispers.

My eyes snap to hers, and instantly she moves farther away from me, fear flashing over her face.

Few people in this world have seen me angry. Most of them are dead.

I might be the cool-headed one among my friends, but once I lose my shit, I fucking lose it completely.

Calm down. Tiana's terrified enough.

Knowing I'm scaring Tiana, I grumble, "I won't hurt you. I'm just fucking angry that you were hurt."

Her eyes remain glued to my face until I regain complete control over my emotions.

I gesture for her to sit as I take my own seat again. After pouring myself a tumbler of whiskey, I drink half of the amber liquid before looking at Tiana.

"We'll have your back looked at once we're at St. Monarch's."

"I'm okay." The caution doesn't leave her eyes, and she looks exhausted.

"Try to get some sleep."

She shakes her head and turns her head to stare out of the window.

Wanting to take her mind off everything, I say, "I told my mother about you. I think the two of you will get along. She loves to cook and bake, as well."

Hesitation tightens her features before she asks, "Does she live with you?"

"No. She lives with her sister, not too far from my apartment. I'm sure I mentioned it to you at the wedding."

"Right." Tiana nods as she inhales deeply. "I remember now." Her tongue darts out to wet her lips. "What will you expect…of me once…we're…ahh…married?"

"Have something to drink, *piccola.*"

She helps herself to a bottle of water, and I wait until she's quenched her thirst before I say, "I expect loyalty."

When I don't add anything else, her eyes flit to my face. "And?"

I stare at her before saying, "Why don't you tell me what you're worried about so I can set your mind at ease."

"I just want to know what's expected of me, so I don't do anything to upset you."

I let out a heavy breath as I shake my head. "It takes a lot to upset me. As long as you're faithful to me, we'll be fine."

"Will the same count for you?"

I can see the regret in her eyes the moment she's done asking the question.

I know how a mafia and bratva princess is trained. Be a good little obedient wife, don't ask questions, and expect to share your husband with every piece of pussy he feels like fucking. That kind of shit doesn't sit well with me.

"Yes. I'll be faithful to you."

Her eyes sharpen on me as if she's trying to see the truth of my words on my face.

"My father cheated on my mother, and I saw how much it hurt her," I explain. "I won't tolerate it in our marriage."

Tiana nods quickly. "Okay."

When she stares out the window again, I relax in my seat. My eyes lock on the bruises covering her neck, and I vow to cut off each of the fucker's fingers.

Chapter 11

Tiana

To say I'm overwhelmed is the understatement of the year.

Holy crap. Misha arranged for me to marry Armani?

I can't believe it.

There are so many thoughts whirling in my head it's hard to focus on anything for long. It feels like I'm stuck in a daze.

After Armani looked at my back, he was so angry it scared the shit out of me. It's freaking terrifying how he can go from being a perfect gentleman to a lethal mafioso in a split second.

But no matter how scary he is, he came to help me when I needed him, and not once has he yanked me around like I'm nothing but a rag doll.

As I walk up the steps of St. Monarch's with my hand firmly in Armani's grasp, I worry about what will happen.

"I need to call Misha," I say.

"I've left messages for him. Once he gets them, he'll come back," Armani informs me.

We pause so Armani can hand his weapon to the guard because no guests are allowed to be armed on the premises.

Alek emerges from the dining hall, and surprise flickers over his face when he sees me. "This is a surprise. What are you doing here?"

He gives me a quick hug, then exchanges a questioning look with Armani.

"Your father arranged a marriage for Tiana, so I went to get her," Armani sums up the crazy week I've had.

A dark frown forms on Alek's forehead. His eyes swing from Armani to me. "Why didn't you call me?"

"I didn't want to cause more trouble between you and your father. Things are strained as is," I answer.

Alek shakes his head at me. "Nothing you do can make things worse between my father and me. You should've called me, Tiana."

Alek only calls me by my name if he's upset. My stomach sinks because it feels like no matter what I do, it's never the right thing.

"She's had a rough night, Alek. Ease up on her," Armani says with a tone of warning lacing the words.

The two men lock eyes, and for a moment, I worry there will be a fight, but luckily Alek doesn't push things. "I'll let you handle things, brother. Let me know if I can help with anything."

Alek gives my shoulder a squeeze, then walks off. My eyes follow him until he disappears up the stairs.

Armani tugs at my hand to bring my attention back to him. "Let's go to the infirmary so the doctor can look at your back."

I'd much rather shower and crawl into bed, but I follow Armani down a hallway.

I was nervous in Armani's presence before I learned about the arrangement between him and Misha. Now I'm an anxious mess.

I'm highly conscious of his strong fingers that are wrapped around mine. His body moves with predatory grace, but I'm starting to get the feeling it's all a mask to hide the mafioso who won't hesitate to maim and kill whoever gets on the wrong side of him.

Entering the infirmary, Amani addresses the doctor. "Examine Miss Petrov's back." His eyes flick to my face. "Is there anywhere else the doctor should look?"

I'm about to shake my head when I remember the tumbler incident. "It's probably nothing, but a glass was thrown at my head." Extreme self-consciousness and shame engulf me as I say the humiliating words.

In a heartbeat Armani's features darken, changing him from calm to looking like a killer with an unquenchable thirst for blood and violence.

Dear God.

My body shrinks beneath his vicious gaze while my heartbeat and breaths speed up.

Until now, Armani has treated me with respect, but seeing this aggressive side of him makes me wonder whether he's just like any other man in the bratva and mafia.

Once again, he reins his temper in, and his features relax, but his voice has a biting edge to it as he says, "Check Miss Petrov's head as well."

The doctor gestures for me to take a seat on one of the empty beds. "Let's take a look at your head," the doctor says.

I point out where the bump is and lower my eyes while he inspects it.

"There's a small cut. I'll clean it, but I don't think the injury is serious." The doctor looks at Armani. "Just keep an eye on her for the next twenty-four hours. She might have a concussion. If she starts to vomit or experience severe headaches, bring her back to me."

"Yes, sir."

"Turn so I can check your back," the doctor instructs.

I do as I'm told, and when he lifts my top, I help to hold the fabric in place.

Armani takes a sharp breath, and I can feel his eyes burning on my skin. "It looks worse than before."

"Please remove your shirt," the doctor asks.

Feeling shy as hell, I pull the fabric over my head and cover my front with it. The doctor's fingers probe my back, and he smears something over the welts.

I clench my teeth when my skin burns from all the touching.

"Do you experience any pain when you breathe?" he asks.

"No, Doctor."

"Any pain in your neck?"

"No."

He presses on a couple of spots, checking if it causes me discomfort, then says, "Just apply the ointment after every bath. I'll give you something for pain."

I want to tell him it's not necessary but keep quiet.

"You can put your shirt on, Miss Petrov."

I quickly pull the top over my head and cover myself. When I turn around, Armani looks like he's about to kill someone.

When his eyes lock with mine, he visibly calms down again. It amazes me how much control he has over his emotions. I wish it were that easy for me.

While waiting for the doctor to bring the painkillers and ointment, I get lost in my thoughts, worrying about how much trouble I've gotten myself into. A sore back and a bump on my head are the least of my worries.

Last weekend all I had to worry about was being alone, and now my entire life has been upended. I always knew I'd have an arranged marriage and it might not all be sunshine and roses. I thought I could handle it like so many women before me.

But things are always easier said than done.

Maybe Armani won't be as abusive as Karlin. After all, Armani is one of Misha's best friends. My brother would never set up an arranged marriage with someone who would hurt me.

I trust Misha to do what's best for me.

"Tiana." Armani's fingers wrap around my bicep, and I flinch as it rips me out of my worried thoughts.

Immediately he lets go of me and takes a step back. His eyes narrow on my face, but he doesn't comment on my startled reaction.

He jerks his chin toward the door. "Let's go."

I spare the doctor a smile. "Thank you."

Following Armani out of the infirmary, I stick close to his back. It's only when we head up the stairs that I realize I have nothing with me but my purse.

How am I going to get any of my clothes and my personal belongings?

Armani opens a door and waits for me to enter. It's not the same suite I stayed in last weekend.

"You can freshen up in the bathroom while I order something for dinner," he says.

I feel painfully shy as I walk to the bedroom, and when I see men's clothing in the walk-in closet, I realize this is Armani's suite.

My eyes lock on the bed, and my cheeks go up in flames as the full impact of an arranged marriage with Armani hits. He made it clear we'll be loyal to each other, which means he won't look for pleasure elsewhere.

He expects the marriage to be consummated.

Goosebumps spread over my skin, and I turn around to look at the man who'll become my husband.

He's busy pouring himself a drink, looking coolheaded and in complete control of his surroundings again.

Armani is as handsome as they come, and if I only consider the physical aspect, the thought of sex with him doesn't scare me.

But being physically attracted to someone is not the only thing that matters.

Will Armani learn to love me? Will he be able to think of me as a woman instead of his friend's little sister?

Will he see me as an adult or a child he's stuck with?

Armani's eyes flick to me, and for a moment, we just stare at each other.

His voice is patient and soft as he says, "You can ask me anything."

Nothing is set in stone yet. I might still end up marrying Karlin, so it's no use asking such personal questions.

"Am I going to stay in this suite…with you?"

He nods. "I'm not letting you out of my sight until Misha's back." The corner of his mouth lifts in a comforting smile. "It's for your protection. I'll sleep on the couch."

My eyes dart to the couch that's too small to fit Armani's body. "I'm smaller. I'll take the couch."

He shakes his head. "It's not open for discussion."

I search Armani's face wondering who he really is – the gentleman or the mafioso.

Not finding the answer I'm looking for, I say, "Thank you for everything you're doing for me."

He nods, the corner of his mouth lifting again. "Take a shower and relax, *piccola mia*. You're safe with me."

You're safe with me.

The words make me feel strangely emotional as I walk into the bathroom. I shut the door behind me and draw my bottom lip between my teeth.

I've only truly been safe with Misha, and to hear those words from another person makes me feel not so lonely anymore.

If everything Armani has said is the truth, then a marriage with him will be what I prayed for.

Home. It's the one thing I want more than anything. A husband I can love. Children I can give the world to. A house I can call my own. To many, it's a stupid wish, but to me, it's everything.

I can cultivate a friendship with Armani, and even if he can't fall in love with me, it doesn't mean I'm not allowed to love him.

The only problem is whether Armani will be happy with a loveless marriage.

Chapter 12

Armani

When Tiana emerges from the bathroom, dressed in the clothes she wore when we arrived, I can kick my own ass.

She has nothing clean to wear.

Upset with myself, I stalk into the bedroom and yank one of my shirts off a hanger. I hold the shirt out to her. "Wear this to sleep in. I'll get you clothes first thing tomorrow morning."

Her cheeks flush as she takes the fabric from me before darting back into the bathroom.

There's a knock at the door, and I open it for the server, who pushes a cart into the living room. I sign the receipt to add the charge to my account and shut the door behind him.

I didn't know what to order for Tiana, so I got a variety of foods.

I hear movement behind me, and when I glance over my shoulder, my heart stutters and my jaw drops.

Gesù Cristo, I didn't think this through.

The shirt engulfs Tiana's petite frame, the fabric stopping above her knees. Her wet hair hangs down her back, and her makeup-free face is a picture of pure innocence.

The sight of her in my shirt is borderline erotic. Desire ignites in my veins, and my cock hardens at the speed of light.

She tugs nervously on the hem as she comes closer. "What are we eating?"

"Ah…" Reluctantly I tear my eyes away from her and lift the lids off the plates. I keep one of the lids positioned in front of my crotch so Tiana won't see the hard-on she's given me. "I wasn't sure what you like, so I got a variety of dishes. Help yourself."

Tiana looks at all the food, and for the first time, a smile that's not forced spreads over her face. Gratitude shines from her eyes as she says, "Thank you, Armani."

Misha told me about their years in the orphanage, so I know how important food is to Tiana.

Now that I've seen what she looks like and I'm getting to know her, it breaks my fucking heart picturing her as a little girl who almost starved to death.

"You're welcome, *piccola mia*," I murmur, affection softening my tone.

Her smile falters, and while she picks up a plate of roasted vegetables and grilled chicken thighs, she asks, "Why do you call me little girl?"

It's the second time tonight she's bringing up this subject. Tilting my head, my eyes search hers. "Because you're so small. Does it bother you?"

Tiana sits down on the couch, and keeping her eyes trained on the food, she whispers, "I'm not a little girl."

A frown forms on my forehead. "I know. I don't mean it condescendingly. It's a cute nickname."

I help myself to a plate of slow-cooked lamb and take a seat across from her.

"People tend to treat me like a child," she admits. "It's very frustrating."

Trust me, I won't treat you like a child. Especially if you keep wearing my shirt.

"I'll never do that." Giving her a reassuring smile, I say, "I'll pick a new nickname for you."

Her cheeks flush pink. "You don't have to."

"*Bella*? It means beautiful."

Tiana's eyes flick to mine, and the pink on her cheeks deepens in color. "I like that."

A satisfied smile spreads over my face. "Eat your food, *bella*."

My eyes lower to her sexy as fuck legs and get stuck on her thighs, that are exposed because the fabric has ridden up.

She's already uncomfortable enough. She doesn't need you eye-fucking her.

I force my gaze to her face and say, "We should get to know each other better. What else do you dislike?"

She swallows the bite she took and licks her lips. "Ahh…"

The nervousness is back on her face, and I don't like it at all.

"I don't like being yanked around," she admits. Her eyes fill with caution. "If I'm told what to do, I'll do it. I don't need to be slapped."

Christ, give me strength.

"I'll never hit you, Tiana," I assure her. A pleading expression tightens her features, and it has me adding, "I promise. I'll never be violent toward you."

She stares at me briefly before asking, "Do you have any rules?"

I cut a piece of meat. "Just the loyalty one. No man is to touch you, and you're not allowed to be alone with one." Before I pop the bite into my mouth, I add, "That excludes Misha and Alek, of course."

Tiana nods obediently. "What about the chores I have to do? Do you want me to stay out of your way when you're home? Is there a specific way you like your food to be prepared? Will I do the shopping? Do you–"

I hold up a hand to stop the questions and swallow the food before I chuckle. "I don't want you hiding whenever I'm home. I'll eat whatever you prepare, and I'd appreciate it if you'd take care of the house and shopping."

An emotion I can't place trembles in her eyes as she asks, "Will I be allowed to make your apartment my home?"

God help me. I hate the fucked up life this angel had to endure.

I take a deep breath before letting it out slowly. Setting the half-eaten plate of food on the coffee table, I wipe my mouth with a napkin while I fight to control the anger threatening to fill my chest.

My eyes lock with Tiana's as I tilt my head. I hope she can hear the compassion in my voice as I answer, "Once we're married, the apartment will be *our* home. I don't want you to ask permission for anything. I want you to make the place your own. I don't believe in divorce, so we'll spend the rest of our lives together. It will take a lot of work, but I believe we can be happy."

Heartbreaking emotion washes over her face, her chin trembles, and she struggles to keep the tears back. Her breathing speeds up as her eyebrows pull together.

She doesn't try to hide her strong reaction to my words as she asks, "Will you really be happy having me for a wife?"

Only time will tell. It's a bit too soon to answer that question.

"As I said, it will take some work on our part. We're already becoming friends, so I believe if we continue to get to know each other, we'll be able to have a successful marriage."

I can see there's something else she wants to ask, so I wait patiently until she'd ready.

"What about children?" Tiana's eyes fill with hope.

"God willing, we'll have children." I smile at her and ask, "How many do you want?"

Happiness pours over her face, and I feel like a king for being the one to make her feel this way.

"I don't care how many we have. I just want to be a mother."

Her emotions seem to settle, and when she continues to eat her food, I get up to pour myself a drink.

"I'm a morning person," I start to tell her about myself. "I love getting up at dawn when everything is quiet. My apartment has a private courtyard by the entrance where I like to sit and have my morning coffee." I glance at Tiana. "Are you a coffee or tea person? Or neither?"

"It doesn't really matter. I like tea and coffee." She takes the last bite, and getting up, she collects my plate and places the dirty dishes on the cart.

"What do you like to drink?"

"Lemon water. Any juice." She tugs at the hem of the shirt. "I'm not picky."

I take a bottle of orange juice from the bar fridge and hand it to her.

"What do you like to eat?"

"Anything but bread." Her eyes rest on mine. "And you?" Suddenly her eyes widen, and she starts to ramble, "I mean, what do you like to eat, not that I'd like to…eat you." She lets out a mortified groan, her face bright red, before she covers it with her hands. "*Pizdets.*"

I chuckle at her cute reaction. "It's okay. I understood what you meant."

She lowers her hands while inhaling deeply. "Sorry about that."

Answering her question, I say, "I love any home-cooked meal."

A smile tugs at her mouth, and as she's about to ask another question, my phone starts to ring.

I pull the device out, and seeing Luca's name flashing on the screen, I answer quickly. "Yes, sir?"

"Viktor and I are on our way. He talked to Aslanhov and Makarova. We'll meet at St. Monarch's to discuss this mess."

"Yes, sir."

"Keep the girl there. Don't you dare run off with her," he warns me.

"Yes, sir."

The call ends, and I check to see if any of my texts have gone through to Misha. They're still marked unread, so I dial his number again to leave another message.

"I have Tiana. Luca and Viktor are on their way to St. Monarch's for a meeting with Aslanhov and Makarova. I hope you get this message soon and get your ass back to Switzerland. If you don't, I'll handle everything."

I place my phone back in my pocket, and looking at Tiana, I see the worry is back in her eyes.

"The meeting is inevitable," I inform her. I wish I could put her at ease, but wanting to prepare her for the worst, I say, "Viktor will have the final say about who you'll marry."

The blood drains from her face. "Oh, God. What if he chooses Karlin?" She paces away from me while shoving her hands into her hair. "He's going to choose Karlin. The bratva wants his business." Panic tightens her voice until she sounds frantic. "This is going to be so bad. I'll probably get punished for running away."

Walking to Tiana, I take hold of her shoulders, spin her around, and press her to my chest. "Viktor isn't an unreasonable man." I lean down so I can see her face. "Tell him everything Karlin did to you. Leave nothing out. The Vetrovs disapprove of women being abused. It will count in your favor."

Tiana nods, her eyes jumping over my face. "Do I have any say in this? Do you think it will help if I tell Mr. Vetrov I want to marry you?"

"Definitely."

"Do you think Misha will get back in time?"

I let out a sigh as I hold her to me again. "I don't know. Try not to worry too much. I'll do everything in my power to keep you with me."

Tiana wraps her arms around me, pressing her face hard into my chest. Her words are mumbled against my shirt as she pleads, "Please, Armani. I want to stay with you. I know it's asking a lot, but I can't marry Karlin."

I press a kiss to her hair and wrap her so tight against me it will take an army of men to pry her from my arms.

There's no way on this godforsaken earth Tiana will marry Makarova. Over my dead body will I allow that to happen.

Chapter 13

Tiana

Armani puts on the TV to try and distract me, but it doesn't work. It's impossible to focus on anything but the sword hanging over my head.

Please, God. Please, please, please, let me marry Armani and not Karlin.

"Let's get some rest," Armani murmurs as he switches off the TV.

"I'll take the couch," I try again, not wanting him to struggle with the small space.

He shakes his head and nods toward the bedroom. I follow him, and he points to the bed. "Get in. I'm just going to shower, then I'll be out of your way."

"Take your time. I'm invading your space," I say as I inch closer to the bed. On the spur of the moment, I add, "The bed is big enough for both of us."

Armani comes out of the walk-in closet with a pair of sweatpants in his hand. He stares at me for an intense second, then says, "I don't think that's a good idea. You've had one hell of a day, Tiana. Get some sleep."

Nodding, I pull the covers back and climb into bed. Armani walks into the bathroom, shutting the door behind him.

I lie down and stare up at the ceiling while I listen to the shower running.

Why did the thing with Karlin have to happen? Sometimes I don't understand why life has to be so hard.

Even though there were times tonight when Armani downright terrified me, I'll pick him a thousand times over Karlin.

Where Karlin spoke to me as if I was shit under his shoe, Armani has only treated me with respect and kindness.

Please, God, I'll never ask for anything ever again. Let me marry Armani.

When the bathroom door opens, my eyes dart to Armani. He's only wearing a pair of sweatpants, making my eyebrows fly into my hairline. His chest, abs, and a V curving into the waistband is the most attractive thing I've ever seen.

Sweet mother of God.

I blink a couple of times as I stare at his chest. His muscles aren't overly defined and bulky. No hard ridges of abs. Instead, golden skin runs smoothly over what I'd call pure perfection.

He walks closer to the bed, and staring down at me, the corner of his mouth lifts. "Try to get some sleep, *bella*. If you need anything, just wake me."

I nod, and when he leans down and presses a kiss to my forehead, my heart flutters in my chest.

He smells heavenly, like wild spices and calm waters. I don't know how else to describe the scent, but I think it fits him perfectly.

"Good night, Armani," I murmur before watching him leave the room. Then my eyes get stuck on his shoulders and back.

Dear, God.

His back is a work of perfection. Strength ripples beneath his skin, and his shoulders are broad, giving me the impression he can carry the weight of the world on them.

The mafia-related tattoos on the back of his hands only add to how hot he looks.

Armani switches the lights off, and I turn onto my side, snuggling into the pillow where I can smell his lingering scent.

Surely Armani can have any woman he wants. Why did he agree to an arranged marriage with me?

I can hear him moving in the living room, so I climb out of bed and walk to the doorway. He's standing in front of the floor-to-ceiling windows, staring into the dark night.

"Armani?"

He turns his head. "Yeah?"

"Why did you agree to marry me?" I ask the very important question.

I hear him inhale deeply before exhaling, then he walks toward me. He stops close to me, enough that I can smell his body wash and cologne.

Don't stare at his chest. Eyes on his face.

It's not easy meeting his intense gaze as he finally answers, "There was a moment we were in shit, and Misha asked me to take care of you should anything happen to him."

So it was a heat-of-the-moment kind of promise?

"Did you know anything about me?"

He shakes his head. "Not much. After I made the promise, Misha told me about your time in the orphanage."

He only knows the worst part of my past. That sucks.

"Isn't there another woman you'd rather marry?" My teeth worry my bottom lip, then I add, "Someone you love?"

Again he shakes his head. "I'm a man of my word, Tiana. I never break a promise."

I let out a sigh. "You might not have a choice. If Mr. Vetrov gives me to Karlin, you'll be free from your promise."

Instead of commenting on my statement, he whispers, "Get some sleep, *bella*."

Armani's phone starts to ring, and it tears his attention away from me. He walks to where the device is lying on the coffee table and says, "It's Misha!"

I rush closer while Armani answers, "Fucking finally, brother." There's a moment's silence, then he says, "Yeah, she's here. I'm putting you on speaker."

A second later, I hear Misha's voice. "Tiana?"

Tears jump to my eyes as intense relief fills me. "I'm here."

"How are you holding up?" he asks.

"Honestly?" Armani gives me a compassionate look, and I can't keep the tears from falling. "I'm scared, Misha. I hate asking this of you, but please come to St.

Monarch's." A sob fills my throat, and my words are strained as I whimper, "I don't know what to do."

Armani wraps his hand around the back of my neck and pulls me against his bare chest.

"We're at the airport. The flight leaves in an hour, but it's a thirty-hour trip," Misha informs us. "Just stay with Armani."

I nod even though Misha can't see me.

"Brother," Misha says to address Armani, "Don't leave her alone. Don't allow Makarova close to my sister."

"Don't worry," Armani answers, "They'll have to pry her from my dead arms."

Jesus.

I tilt my head back to look up at Armani's face, and seeing the dark expression, filled with rage and violence, I'm not afraid, unlike the times before.

"Let's hope it doesn't come to that," Misha mutters, sounding tired and upset. "Did Luca say what time the meeting is?"

"No. Once they get here, I'll tell them you're on your way. I'm sure they'll wait."

"I'm going to call Viktor quickly. If I can get ahead of this shitstorm, we might not need to have the fucking meeting."

"That's a good idea." Armani gently rubs his hand up and down my back, avoiding the lower part where I'm hurt. "Let me know how the conversation goes."

"Will do."

"Tiana," Misha says, concern making his voice rough, "There's no way you're marrying that fucker. Don't worry about a thing."

"Thank you, Misha," I mumble from where I'm still pressed to Armani's chest. "I'm sorry I ruined your honeymoon."

"Don't apologize. None of this is your fault."

The call ends, but Armani doesn't let go of me. Instead, he drops the phone on the couch and wraps me up in a tight hug.

"You're going to be okay," he whispers.

I nod, my cheek rubbing against his warm skin.

God, it feels incredible to have his arms around me.

We stand still for a minute or so before he pushes me back. "Go to bed. You need your rest for what's to come."

Letting out an exhausted sigh, I walk to the bedroom and climb back into his bed.

Clinging to the pillow with my eyes locked on the doorway, I must admit I feel a little better now that I know Misha is on his way.

It gives me more hope that I'll marry Armani instead of Karlin.

God, please.

I wonder what it will be like to be Armani's wife. I think he'll be supportive, and our home life will be as calm as he is.

Like I've done almost every night since I was a teenager, I create a fake scenario in my head so my mind will stop racing and I can fall asleep. This time Armani is the star of my fantasy.

Wishing we had met under different circumstances, I picture us running into each other at a bakery. I'm the owner and have just placed a fresh batch of muffins on the display counter.

Armani comes in, and his eyes are drawn to me. It's love at first sight.

A shy smile spreads over my face as I imagine what it would be like to be kissed passionately by him.

When I think about our wedding night and consummating our marriage, my face goes up in flames, and I bury it in the pillow.

Will the sex be clinical, awkward, or both? Having zero experience, I don't know what to expect.

I actually don't care because whatever happens during your first time together will be infinitely better than sleeping with Karlin.

I force my thoughts away from Karlin and think about how kind Armani has been.

With the man I'm crushing on filling my mind, I finally drift off to sleep.

Chapter 14

Armani

Tension is running high at St. Monarch's as we wait for Misha to arrive.

Yesterday I got Tiana a couple of outfits, and once I'm free to take her home, I'll fill up her closet.

She's been a nervous wreck, and nothing I say can calm her down. I understand why, though. Her entire life hangs in the balance, and she has no say in what happens. It fucking sucks, and that's why I'll fight for her.

I'm sitting in the dining hall with Tiana, where we're having brunch, when Mr. Aslanhov walks in. The moment his eyes land on Tiana and he starts to walk toward us, I rise from my chair.

"Aslanhov is here," I murmur to Tiana.

Her head snaps to the side, and she quickly scrambles to her feet.

When he reaches her, and his arm rears back, I dart forward. My hand clamps around his wrist, effectively stopping the slap he was going to give Tiana.

Our eyes lock, and the air tenses.

Shaking my head, I say, "No one will touch Tiana. She's under my protection."

"Not for fucking long," he hisses at me, a storm brewing in his eyes.

Alek is a good friend, but so help me God, I will knock his father on his ass if he tries to touch Tiana.

Aslanhov rips his arm out of my hold and glares at Tiana. "I took you in when you had no home. I fed and clothed you. This is how you repay me?"

"I'm sorry, Papa," she mumbles, her features tight with guilt.

"Don't call me Papa. You've disgraced me."

Without another word, he turns around and stalks out of the dining hall. Tiana slumps down in her chair while covering her mouth with a trembling hand, absolute devastation on her face.

Taking the seat next to her, I wrap my fingers around the back of her neck and pull her to me. Holding her tightly with my mouth by her ear, I say, "I'm sorry, *bella*. Misha will be here soon."

Just then, we hear Misha roar, "How dare you fucking pawn my sister off to that fucker?"

Rushing to my feet, I yank Tiana up by her hand. We jog out of the dining hall, and the instant she sees her brother, she pulls free from me and runs toward him.

"Misha!" she gasps before throwing herself at him.

My friend's eyes burn with barely controlled rage on Aslanhov while he hugs Tiana tightly.

Aslanhov glares at them, but not staying to face Misha's wrath, he walks away, heading toward Director Koslov's office where Viktor and Luca are waiting.

Alek and Aurora stand by the castle's front doors, watching the shit show go down. Misha probably asked him to stay with Aurora while he deals with the problem.

I agree. It would be better to keep Alek out of the meeting. The last thing he needs right now is another reason for him and his father to have a go at each other.

Misha frames Tiana's face with his hands, his eyes scanning over every inch of her. "Are you okay?"

She nods quickly. "Thank you for coming."

Misha pulls Tiana out of the castle and bums a cigarette from Alek. I know he only smokes when he's stressed.

As he exhales a cloud of smoke, he looks at Tiana. "Why did you wait a week before calling Armani?"

She gives me a guilty look before answering, "He's not in the bratva. I didn't want to cause trouble."

Misha shakes his head at her. "So you let a man hurt you? You know better than that, Tiana. What have I taught you? If you can't win the fight, you fucking run."

"I know." Frustration forms a frown on her forehead. "I was thinking of you and Aurora, as well. I didn't want to ruin your honeymoon."

"Stop putting everyone else first!" Misha snaps at her.

I take a step closer, but Aurora speaks before I can open my mouth. "Stop yelling at Tiana. You don't know what it's like being a woman in the mafia. Things are easier said than done."

Misha takes another drag of the cigarette, and when Aurora wraps an arm around Tiana's shoulders, he lets out a sigh.

"Next time something happens, you tell Armani or me immediately," Misha instructs Tiana.

"Or me," Alek mutters.

Misha glances at Alek. "You have enough shit to deal with."

Alek narrows his eyes on Misha. "It doesn't mean I can't help T. She's like a sister to me."

Misha places his hand on Alek's shoulder. "I know, brother. I'm just looking out for you as well."

A guard approaches us, saying, "The meeting is about to start."

I nod at him. "Thank you."

Alek places his hand on Aurora's lower back, nodding toward the dining hall. "Come. Lunch is on me."

After they leave the three of us, I look at Misha. "Let's get this over with."

"Do you want me to wait with Alek and Aurora?" Tiana asks.

Misha shakes his head. "Viktor wants you at the meeting."

"Oh God," she gasps, the blood draining from her face. "I'm so sorry about the mess I made."

"The only thing you did wrong was not calling Armani sooner," he mutters as he walks into the castle.

I take hold of Tiana's hand, giving her fingers a squeeze before we head to the office. When we reach the door, I pull her partially behind me, and I don't let go of her hand.

When the door shuts behind us, Misha greets Luca and Viktor before he turns a murderous glare on Makarova, who's sitting on one of the couches, looking like he owns the fucking place.

Viktor glances at me, then at Tiana. "Come out of hiding, little one."

I feel the tremble in Tiana's hand as she steps to my side. She's so fucking pale I fear she's going to pass out.

"Just so everyone's on the same page," Luca mutters as he takes a seat, a tumbler of whiskey in his hand, "Misha promised his sister to Armani, and Vincent arranged a marriage with Karlin."

Mr. Aslanhov steps closer to the seating area. "The deal between the bratva and Karlin takes precedence over a promise between friends."

"Like hell it does," Misha snaps. "I decide who my sister marries. I'm her only living blood relative."

"I fucking took you in," Aslanhov roars.

"Silence," Viktor shouts. He looks pissed off as his eyes scan over all of us.

He gestures for Tiana to move closer to him. Cautiously she walks until she's within reaching distance of him.

"Why did you run away, little one?"

Her tongue darts out to nervously wet her lips, and she clasps her hands in front of her.

You can do it, bella. Tell him what happened.

"Mr. Makarova is an abusive man." There's a spark in Tiana's eyes when she sees Viktor is actually listening to her, and it makes her voice sound stronger. "He threatened me and said there would be no children, that he's not interested in a weakling like me, so the marriage wouldn't be consummated."

Viktor nods, then asks, "Is that all?"

Tiana shakes her head, and turning her back to Viktor, she lifts her shirt.

The second Viktor sees the welts on her back, rage ignites in his eyes, and his features turn to stone.

Misha lets out a growl, his hands fisting at his sides. I step closer to him in case he lunges for Makarova. Leaning in, I whisper, "Keep calm. We'll deal with the fucker at a later stage."

Luca stands up and takes hold of Viktor's arm. "We're on neutral ground. Calm down."

If the situation weren't so severe, I'd chuckle.

Viktor's eyes burn on Makarova with unconcealed disgust before he looks at Tiana again. His expression visibly softens as he asks, "Do you want to get married, Tiana?"

Her eyebrows draw together. "Sir?"

"Are you ready for marriage? Is this something you want?" He makes it clearer for her.

Tiana swallows hard. "Yes, sir." She takes a deep breath, then continues, "You said I could call you if I need anything."

Viktor's face softens even more. "I did."

She swallows hard again. "Please, will you allow me to marry Armani?" The air wooshes from her lungs as she lets out a breath. "I'll never ask for anything again."

Viktor glances at Luca, and they have a wordless conversation. When Luca nods, Viktor turns back to Tiana. "Are you sure, little one? Marriage is for life."

She doesn't hesitate to answer, "I'm sure. Please allow me to marry Armani De Santis."

There's a tense minute as Viktor spares everyone a glance, then he nods. "If that's what you want, little one."

"Viktor!" Mr. Aslanhov cries. "The deal with Karlin has been signed. I worked my ass off to bring him into the fold."

Viktor ignores the outcry and steps closer to Tiana. Giving her shoulder a squeeze, he says, "You have my permission to marry Armani. You can leave."

Intense relief washes over Tiana's face, and as if she's caught in a daze, she walks toward me to get to the door. I take hold of her hand, and leaning down, I whisper in her ear, "Go straight to Alek and Aurora. Stay with them until I come to get you."

She nods before exiting the room.

Locking eyes with Makarova, Viktor mutters, "You're a worthless piece of shit. What makes you think I'll give you a bratva princess? You've been nothing but a thorn in my fucking side." His eyes narrow on the man. "If I want your business, I'll fucking take it."

Viktor eyes swing to me, pinning me with an authoritative look. "What have you done to deserve Tiana?"

Nothing.

Absolutely nothing.

I take a step forward. "Give me an opportunity to earn Tiana Petrov, and I won't disappoint you."

I don't miss the corner of Luca's mouth lifting with pride.

Viktor tilts his head, stares at me momentarily, then nods. "The task will be sent to you via a secure message. You'll have a week to get the job done."

"Thank you, Mr. Vetrov."

"This is unacceptable," Makarova says as he rises to his feet. "Are you sure you want to give the girl to the boy? Once I leave this office, the offer is off the table."

A smirk tugs at Viktor's mouth. "The offer was never authorized by me. I'll see you on the battlefield, Makarova. Watch your back when you leave the safety of St. Monarch's."

"You'll regret this, Vetrov." Makarova glares at Viktor, and as he walks to the door, his eyes meet mine.

I'll see you once my bride is settled in her new home.

"For months, I worked to get the deal with Makarova. Tiana was a token of good faith between him and us," Mr. Aslanhov complains.

Viktor shakes his head. "I'm disappointed in you, Vincent. My father spoke highly of you, but to allow a woman who's under your care to be treated like an animal is not acceptable."

It's been ten years since Viktor took over as head of the bratva, but everyone knows his father is still active in the business. If you take on one Vetrov, you face the entire family and the Koslovs who they're close with. And the Cotronis. Fuck, you'd be stupid to piss off Luca or Viktor.

Aslanhov's jaw drops, and his eyes widen, but before he can say something, Viktor continues, "Makarova will never bend the knee. Did you really think giving him a woman would make him bow after a decade of war? If it were that easy, I'd have arranged a marriage a long time ago."

Looking like he just had his ass handed to him, Aslanhov mutters, "I apologize for my mistake."

"We'll talk once I'm done cleaning this mess you've created. Leave."

After Aslanhov exits the office and it's just Misha, me, Luca, and Viktor, I let out a breath of relief.

That's half the battle won.

"Thank you, sir," Misha says, gratitude in his eyes. "My sister means the world to me."

Viktor nods as he walks to the liquor cabinet, and pouring himself a shot of vodka, he says, "There's nothing more important than family." He throws the alcohol down his throat, then continues, "The wedding will be officiated as soon as Mr. De Santis has completed the job."

Looking at Luca, I say, "There's only three months of training left, sir. May I have early leave to do the job, marry Tiana, and return to work?"

Luca's eyes search mine, then he nods. "Once you've succeeded in whatever task I have for you, you may leave

St. Monarch's." He stands up, and closing the distance between us, he takes hold of my shoulder. "Don't fail me."

"I won't."

We look at each other for a moment, then he turns to Viktor. "I think we're done here. Let's go home to our wives."

"Mr. Cotroni," I say to get his attention. "Thank you for settling this issue for us." My eyes move to Viktor. "I appreciate it."

"Clearly, I have a soft spot when it comes to love," Viktor chuckles, the sound deceptive. "But I hope, for your sake, this is the last time I have to leave my wife to clean your mess."

I nod, and only after our bosses have left the office, do I look at Misha. "I'm taking Tiana home. To Venice."

The corner of his mouth lifts in a smile, the tension of worrying over Tiana's future draining from his face. "Thank you, brother." Walking to me, he gives me a brotherly hug. "Tiana will be a good wife. All I want is for her to be happy."

"I'll do everything in my power to give her the life she deserves."

We pull apart, and only then does it sink in – Tiana is mine.

Chapter 15

Tiana

I'm stunned out of my mind as I stare at the glass of water Alek ordered for me.

It was that easy? How? I expected so much worse.

Still, I was a second away from wetting myself. All those powerful men in one room terrified the living hell out of me.

I'm free to marry Armani.

Guilt rears up because not once while I begged Mr. Vetrov did I consider how Armani feels about the arrangement. If Mr. Vetrov had given me to Karlin, Armani would've been freed from his promise.

But this once, I had to be selfish. I took Misha's advice and thought of myself.

I'm sorry, Armani. I promise to be a perfect wife. Maybe you can learn to love me with time.

"That's it?" Aurora asks. "Viktor just gave his blessing?"

"Viktor doesn't fuck around," Alek mutters before popping a piece of crispy bacon into his mouth.

"Yeah, Mr. Vetrov got right to the point. I had braced myself for the men to shout and fight."

Aurora's eyes scan my face. "It's good news, right? You're happy?"

Still stuck in a daze, I nod. "Very happy."

She reaches across the table and gives my hand a squeeze. "Armani is a good man."

I nod again. "I'm lucky."

"Did Viktor say when the wedding will be?" she asks.

Alek lets out a chuckle. "You don't have a lot of time to plan the wedding. Viktor will want the two of you married as soon as possible."

My eyes dart to Alek, and I lean forward. "How long do I have? A week? Two weeks?"

He shakes his head. "A week at most."

Jesus.

How the hell do I plan a wedding in a week?

"You're stressing her out," Aurora chastises Alek. "Viktor gave Misha and me three months. I'm sure he'll do the same for you."

Just then, Misha and Armani enter the dining hall. I jump up from my chair and rush toward them.

"Did everything go okay? What happened after I left?"

"Just bratva business," Misha answers, then he smiles at me. "Congratulations on your engagement, my little sister."

Hearing the words from Misha hits like a ten-pound hammer.

My eyes dart to Armani's face, and I try to read his reaction.

Is he happy? Is this a burden he'll see through because he made a promise?

Clearing my throat, I look at Misha again. "Thank you for choosing a good man for me."

Misha pulls me into a hug. "He'll make you happy, Tiana. All I want for you is to have the life you've always wanted. No one deserves it more than you."

Tears well in my eyes. "Thank you for always looking out for me. I love you."

"Love you too." He presses a kiss to my temple, then pulls back. "You're going home with Armani. Okay?"

I nod quickly, and knowing it's expected of me, I move closer to Armani to stand by his side.

"Oh, all my belongings are still in Russia," I think to mention.

"We'll go get everything before going to Venice," Armani answers.

"I just want a moment alone with Tiana," Misha says.

When Armani nods, Misha takes my hand and pulls me out of the castle. Even though the sun is shining brightly, it's chilly outside.

My brother turns and looks at me with love. "Are you ready for this?"

I nod. "I have to get married at some point. Armani seems to be a good man."

Misha's eyebrows draw together, and his eyes lock with mine. "I only want the best for you. We've been through hell together."

I press my lips against each other as emotion wells in my chest. My eyes sting with tears as I whisper, "Thank you for being the best brother ever. I wouldn't have survived without you."

His features soften as he pulls me into a hug. "I'll always watch over you."

I nod as I hold him, knowing our lives are heading in different directions.

After the emotional moment we just shared, Misha pulls away and brushes a hand over my hair. "Go live the life you've always wanted."

A smile wavers around my lips, and walking back into the castle, I go to the man I'll spend the rest of my life with.

Armani's eyes land on me, and he rises from where he sits with Aurora and Alek.

"I'm taking my wife so we can enjoy the last of our honeymoon," Misha says.

I quickly hug Aurora and whisper, "Thank you for letting Misha come."

"We'll always be there for you, Tiana," she replies.

Before they leave, Armani announces, "We're leaving for Venice. I'll be in touch."

I watch as the men shake hands before I give Alek a hug.

"See you at the wedding, T," he murmurs, giving me a playful wink.

"Can't wait." I keep a smile around my lips, but it wavers when I watch Misha and Aurora leave the dining hall.

That's it. I now belong to Armani.

My heart jumps in my chest before speeding up. Armani takes hold of my hand, and tingles spread up my arm. When we walk to his suite, I'm overly aware of the man next to me.

The man, who likes to wake up early, prefers coffee, and likes home-cooked meals.

The enforcer, who has an eerie control over his temper and emotions.

My soon-to-be husband.

Entering his suite, Armani tugs me to stand in front of him. His eyes lock with mine, and it feels like he's searching my soul for something.

"Do you feel better?"

I nod quickly, then point to the bedroom. "Should I pack your belongings?"

He shakes his head, and lifting his hand to cup my cheek, his expression turns tender. "We're engaged, *bella*. That doesn't mean you're my slave."

With our eyes locked, he begins to lean down. My heart jumps to my throat, and I stop breathing. It feels like all my blood rushes to my head.

Ever so softly, Armani presses his lips to mine. Even though it's only for a moment, the kiss scrambles my thoughts and leaves me completely breathless.

It's so intense my stomach erupts in a kaleidoscope of butterflies, and I swear it feels like the sun is shining in the room. Everything is bright and warm.

Lifting his head, a smile plays around his mouth. *"La mia bellissima fidanzata."*

Before I can ask what it means, he translates, "My beautiful fiancée." His hand moves to rest at the back of my neck. "I thought I'd get the first kiss out of the way so you'll feel more comfortable with me. Once we're home, I'll give you an engagement ring."

This man is so sweet.

"I feel comfortable with you. Thank you for all the effort you're making." Unable to be selfish any longer, I ask, "Are you okay with the arrangement?"

He pulls his hand away from me as he nods. "Yes." I notice a flash of worry in his eyes, then he adds, "We'll take our time. Rome wasn't built in a day."

Is he asking me to be patient with him?

I can do that. I'll give him as much time and space as he needs.

My lips curve up in an empathetic smile. "Yes, there's no rush. We have a lifetime to get to know each other."

He presses a kiss to my forehead, then walks toward the bedroom. "As soon as I'm done packing, we're leaving."

I follow him to the walk-in closet and insist, "Let me help. I'll feel awkward just standing around while you pack."

This time, Armani nods, and as we get to work, the atmosphere between us feels different. I can't place what the change is and assume it's because we're engaged, and Armani needs time to adjust to it.

Chapter 16

Tiana

On our flight to Russia, all the anxiousness bubbled back into my chest.

I don't know if Mr. Aslanhov will be home when I collect my things, and I have no idea how Mrs. Aslanhov will react to the news that I'm marrying Armani.

When I let us into the house, the atmosphere is quiet. Armani sticks to my side as we walk to the kitchen, where we find Mrs. Aslanhov washing dishes.

"Hi, Mama," I say to get her attention.

She spins around, water and suds flying through the air. "You startled me!" Her gaze locks on Armani, then she frowns. "Who's this?"

"Armani De Santis. He's a good friend of Misha and Alek's, and…" I swallow hard, "my fiancé."

Confusion washes over her features. "But you're to be engaged to Mr. Makarova. What's going on?"

"Mr. Vetrov changed the arrangements. I'm to marry Armani," I explain. "I'm sure Papa will tell you everything once he gets home."

"Tsk!" She shakes her head as she dries her hands on a dishcloth. "You know we're never told anything."

True.

"I asked Mr. Vetrov to allow me to marry Armani. Misha already arranged a marriage between us before the deal was made with Karlin," I explain.

Mrs. Aslanhov looks at Armani with narrowed eyes.

He steps forward, holding his hand out to her. "It's a pleasure meeting you, Mrs. Aslanhov."

"Humphf." She shakes his hand but doesn't look happy. "I suppose if Mr. Vetrov issued the order, we'll just have to abide by it."

"Armani is a good man." I give her a pleading look. "I'll be happier with him."

She lets out a sigh as she looks at me. "Happiness has nothing to do with a good marriage." Walking to the fridge, she starts to take out vegetables and meat. "Will you be staying for dinner, Mr. De Santis?"

"No." Armani takes my hand again. "We're here to collect Tiana's belongings. I need to get home."

Shock flutters over Mrs. Aslanhov's face, but she doesn't argue. "If that's the case," she waves a hand to the doorway, "let's pack your things."

Looking up at Armani, I ask, "Do you mind waiting here? I'll be as quick as possible."

"Take your time."

I watch as he takes a seat at the kitchen table before I rush after Mrs. Aslanhov.

I find her in the corridor, where she's pulling two worn bags from the closet.

"Let me help." I take one from her and go to my room.

There's an uneasy silence between us as she starts to take my clothes from the closet, folding everything neatly before placing them in the bag.

I begin to clear the dressing table, my eyes constantly darting to her.

"I'm sorry it's so sudden," I apologize.

"This is the life we live," she replies. "When is the wedding?"

"I'm not sure."

She lets out a sigh. "Just do what he says. Remember to stay out of his way and make sure his meals are always ready when he comes home."

"Yes, Mama."

"When he comes home smelling like a whore house, don't make a fuss. At least he won't look to you to warm his bed."

"Armani said we'd be loyal to each other," I tell her.

"They always say that, child. It means you must be loyal while they sleep with whomever they want."

Remembering what Armani told me about his parents, I'm sure he'll be loyal to me, but I don't mention it to Mrs. Aslanhov.

She folds up one of my nightgowns, then pauses to look at me with worry. "The wedding night. Do you know what to expect?"

Oh crap.

I only know what I've seen on TV and heard other girls talk about when I was in school.

My cheeks go up in flames. "I think so."

"Make sure to wash before the… act." She quickly stuffs the nightgown in the bag. "The first time is always painful. Try not to cry."

This is really not a conversation I want to have with her, but I listen obediently.

She packs quicker, clearly uncomfortable as well, but still, she continues, "If you fake that you're enjoying it, it will be over sooner. Just pretend you're climaxing."

I've tried to masturbate but could never make myself orgasm, so I figured I'd have to fake it anyway.

"Take a warm bath afterward. It will help lessen the pain."

"Yes, Mama."

"Men also like it if you praise them."

"Okay."

"Never nag him. They have stressful jobs and will take it out on you."

I nod, and having cleared my dressing table, I dart into the bathroom to get my toiletries.

Mrs. Aslanhov comes to stand in the doorway, a sad expression on her face. "I loved having you here. The house will be empty without you."

"Oh, Mama," I gasp, emotions rising in my chest. I hurry forward and wrap my arms around her. "Thank you for everything you've taught me. I'll try to visit."

She pats my back between my shoulder blades. "Don't forget to add cinnamon in the honey cake."

"I won't." A tear spirals down my cheek. "I'll call as often as I can."

She nods as she pulls away, and sniffing, she returns to the bedroom to pack the last of my clothes.

The atmosphere feels heavy between us as we carry my luggage down the stairs.

"Be a good wife, Tiana. Make me proud," she whispers before we reach the kitchen.

"I'll do my best, Mama."

Her eyes meet mine. "Try to have a baby as soon as possible. It will give you something to live for."

I nod again.

Rubbing my shoulder, she says, "You'll be fine."

It sounds like she's trying to reassure herself.

"I'll call often," I remind her.

When we walk into the kitchen, Armani stands up. "That was quick."

"It's best you leave before my husband gets home. I'm sure he's not happy about the deal with Mr. Makarova falling through," Mrs. Aslanhov says, already ushering us to the front door.

I give her another hug, and feeling sad for leaving like this, I step out of the house. The cold wind whips around us as we walk to the rental car.

After the luggage is loaded into the trunk, I look at the house where I spent my teenage years. Waving at Mrs. Aslanhov, I swallow hard on the lump in my throat, then climb into the passenger seat.

This is it. From here on out, I'm dependent on Armani.

The thought makes me feel uncomfortable, and while he reverses the car out of the driveway, I steal a glance at him.

Like always, he looks calm and collected. Having exchanged the combat uniform for a suit, he's a million times more handsome.

His eyes catch mine before he continues to drive down the street. "Are you okay?"

I turn my attention to the other houses, thinking it might be the last time I see this neighborhood.

"Yes." Feeling nervous about my future with Armani, I ask, "What is it like in Venice?"

A warm smile spreads over Armani's face. "Unlike here, our streets are water canals. There are sidewalks, but most people use the canals to get around." His eyes flick to me before he continues, "It's not a big city, so you'll get used to seeing the same faces every day."

My mouth curves up at the sides. "Are there cars in Venice?"

Armani shakes his head. "No, it's not allowed within the city. You can only move around by boat or on foot." His smile widens. "I think you'll love it there. You'll get to know my mother and aunt, so you won't be alone when I'm away for work."

"Don't worry about me."

We pull up to the airfield where the private jet is waiting. Only when he's switched off the car, does he say, "It's my job to worry about you."

Job. That's the last thing I want to be.

Chapter 17

Tiana

By the time we land in Venice, I'm exhausted from all the traveling.

Our luggage is loaded onto a boat, and soon we're speeding across the water toward the city that will become my home.

It's almost eleven at night, and as we're steered around a bend and into a narrow waterway, I stare at a little café where chairs are propped up on tables. Everything looks magical, the old buildings bathed in a soft, warm yellow light.

A bridge comes into view, and as we pass beneath it, I tilt my head back, a smile spreading over my face.

Lights twinkle like fireflies on the sides of the canal and passing by an apartment building, I see a couple sitting on a balcony, enjoying a glass of wine.

"It's so beautiful," I whisper, captured in awe of this city of bridges and canals.

"I'll show you around tomorrow," Armani says, his eyes locked on my face.

My smile widens, and excitement bubbles in my chest. I've never really traveled. The two times I left Russia were my recent trips to St. Monarch's. I didn't get to see much of Switzerland.

"Thank you. I'd appreciate it."

The boat pulls up to the side of a building where potted trees stand on either side of a broad door. There's a balcony with flowers around the edges, making the place look like something from a fairytale.

"We're home," Armani murmurs as he stands up.

Home.

My eyes dart back to the beautiful building before I glance up and down the waterway filled with parked gondolas and small boats. The atmosphere feels relaxed and peaceful.

Never in a million years did I dream of such a beautiful home.

Armani holds his hand out to me, and when I place my palm in his, he helps me out of the boat. There are steps leading up to the entrance, and a boat is tied to a pole next to the small docking area.

We take our luggage, and while Armani says something in Italian to the man, I walk closer to the door. I watch as the boat speeds off, then look at Armani.

His eyes search my face before he unlocks the door and holds it open for me.

I take a deep breath, then step inside a courtyard that steals the air from my lungs.

Oh my God.

There's so much greenery, two wrought-iron benches, and a staircase made of the same stones used for the walls. A statue of a woman without arms stands against one wall, and looking up, I can see the sky.

"Is this where you drink your morning coffee?" I ask as I follow Armani to the stairs.

"Yes. I leave the door open and watch as the city wakes up."

It sounds so lovely.

Entering through another door, we step into a foyer. Armani drops his keys in a wooden bowl situated on a glass stand.

My eyes keep darting around as I try to take in everything. We pass a kitchen that looks warm and inviting with a large wooden table and bench seats. Through the windows, I see a balcony with small pots of herbs.

My heart swells at the happy sight.

This is where I'll spend most of my days, cooking and baking. I can't wait.

As we move through the apartment, there are wooden beams for a ceiling, contrasting with the stone walls and floors. Potted plants lend color to the otherwise white and black décor.

I can feel Armani's personality in the air, everything is calm and collected.

He'll probably notice if something is out of place.

Entering a bedroom, I stop midway when I realize it's where Armani sleeps. He sets his luggage down near an open walk-in closet before coming to take my bags.

Suddenly he pauses and asks, "Would you like to stay in one of the guest bedrooms until you're more comfortable with me?"

"Ahh...no. The sooner I get used to everything, the better."

He sets my luggage next to his, then says, "Make yourself at home, Tiana."

I stand awkwardly for a moment, then move closer to the closet. "I'll unpack...unless there is something else you want me to do."

"Move my clothes over to the right side to make space for your things."

Nodding, I watch as Armani leaves the bedroom before I take a good look around. The bed is massive, with black covers and pillows. There are two bedside tables, the one nearest to the door has a book, lamp, and a small clock.

There's a balcony outside the windows with a small, round table and chairs.

A smile spreads over my face again as I picture Armani and me sharing a glass of wine while watching the waterway below.

It would be so romantic.

Walking into the closet, I make space on the right side before moving Armani's suits. His scent drifts around me. I make sure everything looks neat before I unpack my clothes.

A smile keeps playing around my lips, and I don't feel the time pass.

"Are you almost done?" Armani suddenly asks behind me.

"Yes." I quickly place the stack of leggings on a shelf, then turn to him. I gesture at his clothes. "Is everything where you want it?"

He doesn't even look at his side of the closet as he nods, then he holds his hand out to me.

I place my palm in his, and he pulls me out of the bedroom. We head to the living room, and before I can glance around, I'm tugged out onto a balcony.

I glance up and down the waterway, then look up at the stars above us. "You have such a beautiful home, Armani."

"I'm glad you like it."

When I look at him, he takes hold of my left hand.

"This was my grandmother's ring." His eyes lock with mine. "Even though this is an arranged marriage, I want you to be happy, Tiana."

My lips part, and in absolute surprise, I watch as he pushes a vintage ring onto my finger. The diamond is huge and set in gold that's been shaped into a rose.

"Thank you," I breathe. My eyes dart to his. "For everything. I won't disappoint you."

I can't read the expression on his face. It almost looks like he's in two minds about something.

I'm still trying to get a read on his emotions when his hands settle on the sides of my neck, his thumbs caressing my jaw. Slowly he leans down until his mouth brushes against mine.

Just like the first time, my heart sets off at a crazy pace, and my stomach flutters up a storm.

Then something very unexpected happens, and Armani deepens the kiss. His tongue brushes against my bottom lip, and instinctively I open for him.

An intense wave of tingles hit so hard I lose my ability to think and breathe.

His tongue brushes over mine, then he tilts his head, and I have to grab hold of his sides to remain standing as he kisses me as if he's attracted to me.

As if he could one day fall in love with me.

When he ends the kiss, I don't know what to do with all the emotions he awakened in me.

He pulls me to his chest and holds me while I come down from the dizzying heights the kiss took me to, thinking it will be as easy as breathing to fall in love with this man.

Chapter 18

Armani

Watching Tiana experience Venice for the first time was nothing short of awe-inspiring. The way her face lit up and her eyes shone like stars. Christ, it was a breathtaking sight.

Even though she still has a cautious air about her, she seems to be relaxing in my presence.

After I put my ring on her finger, I intended to give her a peck on the lips. All my good intentions flew out the window the moment my mouth touched hers.

The way she held onto me as if she needed me to keep her standing filled me with an overpowering need to protect her with my life.

She let me take the lead, and I get a feeling it's because she's inexperienced. Not that I have a problem with it. Quite the opposite.

Wanting to know precisely what I'm dealing with so I don't push her too hard, I ask, "Have you had a boyfriend before?"

Tiana pulls out of my arms and shakes her head. She takes hold of the railing, her eyes feasting on our surroundings.

"Misha made sure I stayed single throughout my teenage years. He wouldn't allow anyone near me."

A smile curves my lips, knowing I would've done the same if I had a sister.

"Who was your first kiss?"

Her eyes dart to my face before she looks down at the water. "You."

I'm an asshole because my smile grows, and satisfaction pours into my chest.

"Yesterday?" I check to make sure.

Tiana nods, then nervously rambles, "Misha made sure I remain untouched for my wedding day." Her fingers fidget with the railing. "He did everything he could to keep me safe."

I know. Misha told me how he never let Tiana out of his sight while they were in the orphanage. He was scared some fucker would try to rape her, so he guarded her with his life.

To know my friend entrusted his virgin sister to me means a hell of a lot. I'll repay the favor by giving Tiana the world.

Stepping closer to her, I place my hand on the railing, an inch away from hers. Once again, I notice how much smaller than me she is.

I turn my face to her as I promise, "We'll take it slow. If you're not ready to consummate the marriage on our wedding night, I'll wait."

She tugs her bottom lip between her teeth, the sight making desire stir in my blood.

Freeing her lip, she lifts her eyes to mine. Her voice is steady and sure when she says, "I'm ready. I want to consummate our marriage. It's important."

Nodding, I lift my other hand and brush a couple of strands away from her face. "I have a job to do. I'll probably be gone three days at most."

Surprise flutters over her face, but she doesn't argue.

"Viktor wants us to get married as soon as I'm done with the job," I explain.

This time her eyes fill with shock. "So we're getting married in three days?"

"We'll get married on Saturday. I'll make all the arrangements tomorrow morning," I say, hoping it will lessen the blow if she knows I don't expect her to arrange everything.

"Oh wow," she breathes. "A week."

Leaning down to see her face better, I ask, "It will be an intimate wedding. I was thinking we can have it in the courtyard. Just my mom and aunt on my side and Misha, Aurora, and Alek and his parents on your side. Will you be okay with that?"

Tiana nods. "I'm good with whatever you want."

I shake my head. "It's not what I want, *bella*. It's what Viktor ordered. I wish we had more time to get to know each other better."

Her features relax, and she places her hand on my arm as if she's trying to offer me comfort. "I understand. Let me know if there's anything I can do to help with the arrangements."

My eyes search hers. "Are you okay with the wedding happening so soon?"

She nods again. "I am. Please don't worry about me."

"You're mine to worry about." I can't keep the possessiveness I feel for her out of my tone.

Tiana turns to face me, her eyebrows drawing together. "I don't want to be a burden to you, Armani. I want to make your life easier. It's the least I can do to repay you for your kindness."

"I don't expect you to repay me for anything." Resting my palm against the side of her neck, my thumb brushes over the marks that are fading. "And you're not a burden."

My phone beeps, drawing my attention away from Tiana. Pulling the device out of my pocket, I read the encrypted message that's been sent from Luca.

You have a week to complete the task. Don't fail me.

There's a list of names and the amounts they owe to the mafia. I have to collect every last cent.

I browse the nine names and where they live, already planning where I'll start and who'll I'll leave for last.

"Is everything okay?" Tiana asks.

Locking my phone, I tuck the device back into my pocket. "Yes." I nod toward the living room. "Let's get ready for bed."

I lock the doors behind us and switch off the lights as we head to the bedroom.

For the past two nights, I've slept on the couch. Let's just say it wasn't fun. Tonight we're sleeping in the same bed because I need my rest.

"You can use the bathroom first," I say while I plug my phone into the charger next to the bed.

Tiana grabs clothes from the closet along with her toiletry bag and disappears into the bathroom.

Walking into the closet, I look at her collection of clothes to see if she needs anything. She seems to have enough, and as I turn around, my eyes catch on an old shoe box pushed into the corner of the closet.

Don't you fucking dare invade her privacy.

I stare at it for a moment longer before grabbing a pair of sweatpants and heading to the other bathroom.

I'm done showering before Tiana, and placing my loaded gun on the bedside table, I throw the covers back and lie down.

Just as I'm about to pick up my phone, so I can check the list Luca sent me, the bathroom door opens. Tiana comes out wearing a pair of leggings and a plain black T-shirt. It sits tighter than my shirt did, and it's clear she's not wearing a bra.

When I say tight, I mean *tight.*

I can see the outline of her areola and hard nipples, and of course, my cock stands at attention in less than a second.

"Did you shower?" she asks as she places her toiletry bag back in the closet.

"Yes." I point to the bag. "Leave your things in the bathroom."

She does as I say, then walks around the bed to climb beneath the covers. Her eyes dart to me while she keeps a gaping distance between us.

"I don't bite."

She scoots closer, a smile playing around her lips.

I switch off the lamp before turning on my side to face her.

"Are you nervous?"

"No."

A grin spreads over my face. "I'm going to hold you. Don't panic."

"Okay."

While my eyes adjust to the dark, I move closer before slipping my arm beneath her head and pulling her to me. Tiana rests her cheek against my chest, and I feel her hand hover above my waist.

"Get comfortable, *bella*. It would be nice if you held me," I murmur.

Her fingers brush over my side, then she wraps her arm around me, settling her palm in the middle of my back.

"That's better."

She snuggles into my chest, making my smile widen.

She feels good in my arms. As if she was made for me.

"Armani," she whispers.

"Yeah?"

"Is the job you're going to do dangerous?"

Yes.

"No." The lie slips easily over my lips. "It just involves a lot of traveling."

She tilts her head back, and I see her eyes shining. "As long as you're safe."

That's the last thing I'll be, but I'm not about to tell her that. Instead, I close the distance between us and press my mouth against hers.

With every kiss, the possessiveness and protectiveness I feel for this woman keep multiplying inside me.

I can already tell I'm going to be a jealous husband.

Not wanting to risk losing control with her, I don't deepen the kiss.

Trying to take my mind off my desire for her, I ask, "What dreams do you have?"

She snuggles against my chest again, and I can hear the smile in her voice as she answers, "I have three dreams. I've always wanted a home I can call my own, a husband I can love, and children I can give the world to."

My arms tighten around her. "You're missing something."

"What?"

"A husband who loves you."

She's quiet for a moment, then replies, "Being a bratva princess, I've been taught not to expect that."

A frown forms on my forehead. "What else have you been taught."

"Basically, everything that's needed to be a good wife."

Yeah, I'm curious about what *everything* entails. I have a feeling I'm not going to like any of it.

Deciding to leave the conversation for when I get back from the job, I press a kiss to her hair and whisper, "Sweet dreams, *bella*."

"You too."

With her cheek pressed to my chest, I feel her breaths brush over my skin. I focus on the feel of her petite body until I drift off to sleep.

Chapter 19

Tiana

I wake up to Armani's body lying half over mine, his face pressed into my neck, and his arms locked around me.

It's still dark in the room. I wanted to get up early to make coffee and watch the city come to life with him, but I don't dare move a muscle.

Not because I'm scared I'll wake him but because I'm enjoying the moment. This is my first time waking up next to a man, that's not my brother guarding me, and I love it.

If Armani's holding me so tight in his sleep, it means he likes me, right? Maybe he will learn to love me and not just think of me as Misha's little sister that he's stuck with.

And he kissed me three times out of his own free will.

Did I overthink our arrangement and create worries that aren't there?

Armani's arms tighten around me, and his groin presses against the side of my thigh. All my thoughts come to a sudden halt when I feel his hardness. My heart sets off at a crazy pace, my eyes wide open.

Even though I know it's a typical morning reaction for men, my body doesn't seem to care. My abdomen clenches, and heat pools in my core.

My mind runs away with me, and I imagine Armani crawling over my body, and while he kisses me deeply, he makes love to me.

My cheeks flush, and my heart races faster. There's a needy sensation between my legs.

Yeah, I don't think consummating the marriage will be a problem. Not on my part, at least.

He stirs again, and letting out a soft groan, his hardness rubs against my thigh. He pulls an arm back, and his hand lands on my right breast.

Oh, Jesus.

Then he freaking squeezes my breast, and it sends a shockwave of tingles through my body. I gasp from how good it feels while fighting the urge to move.

With my breast firmly in the grip of his hand, I start to tremble, wishing he would squeeze or rub me again.

Instead of getting my wish, his hand travels down to my stomach. I feel his breathing change against my neck and how his body tenses.

Closing my eyes, I pretend to be asleep, which is actually stupid because I'm pretty sure he can feel my racing pulse.

Armani doesn't pull away from me but instead relaxes again. "Morning, *bella*."

My voice sounds hoarse as I whisper, "Morning."

"Did I grope you?"

The direct question has a blush forming on my face. "No."

"Either I had one hell of a good dream, or you're lying."

Wanting to set him at ease, I say, "It's okay if you touch me. We're engaged."

Armani lifts his head, his tousled hair looking dangerously hot first thing in the morning.

I can get used to waking up like this.

His eyes search my face, then the corner of his mouth lifts. "I'll remember that next time."

I begin to wiggle out from under him, saying, "The sun is coming up. I'll prepare coffee quickly." Climbing out of bed, I think to ask, "How do you like your coffee?"

"Sweet like you." A grin spreads over his face as he stretches out. "Two sugars and cream."

Walking out of the bedroom, I feel a burst of happiness in my chest. It's such a rare emotion, it makes my eyes sting with tears.

I find my way to the kitchen in the three-story apartment, and checking all the cupboards, I try to remember where everything is.

Suddenly I pause as another wave of happiness hits. Turning in a circle, I look at the beautiful kitchen. I inhale the new smell of my home.

Home.

A tremble racks hard through me, and I take a quivering breath.

Thank you, God, for answering my prayer.

With a massive smile on my face, I grab two cups from the cupboard. Making coffee was always a routine kind of thing, but this morning, I take extra care. As I'm stirring the warm liquid, strong arms circle my waist, and a kiss is pressed to the side of my neck.

I didn't even hear Armani come into the kitchen.

God, this feels like a dream. If it is, I never want to wake up.

I set the spoon down, then Armani asks, "Which one is mine?"

"The one on the right."

He picks up the cup and takes a sip. My eyes are locked on him as I try to figure out if I made it right.

Armani winks at me. "Perfect."

With my steaming mug of coffee in hand, I follow him to the courtyard and take a seat on one of the benches while he opens the main door leading to the waterfront before coming to sit next to me.

We drink our coffee as the sun starts to rise, and when a gondola passes by our entrance, I say, "Venice feels magical."

"There's no place like it on earth," Armani murmurs. Lifting his arm, he wraps it around my shoulders. "It's cold."

I set my cup down on the floor, and darting back up the stairs, I rush to the bedroom and grab the covers off the bed. When I get back to the courtyard, Armani lets out a chuckle.

We snuggle under the covers, and I lean against his side, my coffee forgotten.

Thank you, Misha. You chose such an amazing man for me.

I don't know how much time passes before Armani lets out a sigh. "We need to get ready for the day. My mother is expecting us for breakfast."

I dart upright. "I'm meeting your mother today?"

Armani picks up my cup and rises to his feet. "Yes, I can't go away for three days and leave you all by yourself."

I gather the bedcovers in my arms and follow Armani back into the apartment with nerves spinning in my stomach.

I hope Mrs. De Santis will like me. Wait, is that even what I should call her?

Just to be sure, I ask, "Do I call your mother Mrs. De Santis?"

Armani places the cups in the sink, then replies, "You'll call her Signora until she tells you otherwise. The same counts for my aunt."

"Signora," I test the word, getting a nod of approval from Armani.

When we return to the bedroom, I quickly place the cover back on the bed and set the pillows in neat rows.

Armani pulls a pair of jeans and a comfy sweater from the closet, grabs the gun from the bedside table, then disappears into the bathroom.

Deciding to wear something similar, I quickly strip out of my leggings and T-shirt and get dressed.

Not knowing whether we'll do a lot of walking today, I put on a pair of comfortable shoes. When I'm ready, and

Armani's still in the bathroom, I head back to the kitchen to wash the cups.

"I'm just going to introduce Tiana to my mother before leaving to take care of the job," I hear Armani say as he comes down the hallway. "Yeah, we had a good night. I gave her an engagement ring."

I stand still in the kitchen, shamelessly listening to his conversation.

"She looks like she's adjusting." There's a pause, then Armani mutters, "Stop worrying, Misha." ... "No, I don't need backup. I have to do this on my own." ... "I'll be fine." ... "You know I can't tell you what the job is. This line isn't secure." ... "Tiana will be fine. Look, I have to go. I'll call if I run into trouble."

Armani lets out a sigh and mutters, "*Cristo*, he's like a mother hen."

He comes into the kitchen and glances at me. "Go get ready."

I rush to the bathroom and hurry through my routine of brushing my teeth and hair. I wash my face and steal a few minutes to put on moisturizer, mascara, and lipstick.

When I walk back into the kitchen, Armani's leaning against a counter while studying something on his phone.

He looks so serious and hot, the sight has a wave of attraction spreading through my abdomen.

"Is everything okay?" I ask.

His head snaps up, and he tucks the phone into his pocket. "Yes, Misha just called to check in on you." He lifts an eyebrow at me. "Ready?"

I nod quickly. "Yes."

Armani comes to take my hand and leads me down to the courtyard. We exit through a different door, and I find myself on a narrow street.

With Armani showing the way, I glance around at all the old buildings.

A door opens, and an old woman sweeps dust out of the house. Her eyes land on us, then a friendly smile spreads over her face. "*Signor* Armani…" I don't make out the rest of her sentence, but I assume she's greeting him.

They exchange words, then Armani says, "My fiancée, Tiana Petrov."

I smile at the woman. "It's nice meeting you."

"She doesn't speak much English," he informs me.

I need to learn their language.

We continue down the narrow street before turning up another and crossing over two bridges.

It really feels like I'm in a fairytale.

Chapter 20

Tiana

Without bothering to knock, Armani lets us into a house, then calls out, "Mamma?"

"*Dio, Dio, Dio*," I hear an excited voice right before a woman comes barreling toward us. "*Cuore mio*."

Armani lets go of my hand and hugs the woman tightly before smiling at me. "Tiana, this is my mother."

I reach a hand out as I say, "It's a pleasure meeting you, *Signora* De Santis."

The next second I'm yanked into a smothering hug, a kiss pressed to both my cheeks. "Tsk, call me Mamma. You'll be my *figlia* by the end of the week."

It's going to take me a while to get used to calling her Mamma, but for Armani, I'll pretty much do anything.

Another woman comes to join us, who Armani introduces to me as *Zia* Giada.

Zia Giada and Mrs. De Santis are like two whirlwinds as we're ushered into a kitchen where the delicious aroma of baking hangs in the air.

I'm pushed down into a chair, then a cappuccino and a croissant with condiments are placed in front of me.

"*Mammamia*," Mrs. De Santis exclaims. "You're so tiny. Eat, *piccola*."

Armani chuckles from where he's sitting next to me while lathering his croissant with jam and cheese.

I do the same, my eyes darting between the two women who seem to be doing a lot and nothing at the same time.

Finally, they come to sit at the table, and as I take a bite, I'm peppered with questions. "Where in Russia are you from? Who are your parents? Have they given their blessing for the wedding? We don't have much time to prepare. Will your mother come help with the arrangements?"

My eyes dart to Armani, and it has him answering, "I'll take care of the wedding preparations once I'm back from work."

Mrs. De Santis' eyes widen like saucers. "Work? You're leaving again? But you just got home!"

Armani shrugs. "When Luca gives an order, I have to carry it out. You know this."

"But…" Mrs. De Santis starts to argue.

Armani shakes his head.

A frown settles on her face, then she mumbles, "Luca could at least give me time with my son before sending him away again."

Armani helps himself to another croissant, and I make a mental note to learn how to make them.

"I have to leave after breakfast. Please check in on Tiana while I'm gone," he says before devouring the pastry.

God, even the way he chews is hot.

Both women nod, and Mrs. De Santis answers, "We'll take good care of her."

Even though I feel out of place, I'm thankful for the warm welcome I'm given.

Mrs. De Santis' eyes settle on me, then she says, "We'll look for a wedding dress while Armani is away at work."

"Thank you." The cappuccino is too sweet, but I drink every last drop.

"Where will the ceremony be held?" Mrs. De Santis asks.

"It will be intimate with only our close loved ones," Armani answers. "We can have it in my place in the courtyard."

"How many people?" Mrs. De Santis demands to know before looking at me. "We'll cook and bake all of Friday."

"Seven," Armani answers. "That's excluding Tiana, me, and whoever's officiating the marriage, but don't worry about cooking, Mamma, I'll book a restaurant for the celebration."

"Oh, okay. I'll speak with Father Moretti," Mrs. De Santis says. "He baptized you, he can marry you."

The moment we're done eating, Armani stands up. "I'm sorry the visit is so short, but I must take care of urgent business."

Mrs. De Santis waves a hand in the air. "You forget I was married to your father for thirty years. I'm used to it."

When *Zia* Giada starts to clear the table, I notice she's been quiet and wonder if she's just as shy as I am.

"Don't get hurt," Mrs. De Santis tells Armani.

"I won't." He hugs his mother and aunt, and I quickly do the same before we leave the house.

The breakfast felt rushed, and I didn't actually get to talk to the women, but I'm sure I'll spend time with them over the next three days.

"I'm sorry the visit was so quick," Armani says as if he's reading my thoughts.

"I understand you have to get to work."

His hand slips into mine, and he gives it a squeeze. "There will be plenty of time for you to get to know my family."

We take a different route home, and soon Armani points out a bakery, a couple of cafés, a deli, and a store where I can get the basics. He also shows me which direction to go to reach a general shopping area.

I'll explore Venice later this afternoon.

When we get home, Armani heads straight for the bedroom, where he takes a black suit from the closet.

Instantly, I turn around and head for the kitchen to give him some privacy.

I open the fridge, and seeing it's practically empty, I take my phone from my pocket to make a shopping list.

I inspect the cupboards again, adding more things to my list. When I'm sure Armani's had enough time to change into the suit, I head back to the bedroom to show him what we need.

The moment I enter the room, my mouth drops open, and my eyes widen. There's an array of weapons on the bed, and Armani's checking a set of knives.

Reality sets in hard and fast, sending a tremor through my body.

He's been so kind to me that I've forgotten he's an enforcer for the mafia. He gets paid to hurt people who owe the mafia money.

He straps on an armored vest with pockets and slits for his guns and knives before he shrugs on his jacket to conceal everything.

And just like that, he's gone from the perfect gentleman to a ruthless mafioso.

When he glances at me, I step closer, clasping my phone in my hands. "I made a shopping list for you to look at."

A frown mars his forehead, then he pulls his wallet out and hands me a black credit card. "Charge anything you need to the card."

I nod, then ask, "What's the monthly amount for food and cleaning supplies?"

"Try to keep the expenses below ten thousand."

My eyebrows draw together. "We're just two people. Our food will never be that much."

Armani comes to stand in front of me, and somehow he feels taller with all the weapons strapped to him.

"The ten thousand is for whatever you need, *bella*. It's yours to spend on anything you want."

I blink a couple of times before his words sink in.

He's giving me an allowance?

I'll never spend that much, but I'm still grateful for the gesture. Standing on my tiptoes, I press a kiss to his cheek, but before I can pull away, his arm wraps around me.

"I'm leaving for three days, *bella*. Say goodbye like you'll actually miss me."

Resting my hands on his shoulders, I push up and press my mouth to his. Armani tilts his head, and when my tongue peeks out, I feel him smile before he takes control and kisses the living hell out of me.

He devours me with so much need it makes my mind cloud over. Our rushing breaths mingle, and an intense longing for more than just a kiss, pools between my legs.

When Armani lifts his head, his eyes are dark with lust, and I think it's safe for me to hope he can love me one day. After all, attraction is the start of love, isn't it?

"I won't be able to call," he says as he lets go of me. "But I should be home in three days. If there's any trouble, call Misha or Alek."

I nod. "Please stay safe." My eyes lock on his. "I really want to marry you on Saturday."

So I'm not forced to marry someone else.

The corner of his mouth lifts. "That's why I'm doing this job. It's my payment to get you as my wife."

What?

Armani kisses my lips once more, then says, "It's time for me to go. I'll see you soon, *bella*."

He grabs a bag off the bed, and I follow him to the courtyard and out the doors, then watch as he climbs into the boat.

When the engine roars to life, Armani takes one last look at me before steering the boat down the waterway.

My eyes follow him until he disappears around a bend.

Keep Armani safe, and bring him back to me.

Chapter 21

Armani

First on the list is Fontana. He's been dealing drugs in Italy for the past year, thinking he could hide his business from the mafia.

Seventy-two hours.

I set the alarm on my phone before driving from Marghera to Bari, that's on the other side of Italy. Fontana deals from a 'Cash and Carry' warehouse where everything is low priced. Except for the drugs, of course. You pay through your ass to get high.

The eight-hour drive is tedious, but when I pull up to the warehouse, I'm alert and ready to start the job.

I put the car in park and dig the machine gun out of my bag of toys. Climbing out of the vehicle, I pull the weapon's strap over my shoulder before putting on my jacket so it's concealed.

Walking toward the back door, because it's eight at night and the place is closed to the public, I lift my chin to the two guards, playing a game of cards.

"Is Fontana here?" I ask.

The one guard stands up, a frown forming on his face. "Who's asking?"

"De Santis."

"Never heard of you," he mutters. "We only open at ten. Fuck off."

He sits down again, grumbling as he picks up his hand of cards.

"That's okay," I chuckle. "Soon, everyone will know the name."

Pulling two K-Bars out of my armored vest, I roll my shoulders as I walk closer.

Both guards jump up, their chairs falling backward. "You're dead," the bigger one growls as he stomps toward me.

When he takes a swing at me, I duck and plunge one of the knives into his armpit. Ripping the weapon out, I move quickly, slitting his neck open from ear to ear.

"Motherfucker," the smaller one shouts as he yanks his gun from where it's tucked into his pants.

I throw my knife before he can get his finger on the trigger, burying the blade in his left eye.

Stalking to the fucker, I crouch over him and pull the knife out. I wipe it clean on his shirt, then get up and kick a metal door open. It shudders on its hinges.

Holding the knives ready, I move into the back of the warehouse.

I see people packing drugs into small bags on the other side of the building. I keep walking as if I don't have a care in the world, but instead, I'm ready for an attack.

When I near an office, lights from the windows shining into the main part of the warehouse, I hear someone say, "We had good sales this month."

I appear in the doorway and watch as four men count stacks of cash. Fontana is sitting behind a desk, reading something on his laptop.

"I'm here to collect what you owe Luca Cotroni."

My voice sends shockwaves through the office. Fontana is the first to move, rising from his chair.

When one of the four jumps up, I throw my knife into his chest. I twirl the remaining knife between my fingers as I step into the small space.

"You've been trading in Cotroni's area for eight months without paying a dime."

Fontana starts to laugh as if I told him the joke of the century while the other three men take fighting stances.

I throw my other knife, hitting Fontana in the shoulder while swinging my machine gun up and firing several shots.

"*Gesù Cristo*," Fontana shouts, shock and fear bleeding over his face.

The three bodies drop to the floor, and shaking my head, I give Fontana a bored look as he rips the blade out of his shoulder.

"Fucker," he hisses.

Lowering the machine gun, I step out of the office and shout to the people packing drugs. "Unless you want to fucking die, get your asses out of here in the next minute."

I keep an eye on Fontana, who's glaring at me, while the packers run toward the entrance.

Kicking the office door shut behind me, I turn my full attention on Fontana. "I have to admit, I'm disappointed. I expected more action." I walk closer to the desk that's between us. "How the fuck do you run a drug business with only six men guarding the stock?"

"How did you find out where I work from?"

Chuckling, I move closer. "Did you really think you could trade in Italy and the mafia wouldn't know?"

He doesn't answer me but just continues to glare at me.

Letting out a sigh, I say, "You will pay twenty percent of your gross profit to an account at St. Monarchs. Don't miss a payment, because if I have to come back, I will take a pound of flesh for every cent owed."

In other words, you'll be nothing but a pool of blood once I'm done with you.

I pull the black card with the account number from my pocket and drop it on the desk. "You've made a gross profit of fifty-nine million euros over the past eight months. Transfer eleven-million-eight-hundred."

There's a stubborn light in Fontana's eyes as he tries to stare me down. Not having any time to waste, I pull my Glock from behind my back and shoot the fucker in the left knee.

He drops to the floor with a cry, then a string of curses rattles from him. "Fucker. MotherFUCKER."

"Transfer the money or lose your right knee, as well."

He struggles to climb up so he can sit on his chair and makes the transfer.

Taking my phone from my pocket, I wait for the message to come through from St. Monarch's, letting me know the funds have been paid to Luca's account.

€11800000-00 DEPOSIT RECEIVED

A smile curves my lips as I say, "It was good doing business with you."

I collect my knife from the floor and the other from the dead guy's chest, then leave the office.

Fontana's curses and fit of rage fade behind me as I leave the building and head to my car.

One down. Eight to go.

Fontana was the easiest of the nine. He's still learning the trade.

Prodi, whom I'm keeping for last, will be a fucking nightmare.

But Tiana is worth every drop of blood I'll spill, and once I'm done with this job, every fucker in Italy will know the name De Santis.

Chapter 22

Tiana

The house feels empty without Armani.

Wow, I've become used to having him around in such a short space of time.

If I'm honest with myself, I think I'm already in love with him.

Maybe it was love at first sight, the weekend of Misha's wedding?

While I check the shopping list again to make sure I left nothing out, I think about the kisses we've shared. I'm starting to believe I might've read the situation wrong because Armani wouldn't kiss me like that if he weren't attracted to me. Right?

I'm lost in my thoughts, reliving how it felt to be in his arms. Kissing him always leaves me in a daze. A happy one.

Not once has he manhandled me, but instead, he treats me like I'm a treasure he has to safeguard.

A frown forms on my forehead.

Were all the things Mrs. Aslanhov taught me wrong?

The Aslanhovs' marriage was the only example I had, so I believed everything I was shown and told.

Armani has not once been annoyed with me. Although I've only seen him angry maybe twice or three times, he never took it out on me.

The man is perfect – everything I could wish for.

"*Piccola*," I hear Mrs. De Santis call from the direction of the courtyard. "Tiana?"

I open the door and smile when Mrs. De Santis and *Zia* Giada come up the steps. "Hi."

"Our meeting at breakfast was so short," she mutters with a frown on her face. "We didn't even get to talk."

They come inside and head straight for the kitchen. "We'll have coffee, *piccola*."

I rush after them and quickly take cups from the cupboard. "How do you like your coffee?"

"Sweet and creamy," Mrs. De Santis answers.

Just how Armani likes his.

While I'm preparing three coffees, I say, "Thank you for breakfast this morning. Armani seems to love croissants. I want to learn how to bake them."

Mrs. De Santis smiles widely. "I'll teach you."

I can feel their eyes on me, and as I turn around, *Zia* Giada quickly looks away.

"Armani told me you're sisters?" I comment as I set the cups down on the table.

"I'm the oldest. Giada has always been shy. Don't worry if she doesn't say anything. I talk enough for both of us."

My smile widens. "I was just about to go out and search for the grocery store to get a couple of things. The kitchen is empty."

Mrs. De Santis takes a sip of her coffee, then gives me a nod of approval. "I'll also teach you to make a good cappuccino. We'll drink our coffee, then go with you to the store."

I let out a sigh of relief. "Thank you. I wasn't sure I'd be able to find it again. There are so many alleys and bridges."

Mrs. De Santis sets her cup down, then pins me with a curious gaze. "Tell me about yourself, *piccola*."

"Ah…you asked earlier about my parents," I reply, feeling a little nervous. "My brother and I were in an orphanage until I was eight. Mr. and Mrs. Aslanhov took us in. That's how we came to be raised in the bratva."

"*Dio*, so you have no other family besides Misha?"

I nod. "He's a wonderful brother."

She reaches across the table and pats my hand. "Well, now you have us, too." A smile tugs at her lips. "And hopefully soon, God willing, you and Armani will have many children."

"From your lips to God's ears," *Zia* Giade murmurs, signing the cross over her chest.

Mrs. De Santis stands up, then says, "Let's go shopping and fill the cupboards. Armani will be hungry when he returns from work."

I make sure I have my phone and the credit card before locking the door behind us.

When we walk down the narrow street, Mrs. De Santis says, "Armani loves *pollo alla cacciatora*. It's braised chicken made with herbs, onions, tomatoes, bell peppers, and wine. I'll show you how to make it so you can prepare it for him once he's home."

"That would be wonderful. Thank you."

Reaching the store, *Zia* Giade grabs a cart and follows us up and down the aisles.

I show Mrs. De Santis the list, and soon we're filling the cart with everything I need, and whatever else she feels I should get.

When we turn into the pasta aisle, Mrs. De Santis gives me a rundown of what dishes each of the pastas are used for.

"I won't remember it all," I say, wishing I had thought to record the lesson so I could listen to it again.

"You'll learn with time," she assures me.

As we continue to shop, she asks, "Did Mrs. Aslanhov teach you how to cook?"

"Yes, and I can bake. She taught me how to be a good wife."

"Hmm…" Mrs. De Santis glances at me. "What did she teach you?"

Damn. I think it's too soon for such a personal topic, but okay.

"She told me to always stay out of my husband's way, especially when he comes home from work. His meals should always be ready." I leave out the bedroom stuff because there's no way I'm telling my mother-in-law-to-be about it.

Mrs. De Santis rolls her eyes. "Tsk. So old-fashioned. Don't stay out of Armani's way. He'll think he did something wrong. He wants to spend time with us when he comes home from work. We're the good in his life and there to balance out the bad he deals with."

I take mental notes of everything.

"He likes to have a tumbler of whiskey and relax before having his dinner. Normally, I'd prepare the meat and wait for him to get home before adding the finishing touches. That way, the aroma hangs in the air to welcome him home."

"Yes, Mamma," I say, eager to learn more.

"When he makes it home before the sun goes down, he likes to take a walk and enjoy *chicchetti* with a glass of wine."

"*Chicchetti*?" I ask.

"They're small bite-size snacks you'll get at market stalls along the streets. Meat, or cheese, or fish on bread. It's a nice way to interact with your neighbors because most of them will be out and about on the streets before dinner."

"That sounds nice."

We approach the cashier and wait in line.

"I don't like fish," *Zia* Giada whispers.

I lean into her. "That makes two of us. It tastes funny."

When she smiles at me, it feels as if I'm given a miracle.

After we've paid for everything, we all grab bags and make our way home. The atmosphere is pleasant, and my nerves from earlier are long gone.

I'm going to love living here with Armani.

As the thought pops into my mind, I wonder if he's okay. It's only been five hours since he left, and I already miss him.

Ugh, it's going to be a long three days.

Chapter 23

Armani

I've worked my way from Bari, to Naples, to Rome, to fucking Florence. Finally, I find myself in Bologna, where Prodi lives.

I'm fucking exhausted, but I've managed to recover over ninety-eight million euros for Luca.

Now for the biggest problem.

Ignazio Prodi was a member of the mafia for over thirty years. When shit went down with the Aslanhovs, Alek killed Prodi's eldest son.

Since then, Prodi refuses to work with the mafia because of the brotherly bond Luca has with Viktor. He despises the mafia and bratva working together.

Luca gave Prodi three years to mourn, and his time is officially up.

This is the impossible task I was given. Not the other eight men. They were all child's play compared to Ignazio Prodi.

Honestly, I don't see Prodi bending the knee. Today will end in bloodshed.

Sitting in the car, I brace myself for the battle.

You can't think of the shit they did to Alek. This is not personal. Force Prodi to pay what he owes or kill him and make his youngest son, Lorenzo, pay what's owed to the mafia.

That's it. Get in, get the money, and get out.

If only it were that easy.

Tiana's waiting for you. You're getting married to a fucking angel. Do this for her.

I take a deep breath and look at the villa ahead that sits in a cul-de-sac.

Do this, and prove your worth to Luca.

Getting out of the car, I leave every weapon I own behind and walk toward the imposing gates. I lift my arms to show I'm unarmed, wearing only my clothes and the bulletproof vest that won't do shit if they shoot me in the head.

The gates swing open, and I count three guards at the guardhouse. One walks toward me, and I stop so he can search me.

"Armani De Santis on behalf of Luca Cotroni for *Signor* Prodi," I mutter as his hands pat over my body.

He announces my arrival via a two-way radio and, a moment later, nods. "You'll be received at the front door."

"*Grazie.*" I proceed to walk up the driveway, constantly glancing around and counting how many men there are on the property.

Eight in the front yard.

Probably eight at the back and two of his best men in the house.

Twenty at most.

My mind stills, and an eerie calmness washes over me.

If you take out Prodi, you'll have to deal with the men in the house and the eight at the front as you make your escape.

I'll have to try and reason with the stubborn old fuck.

The front door stands open, a guard waiting to receive me. In a split second, I take in his machine gun, and the Heckler & Koch tucked into the waistband of his pants behind his back.

I step into the foyer, taking note of anything I can use as a weapon while I follow the guard through a sitting room and out onto a veranda.

Ignazio and Lorenzo are sitting at a round, wrought-iron table, enjoying a late lunch.

Ignazio cuts into his *Fiorentina* steak, but instead of taking the bite, his hardened eyes lock on me. "Ahh...*The Reaper*. You know that's what they call you, *Signor* De Santis?"

Lorenzo glances at me, and I notice how the guard, who let me in, positions himself near Lorenzo.

Where's the other guard? There can't just be the one.

Just as I think the question, another guard steps out of the house. He has the same weapons as the one standing by Lorenzo.

"I wasn't aware," I answer Ignazio.

"Your reputation precedes you. The whole of Italy is wondering where you'll pop up next." Ignazio lets out a chuckle. "My phone's been ringing non-stop the past two days. I hear men are paying the mafia in fear they might be next on your list." He takes the bite of meat and slowly chews while gesturing at the open seat.

"*Grazie,*" I murmur as I make myself comfortable. When a server rushes closer, I wave a hand. "Nothing for me. I can't stay long."

"You're getting right down to business," Ignazio mutters. "I hear you're marrying a bratva bitch."

Anger ignites in my chest, but I keep it restrained. The atmosphere tenses, and the one guard shifts on his feet.

"Your intel is wrong."

Ignazio's eyebrow lifts. "You're not getting married?"

"I am." My eyes are locked with his in a wordless battle. "To a bratva princess."

His top lip curls in disgust. "The mafia isn't what it used to be when Lucian Cotroni was in charge."

Loyal until death, I mutter, "Luca has made his father proud by expanding our territories."

"Hmphf," he snorts. "It's unnatural. The mafia and bratva can't co-exist." His eyes narrow on me. "I also hear you're friends with the fucker who killed my son."

Here we go.

Not commenting about Alek, I say, "Luca's given you three years to mourn. It's time to come back into the fold."

Ignazio slams his steak knife down on the table in a fit of anger. My eyes only touch on the weapon for a second before I hold his enraged gaze.

"Over my dead body will I pay a cent to the mafia as long as they're tied to the fucking bratva rats! Are you all fucking blind or just stupid? You're letting the enemy take over everything we bled for."

As Ignazio rages, I see Tiana's face in my mind's eye.

Her expressiveness. The wonder in her eyes every time I kissed her. The flush of her cheeks. Her shyness. How fucking grateful she is for everything.

The way she looks at me as if I'm an answer to all her prayers.

Tesoro mia.

In a heartbeat, I survey the backyard.

Five guards. The two standing by us and the eight at the front.

Fifteen men besides Ignazio and Lorenzo.

My eyes flick to Lorenzo, who looks wary and subdued. He's never been Ignazio's favorite son because he's gay, and Prodi considers him weak, which I think is fucking stupid.

Lorenzo is the calm one in the family and doesn't make any rash decisions.

My eyes swing back to Ignazio as he rages, "You're all fucking traitors! I'll kill that fucking scum who took Riccardo's life, and then I'll make Lorenzo fuck your bratva whore until he learns the value of a pussy. I'll make her brother watch–"

Rage explodes behind my eyes, all my control vanishes, and I grab the steak knife and plunge it rapidly into

Ignazio's neck. Five times the blade tears through his skin, and his blood spurts like a fountain over the floor and table.

My hands and sleeves are soaked in Ignazio's blood as I grab Lorenzo, yanking him to his feet to use him as a shield.

"Wait!" the main guard shouts, his Heckler & Koch trained on us. "Don't kill him. Let's talk."

I press the blade's tip to Lorenzo's neck, and seeing a flash of panic in his guard's eyes, my lips curve up. "Unless you want your lover's blood pooling at your feet, I suggest you lower your weapon."

He places his weapon on the table where Ignazio's head is slumped, his last breath exhaled without us noticing.

With my mouth by Lorenzo's ear, I say, "You're the only Prodi alive, Lorenzo. Will you take over the business and pay Luca what he's owed?"

His words are strained and rushed. "Yes. I'll pledge my loyalty to the mafia."

My eyes touch on every guard, but my main concern is Lorenzo's lover.

"Call off your guard dog," I order.

Lorenzo holds up a trembling arm. "Stand down, Santino."

Santino's eyes are locked on me, rage burning deep in his gaze. He visibly relaxes, and when I push Lorenzo toward him, he catches him.

With my knife in my right hand, I watch as Santino pulls Lorenzo behind his body to shield him.

"Make the payment of one hundred million euros so I can leave," I instruct.

Every muscle in my body is wound tight.

As Lorenzo digs his phone out of his pocket, the other guard's finger slowly inches toward the trigger. Before he can take another breath, I lunge at him. He blocks my first blow, but I catch him with a punch to his gut from my left fist.

"Stop!" Lorenzo cries.

Before his cry is cold, the blade of the steak knife is plunged beneath the guard's ribs, digging deep into his chest.

His blood warms my hand as I watch the life drain from his eyes. Within another heartbeat, I spin around and block the attack from Santino.

Our feet move fast and the blows are even faster as we face off.

Fuck, he's good.

I manage to slice his side, and it has Lorenzo shrieking, "*Dio! Dio!* Stop!"

Santino grabs hold of my wrist, and a power struggle for the knife ensues. For a breathless moment, he manages to turn the blade toward me. Using all my strength against the man, I turn the tables on him, and as the blade touches the spot beneath his ear, Lorenzo screams, "Stop! Don't kill him. I've transferred the money. I swear loyalty. Don't kill him!"

I shove Santino away from me, but he quickly regains his balance. As we glare at each other, Lorenzo darts between us and presses his back to Santino's chest. "I've made the payment. There will be no more killing. Please."

My phone vibrates in my pocket. Breathless from the altercation, I don't take my eyes off Santino as I pull the device out of my pocket. I give the man a look of warning before checking the text.

€100000000-00 DEPOSIT RECEIVED

JOB COMPLETED

Instantly my phone starts to ring, and seeing Luca's name flashing on the screen, I answer. "It's done, sir."

"I noticed. How did you make Prodi pay so quickly?"

"Ignazio is dead. Lorenzo is now in charge, and he's sworn loyalty to you."

There's a moment's silence then Luca murmurs, "It's a pity there couldn't be another outcome. Ignazio will be missed."

I seriously doubt that.

"Give my condolences to Lorenzo and tell him I'll be in touch."

"Yes, sir."

"I'm proud of you, Armani. You've done the impossible."

"Thank you, sir."

Santino gives me an impatient look and jerks his chin toward the front door, signaling for me to get a move on and leave.

"Take two weeks off for your wedding," Luca continues, not knowing how volatile the situation is that I find myself in. "I won't be able to attend the happy celebration, but you'll receive my wedding gift soon. When you return to work, you'll report to Franco Vitale."

"Thank you, sir."

The call ends, and as I tuck the device back into my pocket, I say, "Luca will be in touch." I gesture to the living room. "If I don't make it off the property alive, the Prodi bloodline will be wiped from the face of the planet."

"Make sure *Signor* De Santis is not harmed as he leaves," Lorenzo orders.

If it weren't for the relationship between Santino and Lorenzo, things would've gone down a bloody path. Fuck, that was a lucky break.

"My condolences for your loss," I mutter as I check where every guard is before walking back into the house. The handle of the knife is sticky from the blood that's starting to dry.

As I exit the front door, I pause by a fountain, dropping the knife into the water and rinsing my hands.

Every guard watches me like a hawk as I walk down the driveway. The gates open, and only when I leave the property do I take a deep breath.

The cut on my arm I got from La Russa, who was number six on my list, starts to burn. My bloody clothes make my skin itch.

Exhaustion sinks into my bones from the insane three days I've had.

I climb into the car and let out a sigh.

It is done. Tiana is mine.

Chapter 24

Tiana

I've been alternating between the kitchen and sitting in the courtyard all day long. It's almost midnight, and there's no sign of Armani.

There were many times I almost messaged him, just to check if he's okay, but decided against it because I don't want it to look like I'm nagging him.

God, Armani. Where are you? It's been three days.

Technically it will only be three days tomorrow morning, but I'm anxious to see him.

I got up early this morning and chose a pretty pink dress to wear. I braided my hair and put on makeup. I wanted to look pretty for Armani.

With a heavy sigh, I pick up my empty cup and get up from the bench. Heading to the kitchen, I boil water to make myself tea.

Please, let him be okay.

I've loved the past three days, getting to know where everything is in the apartment and visiting with Mrs. De Santis, who I really have to start thinking of as mamma, and *Zia* Giada, who's coming out of her shell.

I explored a nearby square and had an expresso at a café. I saw a seagull steal a pastry right out of a woman's hand. It was funny, and when laughter bubbled from me, I was shocked.

Before that moment, I can't remember when I last laughed.

Picking up the cup of tea, I turn around. A startled shriek escapes me when I see Armani standing in the doorway. The cup falls to the floor, shattering at my feet, the warm liquid splashing over my bare feet.

My God.

He's dressed in the same clothes he left in, only there's blood. *So much blood.*

Intense worry pours through my body, but the dark and murderous expression on his face keeps me rooted to the spot.

"Why is the door open?" the words rumble from him like thunder.

Crap.

Seeing Armani covered in blood, looking at me like I'm his next victim, fear tightens my muscles and sends a tremble through me.

Jesus, he's a terrifying sight.

There's a tremor in my voice as I say, "I was waiting for you in the courtyard. I wanted to welcome you home."

His hands fist at his sides as he takes a calculating step toward me.

There's no sign of the man I got to know. No calm and patient expression. No tenderness.

"I'm sorry," the words rush from me. "I won't–"

My sentence is cut off when he growls again. Intense fear paralyzes me as he stalks toward me, his large steps eating up the short distance.

Armani lifts his arm, and my heart shrivels as I recoil, turning my face away and bracing for the pain.

Instead of hitting me, his fingers grip my chin right before his mouth crashes against mine.

My mind and panic come to a screeching halt.

I hear the pieces of the mug being crushed beneath his shoes, then he presses his body to mine, tilts his head, and thrusts his tongue into my mouth.

He licks the inside of my mouth and bites my lips, the kiss filled with so much passion I can't catch my breath.

My hands grip hold of his biceps, and I feel his muscles strain as if it's taking all his strength to keep from devouring me.

The fear fades and is quickly replaced with desire for this man who's both a saint and a monster.

His mouth frees mine, only to set my skin on fire with scorching kisses as he works his way down my neck.

"You're mine." The words are rough and demanding.

He's completed the job, and I'm his prize.

"I'm yours," I breathe, my eyes drifting shut when he sucks on the sensitive skin beneath my ear.

Sweet Jesus, that feels good.

My abdomen clenches hard, and a shudder ripples through me.

Suddenly Armani's strong arm wraps around me, and I'm lifted against his body as if I weigh nothing to him. I'm carried into the hallway, where he presses my back to a wall.

Grabbing hold of my dress, he yanks the fabric up and pulls it over my head.

Instantly I feel shy, and when I try to cross my arms over my naked breasts, he takes hold of my wrists and pins them to the wall, leaving me exposed to his eyes that are nothing more than dark pools of lust.

He lets go of my arms, and a gasp rushes over my lips when his knuckles skim over my right nipple.

"I can't wait." His voice is strained with need.

"I'm yours," I repeat what I said in the kitchen.

His palm covers my breasts, and he squeezes hard, making tingles erupt over my skin. "That's right, *tesoro mia*. Saying our vows won't change a damn thing. You're mine for life, and only death will part us."

I nod, my tongue darting out to wet my lips.

Armani lowers his body, and kneeling before me, he says, "Your virgin pussy deserves to be worshiped before I claim you." The words sound dark and filthy, filled with promises of ecstasy, which I've never experienced.

Still stunned by Armani being home and him looking like a murderous mafioso, I don't realize what his words mean until he grips my panties and tears them from me.

Okay, this is happening. Don't be awkward.

My left leg is yanked over his shoulder, and before I can gasp, he buries his face between my thighs and sucks my clit so hard it rips a cry from me.

Oh, Jesus.

My hands slap down on his shoulders, my mouth drops open, and my eyes slam shut.

The pleasure is instant and overwhelming as Armani licks and sucks me like a starved man.

"Ar-man-i," I gasp his name, my fingers digging into his shoulders.

His teeth nip at my clit, and when he sucks the living hell out of me, my core clenches hard, my legs go numb, and something explodes within me.

Pleasure overwhelms me, and all I can do is feel.

My emotions spiral out of control from experiencing my first orgasm. I sink to the floor and press my face against the armored vest Armani's still wearing.

I smell blood, sweat, and something so primal I can't name it.

"All your firsts belong to me," Armani whispers before he slips his arms beneath me, lifting me bridal style to his chest as he climbs to his feet.

I wrap my arms around his neck and bury my face against his skin while he carries me to the bedroom.

Shit, I'm minutes away from losing my virginity.

No, not losing. I'm giving it to Armani.

He lowers me to the bed, and with his eyes locked on my body, he rips the armored vest off.

My heart sets off at a wild pace, fluttering against my ribs while I watch him unbutton his blood-stained shirt.

When he rips his belt through the loops of his pants, I pull myself up the bed, my stomach a tight bundle of nerves.

The zipper of his pants goes down, and a second later, the fabric pools by his feet.

My eyes grow double in size as they lock on his manhood.

Mrs. Aslanhov was right about one thing – it's going to hurt. A lot.

Armani places his knee on the covers, and the expression on his face looks predatory and ruthless. He grips my thighs, his fingers digging into my skin and pulling my legs open.

My breaths race over my lips, my pulse fluttering insanely fast.

His palm brushes up my side, over my breast, then his fingers wrap around my throat. His movements are so slow and in total contrast to the storm raging in his eyes.

I feel like I'm being hunted and that he's going to pounce at any moment.

My instincts are right because his body crashes against mine, his mouth latches onto mine, and his hardness strokes up and down my slit.

Holy shit.

With a growl from deep in his chest, he seems to lose the last of his control.

I try to brace myself as best as I can, but nothing in this world could prepare me for what's to come.

The swollen head of his manhood pushes against my opening. Once. Twice. A sharp burn tears through my core as Armani fills me in a single thrust, his pelvis hitting mine.

I grab fistfuls of the covers, and my back arches while my hips try to pull away from the pain. I bite my bottom lip, and my eyebrows draw together as I try not to make a sound.

Armani's palms frame my face, and his mouth brushes against mine. He keeps still, allowing me to adjust to the invasion.

"I'm sorry it hurts," he whispers.

I nod quickly, just focusing on breathing through the ache.

"Open your eyes, *bella*," he orders.

When I do as I'm told, a tear spirals down my temple. Armani catches it with his thumb and presses a soft kiss to my mouth.

His hips swivel against mine. "I can't hold back. I'm sorry."

It's my only warning before he pulls out and plunges back inside me.

His chest presses against mine, and moving his hands down to my hips, he holds me in place. He thrusts again and again, and soon his pace is brutal, every inch of his muscled body rubbing against mine.

The ache changes from sharp to a warm and full sensation. I feel every hard inch of his manhood as he fills me, and I swear he reaches to my navel.

I'm filled with awe that Armani is making love to me.

His eyes lock with mine, and he notices the pain has subsided. Gripping hold of my thighs, he pulls my knees up until they're resting at his sides, giving him complete access to me.

His mouth slams down on mine with a wild kiss while his thrusts turn borderline savage. His pelvis rubs against my clit, and his balls hit the sensitive skin between my opening and my butt.

It's all so overwhelming, and before I know what's happening, there's an impossible tightening in my core.

"Armani," I beg. "Please."

I have no freaking idea what I'm begging for, but he seems to understand the plea. He pushes a hand between us, and the moment his thumb presses against my clit, his manhood hits me deep and hard.

I gasp, my eyes locked on his in desperation.

"Let me hear you," he demands, looking like the god of thunder and destruction. "Give me your moans and cries."

He rubs the living shit out of my clit as he fucks me senseless. Even if I wanted to, I can't keep the whimpers from spilling over my lips.

Dear God.

Sweet Jesus.

Have mercy.

Fuck.

My entire world explodes, my body convulses, and a hoarse cry is ripped from my throat. My back arches, and every muscle in my body is wound tight.

I'm completely powerless as I orgasm for a second time, this one a million times stronger than the first.

Armani fucks me right through my orgasm before his body jerks against mine and heat fills me.

"*Cazzo.*" He groans as if he's in pain, his forehead falling to my shoulder. "*Madre di Dio.*"

He jerks inside me twice more before he slumps down, squashing me into the mattress.

The full weight of his body feels comforting and warm, and I find I like it very much.

Chapter 25

Armani

My muscles relax, and I finally regain control over my emotions.

I fucked Tiana out of pure need. There was no stopping to think about what I was doing. There was only the relentless desire to bury myself inside her.

Lifting my head, I meet her eyes. "Are you okay?"

I'm filthy, covered in blood and sweat. I fucking ate her pussy like a starved animal and took her virginity brutally.

There's no way she's okay.

But there are no silent tears as she stares at me with wonder in her sky-blue eyes. "I'm okay." She brings her hand to my jaw and brushes her fingers through the stubble. "You looked very upset when you got home. Do you feel better?"

I scared the shit out of her, but the moment I laid eyes on her in that sexy as fuck dress, her legs and cleavage on full display, I lost the meager grip I had on my control.

I tortured and killed for her, and nothing was going to stop me from taking what's mine.

"I'm calm again." I press a tender kiss to her mouth. "Does it hurt?"

I'm still buried deep inside her, not ready to pull out of her tight pussy.

"No, the pain faded," she whispers, her gaze still holding a world of awe.

The bastard in me asks, "Did you enjoy it, *bella*?"

Her cheeks flush pink as she nods.

I pull out an inch before burying myself to the hilt inside her again.

Christ, she's so fucking tight and wet for me.

Tiana's lips part in a gasp, the flush on her cheeks deepening.

"Did you like it when I fucked you?" I rasp, my desire igniting and threatening to strip me of control once more.

Tiana nods again, her demeanor shy and vulnerable. Having this innocent angel beneath me is fucking intoxicating.

I want to brutalize her pussy with my cock so she'll feel me inside her every second of every hour of every fucking day.

I want her to be reminded of who she belongs to when she sits down, when she walks, and even when she's asleep.

Bracing my upper body on my forearm, I cup her breast, watching her reaction as I squeeze and massage her nipple into a hard pebble.

Her pussy contracts around my cock, her body telling me she loves my touch.

I pull out until just the tip remains inside her before plunging back into her wet warmth.

"So fucking good," I groan, the ghost of my orgasm tingling in my balls. "*Cazzo, bella.* Your pussy was made for me."

Tiana's hands find my biceps, and her nails dig into my skin as she lifts her head to pepper kisses along my jaw and neck.

It's the first time she's reciprocating, making my desire burn hotter.

"I've never felt anything like this before," she whispers near my ear. "I can feel every inch of you inside me."

I grind my pelvis against hers, watching as pleasure tightens her features.

"It feels so good," she moans.

"Keep moaning, *bella*," I order. "Let me hear how much you love my cock."

Slowly I pick up my pace, this time fucking Tiana for her enjoyment and not mine.

A sheen of sweat sparkles like diamonds on her pale skin. Her breaths come faster with every thrust.

Lowering my head to her breast, I suck her nipple, my hand feasting on her petite body as my palm slides down to her clit.

Between thrusts, I brush my thumb over her sensitive bundle of nerves, my tongue and teeth devouring her breasts.

"Armani," she whimpers right before her hips start to gyrate.

I slam into her then keep still, allowing her to grind her needy pussy against me.

Lifting my head, I watch her face, taking in how flushed she is and the unadulterated desire brightening her eyes.

She lets me hear every moan and whimper, and as her body tenses, I unleash myself on her, fucking her relentlessly until her cries of ecstasy fill the air.

Once more, I come inside her, all my strength draining from my body as I slump down on her.

I love that she's caged beneath me, unable to get free unless I allow it.

Even though I'm breathless and she's gasping for air, my mouth finds hers. I kiss Tiana as if she's my beginning and my end.

I kiss her like a man who will sacrifice everything for her.

When I finally lift my head, there are silent tears spiraling from her eyes.

Before I can ask what's wrong, she says, "I prayed for you."

A smile curves my lips. "You don't have to worry when I'm at work. I'll always come home."

God willing.

She shakes her head. "No. I mean, I prayed for a man like you. Someone who won't hurt me, who'd give me a home and allow me to love him." Her fingers brush over my shoulder. "You're the answer to my prayers."

My heart swells double its size with affection for her.

I take hold of her wrist, and bringing her hand to my mouth, I kiss her fingers, then chuckle, "Jesus, I'm falling so hard for you."

Surprise flutters over her face. "You don't see me as Misha's little sister you're stuck with?"

I grind my pelvis against hers. "Baby, your pussy is the only place I'm stuck in. I might stay buried inside you until the sun rises."

She grins up at me. "I'm okay with that."

"But I'm in desperate need of a shower and hungry as fuck," I groan as I pull out of her. I press a kiss to her breast, then push my body off of hers.

Glancing down, I see the red tinge of blood coating my cock. Braced over Tiana, I lock eyes with her and say, "Thank you for bleeding on my cock, *bella*. I'll treasure your virginity."

Her eyes widen, and I misread her reaction as shyness, but then she darts up into a sitting position and grabs hold of my forearm. "You got hurt!"

I look at the cut that's crusted with blood and shrug. "It's nothing, *bella*."

"Nothing, my ass," she mutters as she scrambles off the bed. I get a good look at her sexy ass before she darts into the bathroom.

Cute.

Getting up, I join her, and while she's wetting a facecloth, I turn on the faucets in the shower. She moves closer, and as gently as possible, she tries to wipe the blood off. I almost tell her not to worry but decide against it because I love her fussing over me.

Looking down at her, I admire her flawless beauty and fall harder for her. My eyes drift over her naked body, drinking in the sight of her firm breasts, soft stomach, and the perfect V between her legs.

Taking hold of her slender arm, I tug her into the shower and push her back against the tiles. Tiana's eyes dart to my face. "I'm not done cleaning your wound."

I crowd her body with mine and lean down until there's only an inch between our faces. My voice is low and deep as I say, "Forget about the cut. I want to admire every inch of your sexy as fuck body."

Her eyes dart over my face. "You think I'm sexy?"

"I know," I hum as I lean closer. I brush my hands over her breasts and down to her narrow waist before moving back up again. "Jesus, *bella*. I hope you got a lot of sleep while I was gone because I'm going to fuck you until I pass out."

A breathtaking smile spreads over her face. "I like that I have this effect on you." She places her palms on my chest and starts to explore my body.

There's a flash of nervousness on her face when she reaches my semi-hard cock. Her eyes flick to mine before lowering back to my pelvic area, then her fingers wrap around my girth.

Tiana looks fascinated with my cock as she slowly strokes it, and when I grow hard in her hand, she says, "You feel like velvet stretched over steel." Again her eyes dart to my face. "Is it okay that I'm touching you?"

"A little late to ask, don't you think?" I tease.

Before she can pull away, I cover her hand with mine. "Don't you dare stop. You're going to finish what you started, *bella*." I tighten my hand around hers, then order, "Grip me hard and stroke faster."

Her other hand settles on my side as she carries out the instruction like a pro.

"Yes, baby," I groan. "Rub your thumb over the head." My body shudders from the pleasure. "Yeah, like that." I move her hand from my hip to my ass. "Dig your nails into my skin." Our breaths speed up as I start to thrust into her fist. She grips my asscheek tightly, and leaning forward, she sucks and bites my nipple.

"*Cazzo*," I hiss, thrusting faster. "I'm close. Squeeze harder. I like it rough."

She fucking strangles my cock, and with a look of power in her eyes, she says, "Come for me, *moya lyubov'*."

Never has an order sounded hotter. With a grunt, I pound into her fist. I keep my eyes locked with hers as my release hits her hand and stomach in streaks.

"You're fucking perfect, Tiana," I say before I claim her mouth with a thankful kiss.

I don't know what I did to deserve her, but I'll treasure her forever.

Chapter 26

Tiana

There are no words to describe how happy I am, and there's not a single doubt in my mind that Armani is attracted to me.

We only fell asleep in the early morning hours and woke in time for lunch.

I can't stop looking at him or smiling as I make *pollo alla cacciatora* for him.

He's sitting at the kitchen table, watching as I work. "That smells familiar."

"Mamma taught me how to make your favorite dish," I admit with a sneaky grin.

"Hmm." Getting up, he comes to stand behind me and wraps his arms around me. "Was she here every day?"

"Yes. They helped me get the shopping done and showed me around Venice. I had a lot of fun with them."

Mamma said she saw the perfect dress for me and will bring it by for a fitting. It's crazy how quickly everything is happening. I'm marrying Armani in two days.

"I'm happy to hear that," he says.

He kisses the side of my neck, and my chest explodes with warmth.

"My heart is going to burst," I admit as I leave the food to simmer on the stove. I turn around in his arms to face him. "I never thought I'd be this happy."

Armani's mouth lifts with an affectionate smile. "I wish I could change your past." When he sees the question on my face, he explains, "Misha told me everything about your time in the orphanage."

"Oh." I scrunch my nose. "It doesn't matter anymore. It's a long time ago."

"Still, I want you to know I'm here if you ever need to talk about it."

I push myself up on my tiptoes and give him a quick kiss. "Thank you, Armani."

His phone starts to ring, and as he pulls it from his pocket, he sits at the table again. "It's Misha. I'll put him on speaker so you can say hello."

Armani answers, "Hey, brother."

"You're one badass motherfucker. I hear you've been nicknamed *The Reaper*. Apparently, half of Italy shat themselves and paid up. Did you really cut off Sibilia's hand? Brutal man."

Jesus.

Part of me wants to know what Armani does as an enforcer, but then I think I'd rather not know.

"Tiana's listening," Armani snaps. "Say hello to your sister, fuck-face."

"Shit, sorry, Tiana," Misha chuckles. "Did you hear how awesome your man was?"

"You just told me," I answer. "Before I forget, you need to be here first thing Saturday morning. Don't be late."

"I wouldn't miss your special day for the world," Misha replies. "So, Armani, did you really get a promotion?"

Armani chuckles. "You seem to know more than I do."

"I heard you have to report to Franco." Misha is quiet for a moment, then says, "Alek is here. I have you on speaker."

"Thank you, brother," Alek says, his tone tight with emotion. "I owe you."

Owe him? For what?

"You don't owe me shit," Armani replies. "It was long overdue."

I take the food off the stove, and grabbing two plates, I dish up for us.

"Lunch is ready," Armani informs them. "I'll see you on Saturday."

He sets his phone down on the table, and when I place a plate in front of him, he murmurs, "Thank you, *bella*. It looks delicious."

I take a seat across from him and watch as he takes a bite. "Careful, it's hot."

With a smile stretched over his face, he swallows. "It tastes exactly like my mamma's cooking. You're a quick learner."

Beaming from the compliment, I dig into my food.

We eat in silence for a couple of minutes before I ask, "What did Alek thank you for?"

He stares at me for a moment before answering, "I killed Ignazio Prodi."

Shock waves spread through me, not because Armani killed someone, but because I know the name. Prodi's son is responsible for all the heartache the Aslanhovs suffered.

"I'm glad he's dead." My eyes lock with Armani's. "You rid the world of a monster."

"It takes one to kill one," he mutters before having another bite of his meal.

"I've met plenty of monsters in my life, but you're not one of them."

His gaze lifts to mine. "I kill and torture people for a living."

"I know." I twirl my fork in my food. "But you don't prey on the innocent." I scoop up some braised chicken. "Trust me, Armani. You're the farthest thing from a monster there is."

I'm rewarded with a smile from him before he finishes the rest of his food.

Just as I place the empty plates in the sink, we hear Mamma call, "*Piccola*. I found it!"

She barrels into the kitchen with a wedding dress hanging over her arm. Seeing Armani, she shrieks, "Turn around. You're not allowed to see the dress!"

I hurry to take the dress from her and carry it to a guest room.

"Why haven't you told me you're back?" Mamma scolds him.

"I haven't had a chance yet. Come here and let me hug you."

I chuckle as I hear her grumble something before I dart into the room and lay the dress out on the bed. My eyes drift over the white lace, and picking it up again, I hold it in front of me.

Gosh, it's pretty.

There are no frills. It looks like a dress you'd wear to run through wildflowers.

I love it.

"What do you think?" Mamma asks as she comes into the room. She shuts the door. "Put it on so we can see whether I have to adjust it."

"It's so pretty, Mamma," I say as I take off my leggings and shirt. I feel a little self-conscious and quickly pull the dress over my head.

It falls to my ankles, and I wish there were a full-length mirror so I could see what I look like in the dress.

"Oh," Mamma gasps. "You look beautiful, *piccola*." She comes closer to fuss with the fabric around my waist. "I should bring it in an inch. It will sit better."

"Okay." A smile spreads over my face. "Can you take a photo of me so I can see what it looks like?"

"Of course." Mamma takes her phone out and grins at me. "Smile, *piccola*."

I let my happiness show as she takes the photo and rush closer to her to see.

My heart.

My face is beaming, my eyes alight with sparks of bliss. The dress makes me look carefree.

"I love it so much. Thank you, Mamma."

I pull her into a hug, and when her motherly arms engulf me, emotion wells in my chest.

"I'm so happy," I admit to her. "Thank you for accepting me into your family."

"Hush, *piccola*. You're going to make me cry," she sniffles. Her hand brushes over my hair and back. "Make my son happy, and I promise not to be a mother-in-law who nags you all day."

I let out a sputter of laughter as I pull back. "It's a deal."

Lifting her hand to my face, she tucks a couple of loose strands behind my ear. "And give me grandbabies."

"I will."

God-willing.

Chapter 27

Tiana

I'm getting married to Armani De Santis.

Sitting on Mamma's balcony with a cup of coffee, I stare at the dimly lit street.

It's two am. I'm too excited to sleep.

Misha and Aurora will be here at nine, and the Aslanhovs will arrive in time for the ceremony that's taking place at one this afternoon.

I'm getting married.

To an amazing man.

Mamma insisted that I sleep at her house. The groom and bride cannot see each other the night before the wedding. Armani protested but gave in when Mamma threatened to slap him upside the head.

I suppress a chuckle.

"Tiana," I hear a whisper from the street below.

Setting my cup down on the little table, I get up and peek over the railing. I see Armani looking up at me as if we're reenacting a scene from Romeo and Juliet.

Smiling, I wave at him. "Hi."

"Stand back. I'm coming up."

"How? There's no–"

Armani jumps and grabs one of the railing's bars. I quickly move back, and my eyebrows lift when I watch how easily he pulls himself up and over.

That's hot.

He lands on his feet, and with two strides, his hand grips the side of my neck, his body hits mine, and his mouth delivers a scorching kiss.

The fluttering in my stomach is intense, and I push up on my tiptoes as I kiss him back.

His lips knead mine until he lifts his head and looks deep into my eyes. "I can't wait to marry you."

A wide smile spreads over my face. "Me too."

Emotion washes over his handsome features. "I'm going to love you so hard to make up for all the days you felt unloved."

My heart stutters in my chest before bursting. My eyes tear up, and pushing up again, I kiss him with all the happiness he's given me.

In such a short time, Armani has given me more love and respect than I've ever experienced. It feels like a dream, like I'm getting a glimpse of heaven.

I'm pushed into the room, and he begins to tug at my shirt to pull it over my head.

"Mamma will hear," I whisper against his mouth.

Armani pulls back so he can remove his own shirt, then he drops it on the floor. "Then you better not make a sound." He squeezes my breast and presses a kiss to my nipple before I'm pushed back until I sit down on the bed.

When he tugs my leggings off, he grumbles, "I need to be inside you, *bella*."

I scoot back while Armani takes off his sweatpants. Opening my legs for him, he crawls over me, and the full weight of his body pins me to the mattress.

His hands move up and down my sides before he pushes them beneath my butt, gripping my cheeks tightly. His hardness rubs through my slit, the friction on my clit so good I struggle to keep from moaning.

A fire builds deep in my belly, and before it can spread through my body, Armani finds my entrance and thrusts deep inside me. His pelvis hits mine, and I'm so impossibly full, I can't breathe for a moment.

"Home," he groans as he presses his face into the crook of my neck. "You feel like home, *bella*."

I wrap my arms around him, and when he thrusts inside me again, I gasp, "You feel like home for me, too."

Our mouths fuse together, and my hands move over his shoulders and down his muscled back.

God, I love his back. Feeling how his muscles move with each thrust makes me burn hotter for this man.

Then my palms find his ass, and I feel how he flexes as he takes me in slow and torturously deep thrusts.

God.

My legs fall open as wide as they can go. My back arches and I have to bite my bottom lip to keep from making a sound.

Hunger tightens Armani's features right before he braces a hand next to my shoulder and starts to fuck me like a possessed man.

The friction of his manhood stroking the ever-living shit out of me has me coming apart in seconds. As my lips part and my muscles tense, Armani covers my mouth with his other hand.

Pleasure seizes me, and I convulse beneath him. He takes me even harder, and soon he's jerking against my body as he finds his release.

We ride our pleasure together as Armani keeps filling me until he loses his strength and slumps down on me.

Breathless, we lie in the still of the night while tingles keep zapping through me.

Armani pushes his arms beneath me, holding me like I'm his favorite pillow. He presses his face into the crook of my neck again, and still buried deep inside me, he murmurs, "I'll leave before the sun comes up."

I wrap my arms tightly around the man who's digging his way into my heart and press a kiss to his hair. "Sleep, *moya lyubov'.*"

Minutes later, I feel his breaths grow slower, and his body sinks deeper into mine.

My thoughts are filled with how Armani makes me feel. I've never met anyone like him, and day by day, he amazes me.

I already care so much for Armani, it's only a matter of time before I love him.

I'm woken by the feel of Armani rubbing his pelvis against mine. When I open my eyes, the first rays of the sun start to break through the darkness, spilling through the window.

His face is still pressed against my neck, and I feel as he hardens inside me.

Armani never pulled out or moved as we slept.

He lets out a soft moan before he grinds against me again. The friction has need soaking my core, and I clench hard around his manhood.

"That feels so good," I whisper.

I get no reply, and Armani stills again.

Shit, is he asleep?

His breaths are even, and I struggle not to laugh because even in his sleep, he wants to fuck me.

If that's not proof of attraction, I don't know what is.

He stirs against me again, his hand moving to my right breast. He grips it like a lifeline, his hips grinding again.

I'm going to die.

I'm stuck beneath him but try to lift my butt so I can rub against him for some much-needed relief.

God, he needs to wake up. I'm going to go up in flames.

I try to rub against him, but I can't move much, and it has frustration unfurling in my chest.

He lets out a sleepy chuckle. "Do you need me to fuck you, *bella?*"

"No," I mutter. "Turn onto your back." I push his shoulders, and with another chuckle, he rolls over. I rush to straddle him and desperately slide down on his hardness.

"So much better," I sigh before I begin to ride him, searching for the explosion of pleasure only he can give me.

Armani's hands rest on my thighs as I pepper kisses over his chest, my hips swiveling and grinding.

My orgasm comes fast, and with my back arching, I bounce on his hardness, taking what I want from his body.

I feel him jerk beneath me, and opening my eyes, I see ecstasy washing over his face, his gaze burning fiercely on me.

"Such a horny girl," he purrs. "You can fuck me awake anytime you need my cock."

I slump down on top of him and admit, "That's the first time I was able to make myself come. Seems you were the missing piece."

It's the first time I took what I wanted without thinking about someone else.

His arms wrap around me. "You haven't orgasmed before I ate your pussy?"

His words make my cheeks flame up. I need to get used to his direct way of talking about sex.

"No." I shake my head as I catch my breath. "I could never get it right."

Grinning at me, he says, "I like that I'm the only one who can make you come."

"Me too." I push up and crawl off the bed. "You need to go before Mamma finds you in my bed."

I use the bathroom and get dressed in the jeans and t-shirt I packed in my overnight bag. When I walk back into the room, there's no sign of Armani. A single yellow flower lies on the pillow with a note.

I'll see you in eight hours, bella. I can't wait to make you Mrs. De Santis.

Love,

A.

My heart melts, and I read the note a couple of times. Every time my eyes land on 'love,' my smile grows bigger, my world becomes brighter, and my heart beats a little more for the man of my dreams.

Chapter 28

Armani

Opening the door for Misha and Aurora, I hug my friends and let them into my house.

It's the first time Misha sees where I live, and glancing around, he mutters, "Not bad. You've done well for yourself."

I take the compliment. "Would you like something to drink?"

Aurora shakes her head. "Just tell me where Tiana is so I can go to her."

"We'll walk you to my mother's place," I say.

As we head down the narrow street, Misha smiles, a pleased expression on his face. He glances at me. "This is what I envisioned for Tiana."

"She seems happy," I admit. "She's not as cautious and skittish as when we first met."

She's slowly coming out of her shell. This morning when she took her orgasm from me, my chest filled with pride. Little by little, she's changing from a scared little bird into a strong woman.

"I'm relieved to hear that," Misha replies, throwing an arm around my shoulders. "Thank you for everything you're doing for her."

Trust me. It's my pleasure.

"You're welcome."

"Oh my God, I love the bridges," Aurora sighs. "And the balconies with flowers. It's beautiful here." She nudges Misha's arm. "Maybe we should move." Smiling up at him, she rubs her cheek against his bicep. "You know, so we can be closer to Tiana."

"Hmmm." Misha brushes the tip of her nose with his finger, then he teases her, "Right, it's not because you've just fallen in love with Venice."

"Yeah, there's that too," she chuckles.

I open the front door and call out, "Mamma."

"*Mammamia*. Stay here, *piccola*." A second later, my mother comes barreling around the corner. "You can't see the bride."

Chuckling, I gesture to Aurora. "I brought Aurora over."

Mom's eyes dart between Misha and Aurora, then she hurries forward and engulfs Misha in a hug. "Finally, I meet you."

She kisses both his cheeks. "Such a handsome boy." Then Aurora's yanked into a hug and kissed. "Welcome."

Mamma wraps an arm around Aurora's shoulders, and dragging her deeper into the house, she throws over her shoulder, "You can leave. Shut the door behind you."

"I'll come back to check on Tiana," Misha says before letting out a burst of laughter.

Walking back to my place, Misha slaps me on the back. "Tell me everything."

I lift an eyebrow at him. "About?"

"*The Reaper*." Another slap hits my back. "Fucking badass, brother."

I shrug. "I was in a hurry to get back to Tiana."

His eyes search my face then a bark of laughter bursts over his lips. "You've fallen in love with her." He grips my shoulder, tugging me to a stop in the middle of the street. "What did I say? Ha. I was right. You're head over heels for my sister. Aren't you?" He jabs my abs. "Admit it."

I chuckle as I shove him. "Fuck off." We continue to walk, then I admit, "Yeah, you're right." My mood turns serious. "She's easy to love."

"I know." Misha throws his arm around my shoulder. "She'll fucking give everything she has just to be loved."

As we near my place, we see Alek checking his phone where he's standing by the front door.

"Yo!" Misha calls out.

Alek's head snaps up, then he stalks toward us. His eyes are locked on me, and Misha quickly steps to the side right before Alek grabs me to him in a brotherly hug.

It's only for a moment before I'm pushed back, and he says, "Tell me how he died."

I place my hand on his shoulder and lock eyes with him. "I stabbed him with his own steak knife and let him drown in his blood."

Some peace returns to Alek's eyes.

He needed this. More than anything.

"Come on," Misha says, nodding toward the house. "I need coffee."

We head inside, and while I prepare the coffee, Alek helps himself to one of the cupcakes Tiana baked.

"Jesus, I missed this," he mumbles around a full mouth.

"Only you can eat sweet shit so early in the morning," Misha mutters.

We sit down at the kitchen table and sip on our coffees.

"We have an hour before the florist comes to decorate the courtyard," I inform them.

"Is there anything we can help with?" Misha asks.

"No." A grin spreads over my face. "Just keep me from going to Tiana, so my mother doesn't kill me."

My friends laugh at my comment, then Alek says, "After today, I'll be the only single one. I'll have to fuck all the single women on your behalf."

Knowing it's all talk because Alek hasn't been with anyone in three years, I just chuckle and shake my head at him.

We enjoy another cup of coffee before I take them out on the boat to see more of Venice. It's only for thirty minutes, and we return in time to open for the florist.

"I'm going to Tiana," Misha says. He pats Alek's shoulder, "Make sure Armani's at the altar at one."

"Trust me," I mutter. "I'll be there."

Chapter 29

Tiana

Aurora is helping me weave a crown of flowers to wear for the wedding when Misha walks into the kitchen.

Jumping up, I hug my brother, and instantly a wave of emotions hit.

His arms are steel bands around me, still holding the safety I've known all my life.

Letting go of me, he takes my hand and looks at Aurora, "We'll be back in an hour."

She gives him a loving smile. "Take your time. I'll finish the crown."

He pulls me out of the house, and we walk toward the marketplace.

"Thank you for coming."

"Of course. It's your big day." He lets go of my hand and wraps his arm around my shoulders, tugging me against his side, then mutters, "My baby sister is getting married."

His tone is filled with disbelief.

"It's surreal," I admit. "Armani is amazing."

"You have him wrapped around your pinky," he teases me.

"I think it's the other way around." I let out a happy chuckle.

"Damn, I'm good. I knew the two of you would make a great couple," he boasts.

I pull away from him and tease, "I better make space for you big head."

Misha gestures at a café. "Let's sit here."

A server comes, and Misha orders a glass of water and a slice of bread. The server looks at him like he's lost his mind but walks to the kitchen.

Misha's eyes lock with mine. "Remember how fucking cold that room was?"

Even though the morning sun is shining on me, a chill spreads through my body. "I'll never forget."

The server brings the order and places it between us. "Will that be all?"

"Give us ten minutes," Misha answers.

When we're alone, he breaks a piece of the bread off and holds it out to me.

Just like he used to do whenever he could steal something for me to eat.

My eyes fill with tears as I take it from him. Unlike the moldy bread when I was little, the fresh piece tastes delicious.

It's the symbolism that matters.

"This will be the last time I feed you," he says, his features tight with emotion. "From today, Armani will take over all duties concerning you."

Dear God.

A tear spirals down my cheek, and I quickly wipe it away.

"But like a shadow, I'll always be there, Tiana," he continues with a hoarse voice. "Your last name might change to De Santis, but you'll always be a Petrov."

I nod and swallow hard. Unable to say anything because of the lump in my throat, I reach across the table and take hold of my brother's hand.

'*I love you, Misha,*' my eyes say what my mouth can't.

The server comes again, and this time, Misha orders pastries and cappuccinos for us.

In silence, we eat together like we've done hundreds of times before. Our days of starving are long gone, and a future filled with happiness awaits us.

We've come far and survived so much because Misha never stopped fighting for us.

I take a deep breath, and looking at my brother, I say, "Thank you for raising me, Misha. Thank you for never complaining and always doing what was needed to ensure I was safe and cared for." My eyes mist with tears again. "You'll be an amazing father to your children."

He lets out an emotional chuckle. "I've had years of practice."

We share a smile before he settles the bill, and we head back to Mamma's house.

I spend the rest of the morning getting ready while Misha moves between the two houses to check on Armani and me.

Mamma and *Zia* Giada do my hair, letting it fall in beautiful curls down my back with some pinned up, while Aurora helps with my makeup.

When I step into the dress and adjust the lace around my body, she places the crown of flowers on my head.

"You look stunning, Tiana," Aurora murmurs.

Misha pops into the room, asking, "Ready? Alek is struggling to keep Armani away from you." Humor dances in his voice, then his eyes drift over me, and his features tighten. "Wow." He walks closer and takes hold of my hand. "So beautiful."

"We're ready," Mamma announces. "Let's go."

She hurries out of the room, wiping a tear from her face.

I hook my arm through Misha's, and as we leave the house, I see our neighbors lining the street.

Rose petals are thrown, forming a path, as I walk to Armani's house. The doors to the courtyard are wide open, and I see flowers everywhere.

Piano notes start to fill the air, and I recognize the song. *You are the reason,* by *Callum Scott.*

The lyrics are emotional as Misha walks me down the aisle of white petals. My eyes lock on Armani, and I lose my breath at how handsome he looks.

Of Saints. That's what Armani's last name translates to from Latin.

I'm marrying a saint.

A huge lump forms in my throat, and my emotions are all over the place. I hardly notice Mr. and Mrs. Aslanhov.

Misha hands me to Armani, saying, "I'm giving you my only family."

Armani nods, "After today, she won't be your *only* family. I'll be honored to call you my brother."

God. My heart.

We turn to Father Moretti, who's graciously agreed to wed us.

He reads a passage of scripture, then smiles at us. "Face each other."

I turn to Armani, and my eyes drink in the handsome man who I'll live with for the rest of my life.

Armani takes hold of my left hand and gives it a squeeze, his gaze resting lovingly on me.

"Armani, repeat after me," Father Moretti says.

Armani waits until Father Moretti has recited the vows, then he says, "I, Armani Diego De Santis, take thee, Tiana Petrov, to be my wedded wife, to have and to hold from this day forward, for better, for worse, for richer, for poorer, in sickness and in health, to love and to cherish, till death do us part."

I can't keep the tears back as they spiral down my cheeks.

"Tiana, repeat after me," Father Moretti instructs.

My lips part and my voice is strained and quivering as I repeat, "I, Tiana Petrov, take thee, Armani Diego De Santis, to be my wedded husband, to have and to hold from this day forward, for better, for worse, for richer, for poorer, in sickness and in health, to love and to cherish, till death do us part."

We exchange the rings Armani got for us, then Father Morretti asks, "Armani, do you take Tiana as your wife?"

The corner of Armani's mouth lifts in a hot smirk, "I do."

I try to smile, but I'm way too emotional.

"Tiana, do you take Armani as your husband?"

"I do," the words slip easily over my lips.

A million times, I do.

"I now pronounce you husband and wife. You may kiss the bride."

Overwhelming happiness takes over my entire being as Armani lowers his head, sealing our vows with a kiss.

Alek lets out a holler, then applause erupts.

Looking around the courtyard, I see the neighbors crowding the doorway.

Everyone came to celebrate with us.

My eyes turn back to Armani's face to find him staring at me with awe. "*Mia moglie.*" He pulls me against his chest, his arms locking around me. "My fucking beautiful wife."

I'm tipped backward, and as he kisses me again, more applause fills the air with laughter and whistles.

My smile is wide, and I tremble from all the joy bubbling in me. "My husband," I whisper against his lips.

I give him everything I have.

My heart.

My body.

My soul.

All that I am belongs to Armani.

Chapter 30

Armani

Fuck, I'm a lucky bastard.

It's almost impossible for me to look away from Tiana.

I've booked an entire restaurant in the square where we're celebrating with our family, friends, and neighbors.

I expected the neighbors to join the celebration because we're a close-knitted community, so I made extra arrangements with the restaurant.

Mamma has not stopped stealing Tiana from me so she can introduce her to the neighbors she hasn't met yet.

There's laughter, and the conversation flows, but before the food can be brought out, Mr. Aslanhov comes to me.

"We're leaving," he announces. Mrs. Aslanhov doesn't look happy, but she keeps quiet.

For Tiana, Misha, and Alek's sake, I say, "Thank you for coming today."

His eyes are hard on me. "Don't make the mistake of thinking I'm happy about this wedding. You cost me millions."

I shrug, not able to give two fucks about the loss he suffered. "Have a safe trip home."

I give Mrs. Aslanhov a nod before walking toward my mother and Tiana.

Wrapping my arms around the front of Tiana, I pull her away from Mamma as I playfully say, "You've had her all day. Tiana's mine."

"Tsk," Mamma huffs. "Possessive boy."

"You raised me," I tease her as I lead Tiana to the dance floor.

I pull her against my chest and steer her over the cobblestones.

Tiana's face beams with delight.

"Are you happy, my wife?"

"So very much," she answers, her eyes filled with an emotion I haven't seen before.

Curious, I ask, "What's that look for?"

She shakes her head, a blush staining her cheeks pink. "It's too soon."

"Too soon for what?"

Her eyes flick to mine before she looks everywhere else but me. "I'll tell you in a couple of months."

"No," I chuckle. "You can't say that and expect me to wait. Tell me now."

I twirl her away from me before bringing her back to my chest.

Her eyes fill with the unreadable emotion once more, then she whispers, "*Ya lyublyu tebya.*"

"I don't speak Russian," I complain with a burst of laughter. "That's unfair."

She shrugs playfully, her eyes dancing with mischief.

Jesus, she's incredible.

I dip her backward and seal my mouth to hers, kissing the ever-loving fuck out of my wife.

I lied. I speak some Russian. Enough to understand what she said.

I right her on her feet again, and holding her, we sway on one spot as I whisper into her ear, "*Ti amo.*"

Pulling back to see her face, it's in time to witness the shock washing over her features. Her eyes start to shine like stars, and in this moment that she realizes I love her too, there's nothing more beautiful than her.

I frame her face with my hands, and leaning down, I kiss her tenderly, letting my love flow from my lips to hers.

Suddenly, the emotion floods every inch of my being, and I pull back to look at the woman that's wiggled her way so fucking deep into my heart, there's no removing her without killing me.

The air between us is charged with the intensity of this moment, and Tiana looks at me like I'm her beginning and end.

Like she would cease to exist if I stopped loving her.

"*Sei la mia*," I whisper. That's what she is – my life.

Her fingers brush my jaw, then she presses a soft kiss to my lips.

"Hey," Misha calls out, "that's enough kissing. Let's eat."

I laugh as I gesture for the servers to bring the food.

When I lead Tiana to our table, my phone starts to ring. Pulling the device out of my pocket, I see Luca's name flashing on the screen.

"Mr. Cotroni," I grin into the line.

"Congratulations on your big day, Armani," he says. "You should receive my gift any second."

My phone buzzes with an incoming text, and I quickly check it.

€19800000-00 PAID TO ACCOUNT: AD DE SANTIS

Jesus Christ.

Pressing the phone back to my ear, I say, "Thank you, sir. I appreciate it."

"It's ten percent of what you brought in. I hope it encourages you to continue excelling in the business."

I let out a chuckle, "It does."

"Enjoy your special day with your wife."

The call ends, and I go into my bank account to check my balance and transfer most of the funds into an investment.

"Did you get good news?" Tiana asks from where she's taken a seat at our table.

I sit down beside her. "Yes."

She gives me a questioning look.

I pick up her hand and press a kiss on her knuckles. "Luca sends his regards. He gave me two weeks off to spend with you."

Her face brightens with a smile. "Yay! That's so kind of him."

You have no idea how kind he's been to us, bella.

Soon platters of food are carried out, and our guests begin to indulge in the feast.

The celebration continues well into the night until I decide I've had enough and want my bride all to myself.

Taking a moment to say goodbye to our family and friends, I weave my fingers through Tiana's and walk back to our home. We enter the courtyard that's been cleaned while we were at the reception, and I shut the door behind us.

Finally. Just the two of us.

After the crazy week, I want to relax with my wife and catch my breath before I have to start working again.

We head to the bedroom and change out of our clothes into something more comfortable.

"What do you want to do? Did you eat enough?" Tiana asks as she pulls pins out of her hair before brushing the curls.

There's something so intimate about watching her brush her hair.

I head back into the closet and grab one of my sweaters. Coming out, I say, "Arms up."

Tiana gives me a questioning look but lifts her arms. I pull the sweater over her head, and when her face pops through the hole, I press a quick kiss to her mouth.

Instantly, a smile spreads over her face.

I point at her sneakers. "Put them on, *bella*."

She slips her feet into them then asks, "Are we going out again?"

I nod as I hold my hand for her to take. I weave our fingers and lead her out of the house, where a gondola is waiting for us.

I feel the excitement bubbling in her as I help her to sit. Finding a spot beside her, I cover her legs with a blanket. I nod at the gondolier I arranged everything with.

He gestures to the picnic basket, then says, "Relax and enjoy."

With the lights from apartments and lamps forming a mystical glow on the water, we slowly drift through the waterways.

Tiana's eyes are sparkling with wonder as she experiences Venice at night.

While she admires our surroundings, I stare at her, drinking in her irresistible beauty.

"This is so romantic," she whispers before turning her gaze to me.

Lifting a hand, I brush my fingers over her cheek and jaw. I lean closer, my eyes holding hers imprisoned.

"Was the wedding everything you wanted it to be?"

She nods as she leans her head against my shoulder. "It was so much more. I love how our neighbors celebrated with us."

Taking hold of her chin, I tip her head back. My lips brush over hers. "I've grown addicted to your mouth, *bella*," I groan before I kiss her harder.

With the sounds of people on the sidewalks and the water lapping against the gondola, I savor my wife's mouth.

Time falls away until it's just the two of us wrapped in our bubble of love.

Chapter 31

Tiana

Over the past week, I've learned I'm a morning person.

I mean, when it comes to sex.

And Armani loves it.

Pushing my man onto his back, he lets out a sleepy chuckle. I crawl over his thighs, and rubbing my palms up and down the muscled expanse of his chest, I lean down and lick his shaft from base to tip.

"*Madre di Dio*," he grumbles.

I suck his 'morning glory,' as he likes to call it, deep into my mouth, twirling my tongue around the swollen head, then letting it pop free.

"*Cazzo, bella*," he groans. "So good. Suck me harder."

I take his cock deep again, and hollowing out my cheeks, I suck him as hard as I can

"*Gesù Cristo*," he hisses. "Harder." His hands fist in my hair, and he pushes me down, forcing me to take him all the way to the back of my throat.

I suck once more, then pull free from his hold.

"You little tease," he chuckles.

"You had your turn last night," I say as I straddle his hips. "Now it's my turn."

"I love this new bossy side of you." His eyes feast on my breasts, and reaching up, he pinches my right nipple hard.

With his cock lying on his abdomen, I rub my slit over the hard length and let out a needy moan.

"Hands on the headboard," I order.

I'm still trying to get used to the idea that I'm allowed to have a voice in our marriage. During sex is the only time when I'm brave enough to tell Armani what to do. It's because I can see it's a turn-on for him.

He grabs hold of the wood bedframe, his powerful body stretched out beneath me.

"Such a good mafioso," I praise him.

His nostrils flare, and his features tense as my words make his cock jerk, release already beading on the tip.

I grind my clit up and down his shaft again, and we both moan from the much-needed friction.

"You're soaked, *bella*," he says, his tone hoarse with lust. "Your pussy is dripping for me."

I rub my palms over his chest again, loving the feel of his skin stretched tightly over his muscles. Leaning forward, I suck and lick his nipples as I begin to grind against his weeping hardness.

"*Cazzo*," he hisses. "You're killing me."

"Hmm," I hum against his skin as I move faster, chasing my release that's just out of my reach.

"Tiana," he growls.

Knowing he's reaching his limits, I position his cock at my entrance and thrust down hard, taking all of his shaft.

"*Fuck.Fuck.Fuck*," he shouts as he hammers into me so fast, it sends me over the edge with a cry.

I hear wood crack, then Armani's hands grab me, and I'm thrown onto my back. He slams back inside me and fucks me until I scream from the intense pleasure.

His body strains and I can see the veins in his neck before his mouth drops open, and he jerks inside me as he spills his release.

Instantly, all his strength is drained from him, and he slumps down on top of me, his body still jerking every few seconds.

"Jesus, Tiana," he gasps. "That was fucking intense. You're getting too good at this."

I let out a breathless chuckle, my own body numb from the intense orgasm.

"It's because I have such a good teacher."

Lifting his head, he playfully bites my jaw before he pulls out of me. He climbs off the bed, and I admire his firm ass as he walks to the bathroom.

"Do you want to go out for breakfast?" he calls.

"I'd like that. It took all my energy to torture you," I answer as I pull myself out of bed.

I grab a dress and clean underwear from the closet and join Armani in the bathroom.

Turning on the shower, I glance at him from over my shoulder. "Should we ask Mamma and *Zia* Giada to join us?"

"No. Mamma will insist on cooking for us." He smiles at me. "Besides, I want you all to myself before I have to return to work."

I step into the shower, and Armani joins me.

While we wash our bodies, he asks, "Is there anything you want to do before my vacation is over?"

I shake my head. "Nothing I can think of. I like spending time with you at home."

We finish up and get dressed, and I must admit, I love how comfortable we've become around each other.

How's it possible that you meet a person one day, and the next, it feels like they've been there forever?

When we're ready, we head out of the house. Armani opens the door, and seeing a rectangular box lying on the step, he pauses and gestures for me to wait. "Stay back."

Crouching, he carefully removes the lid, then a frown forms on his forehead. "It's roses. You can come."

As I step closer, Armani takes the note out of the flowers and reads it. His features darken as his controlled demeanor slips, and the mafioso in him rises to the surface.

His eyes flick to me. "It's for you."

"Me?" I gasp with surprise.

Stepping closer, I take hold of his hand and read the note.

My lovely Tiana,
I can't wait to see you again.
I miss the taste of your lips.

xxx

Your one and only love.

Confused as hell, I shake my head. "It must be a mistake. Someone must've left it at the wrong door."

Armani picks up the flowers and walks back into the house. I follow him to the kitchen and watch as he throws them in the trash.

"The note has your name on it." He pins me with an angry look. "Tiana's not a name you'll commonly hear in Italy."

My eyes dart over his face, and fear bleeds into my soul. My voice quivers as I say, "I don't know who sent the flowers."

Armani's features soften a bit, and he comes to hug me. "I know, *bella*. Sorry, I'm not accusing you of anything. I'm worried as fuck you've attracted the wrong person's attention."

Relief pours through me because Armani believes me.

Wrapping my arms around him, I ask, "A stalker? Really? But why?"

"It doesn't take much to catch the attention of a sick bastard. You're beautiful, Tiana. Any fucking man would give his right testicle to have you."

Thinking rationally, I ask, "Maybe it's a prank?"

Armani pulls away from me and reads the note again. "Yeah, it could be a prank." He looks at me again. "Just be careful when you leave the house. If you feel unsafe while I'm at work, ask one of the neighbors to walk you to the store or home. Better yet, ask Mamma and *Zia* Giada."

I nod quickly. "I will."

Armani drops the note on the kitchen table, and taking hold of my hand, again, he leads me out of the house.

I notice how on guard he is as we walk to a café and hate that a stupid prankster has ruined our morning.

When we take a seat at a table, I catch Armani's worried gaze and say, "Try to forget about it, *moya lyubov'*. Let's enjoy our breakfast."

He visibly relaxes and gives me a smile, but the worry's still in his sharp gaze.

Chapter 32

Armani

I've been back at work for a month, and I'm finally starting to get the hang of my new position.

Franco, the boss I'm reporting to, is in his mid-sixties, and he's been around the block a couple of times. He has an easygoing personality, so we get along.

Instead of being an enforcer, like I was before training at St. Monarch's, I now supervise all the shipments coming and leaving the northern area of Italy.

There's not as much action, and I travel more, which means I sometimes have to leave Tiana alone at home for a couple of days.

Not once has she complained, and seeing the happiness on her face whenever I get home makes it all worth it.

It's only temporary. I'll work my ass off for the next promotion, which will put me in charge of the enforcers.

My phone buzzes, and checking the device, I see a text from Tiana. She's sent me a photo of her, Mamma, and *Zia Giada* baking in our kitchen.

Having fun with Mamma and Zia Giada, but I miss you.

I quickly reply that I miss her too, then put my phone away and check the schedule for the next ten days. I make sure no routes have been double-booked. It's a countermeasure we take to ensure if there's a roadblock on a particular road, we don't lose more than one truck.

I check who the drivers will be for the next shipment, transporting weapons and counterfeit money to the rest of Europe.

My phone starts to ring, and seeing Mamma's name, I frown.

"*Ciao*, Mamma?"

"A package was delivered for Tiana. It's a beautiful set of earrings. She's so upset, she threw it in the trash," Mamma whispers, giving me the impression she's hiding while making the call so Tiana won't know.

Cristo.

"Keep the package and note. I want to see it when I get home."

"*Va bene*," she replies, saying okay with a worried tone.

"*Grazie*, Mamma. I'll stop by after work."

We end the call, and try as I fucking might, I can't focus on work. Getting up, I walk to Franco's office.

"Hey, I need to go home. I'll be in early tomorrow morning to make up for the time I'm away from work."

Franco gives me a worried look. "Everything okay?"

"Yeah. An asshole is sending my wife gifts. I need to check if she's okay."

He lets out a chuckle. "I'm sure she's okay. My ex-wife rubbed that shit in my face before I killed her lover and left her without a dime."

"Good for you," I say. "I'm going to kill the fucker when I get my hands on him."

"Good luck."

Heading out of the building, I get into my car and drive from Teviso to where I always park my car. The fifty-minute commute tests my fucking patience, and I start to picture all the ways I will kill whoever's sending my wife gifts.

I'll fucking slice his dick off, piece by piece, and feed it to the bastard.

I'll strap a bucket of rats to him and watch as they eat through his guts.

No.

I'll bury the fucker alive and put a camera in the coffin with him so I can watch as he pisses and shits himself while he suffocates.

Stopping in my reserved space in the car park, *Piazzale Roma*, I get out and walk to the area where I catch a tram to Venice. It's only a ten-minute commute, but it feels like an hour.

By the time I stalk into my mother's house, I'm struggling to keep control of my temper.

"Mamma," I call out as I head to the kitchen.

She comes hurrying toward me, concern etched deep on her face. "Come. I've put it in my bedroom."

Entering her private space, my eyes lock on the box that's lying on her bed. I rip the lid off and see a smaller box, nestled on a bed of rose petals.

Picking it up, I flip it open and look at the diamond earrings that could easily cost over two thousand euros.

What the actual fucking fuck.

I drop the jewelry in the box and pick up the note.

My lovely Tiana,
I still can't believe I finally got to make sweet love to you .
The way you moaned while I filled you over and over will forever be my favorite sound.

Wear the earrings the next time we meet.

Only the earrings.

I want you naked and spread out on my bed as soon as the bastard leaves for work.

xxx

Your one and only love.

I crumple the note in my fist, seeing fucking red. My breaths speed up, and when Mamma tries to lay her hand on my back, I step away from her.

"Give me space," I growl.

"Armani," she whispers. "This can't be true. Right?" I hear her voice tremble.

"I don't know what it is." Rage burns in my voice as I look at my mother.

"Would Tiana–"

"Don't say it," I snap. I suck in a desperate breath of air. "Tiana didn't do anything."

She wouldn't.

Confusion flutters over Mamma's face. "But?"

"It's a sick fucking joke, Mamma. That's all it is." I sit down on the bed and drop the note in the box while trying to regain control over my temper.

I need to think.

What the fuck is going on?

Resting my face in my hands, I focus on my breathing, and when I start to calm down, I can think more rationally.

I'll send the package and note to St. Monach's and ask them to check it for prints. I'll find out who's behind this and fucking kill them.

Now that I have a plan, I stand up and pull my concerned mother into my arms. "Don't worry about a thing. I'll take care of this shit."

"I don't want you to suffer like I did," she sniffles.

Like she suffered when my father fucked everything in sight. It broke her heart.

"Tiana is faithful to me," I say with certainty strengthening my voice.

Mamma pulls back and nods. "You do what you have to do. I just don't want you to get hurt."

I cup her cheek and lean down. "I won't get hurt." I press a kiss on her forehead, then pick up the box and leave her bedroom.

On the short walk to my apartment, I try to process the bomb that was dropped on me.

It's the second gift.

Is there a fucking stalker I have to worry about?

Deciding to check with some of the neighbors, I knock on every other door and ask whether they've seen someone hanging around. Or whether they saw who put the package on my doorstep.

My investigation turns up empty-handed, though. It puts me at ease because our small community would notice anyone who doesn't belong on our streets.

A stalker would hang around. He'd take every chance he could get to watch Tiana. With that suspicion debunked, I'm left only with the hunch that it's a sick fucking prank.

But who?

We get along with all our neighbors. I don't have any jealous ex-girlfriends, and Tiana has no romantic past.

Karlin Makarov wouldn't bother with something so trivial. The man didn't even want Tiana in a sexual way.

So who the fuck is trying to mess with us?

I go through my list of enemies as I open the door and enter the courtyard.

It could be any of the nine men I tortured to pay up.

Jesus, it's going to take a while to work through all of them.

"Mamma?" I hear Tiana call. "Is that you?"

When I appear in the doorway of the kitchen, Tiana drops a pan she is drying. "Jesus!" Her hand slaps over her heart. "You scared me." She lets out a sigh of relief and comes to kiss me. "You're home early?"

Her eyes drift over me, then they lock on the box in my hand.

I watch as the blood drains from her face, and before I can set her at ease, she rambles, "It's all lies. I'd never do that to you. I have no idea who sent it. I'm so sorry." Fear trickles into her eyes. "I promise, Armani. I haven't been unfaithful to you."

When I lift my hand to pull her to my chest, she flinches and stumbles a step back.

I drop the box, and grabbing hold of her, I yank her to my chest and engulf her in my arms. "Calm down, *bella*. I know you have nothing to do with this. I believe you."

A sob is ripped from her, her body trembling hard. "I don't understand…what's happening."

I rub a hand up and down her back to comfort her. "I know, *bella*. I'll get to the bottom of it and deal with the fucker."

She calms down, and when she pulls back, she gives me a pleading look. "I've only been with you. I love you. I'd never do anything to jeopardize what we have."

"Shh," I hush her as I wipe the tears from her cheeks. "I know, *bella*."

When I press a kiss to her lips, she throws her arms around my neck and deepens it, devouring me with so much fucking desperation that the box is soon forgotten, and we're ripping each other's clothes off.

Chapter 33

Tiana

Since we received the second package, I've been on edge. Whenever I go to the store or out to do anything, I find myself checking over my shoulder.

Armani said he'd find out who's sending the gifts, but it's been two weeks since I got the earrings, and we're no closer to getting to the bottom of it. He's even put up a security camera, hoping if the person brings another gift, we'll see what they look like.

I have no idea who would do this to me, and it's making me feel sick to my stomach.

Armani has made it clear he won't tolerate infidelity. What if they keep sending gifts, and he starts to believe the lie?

I love him so much it would kill me if he didn't trust me.

I hope whoever's behind this just disappears.

I bring the cup of coffee to my lips, but my stomach rolls at the smell. Getting up from where I was sitting at the kitchen table, I pour the caramel liquid down the drain and rinse the cup.

Enough thinking about the bastard.

Gathering all the ingredients I'll need, I start to make red velvet cupcakes. They're Armani's favorite, and there's only one left from the previous batch.

My phone starts to ring, and I grab the device from the counter and pin it between my ear and shoulder so I can keep beating the eggs.

"Hello?" I don't hear anything. "Hello?"

The silence continues for a few seconds before the call cuts out.

I check the number, and not recognizing it, I set the device down and continue with my work.

Besides the extremely inconvenient gifts, things between Armani and me are perfect. The past two and a half months have been the happiest of my life.

I've added my touch all over the house. Flowers in the living room. Red throw pillows to add color. Framed photos of our wedding and one of Misha and Aurora, as well.

I finally have the home I've always wanted.

And so much more.

Instead of being married to an abuser, I'm married to a man who loves me and treats me like a queen.

I've given Armani everything I have. I love him like no other.

The muscles in my shoulders relax as I relive the past two and a half months of my life.

It's crazy when I think about how much everything's changed. I never knew such happiness existed.

I mean, I even get along with my mother-in-law. How many women can say that?

My stomach rolls again, and when I feel so sick that I'm sure I might vomit, I set the bowl down and rush to the bathroom.

Dropping to my knees by the toilet, I wait, but nothing comes up.

Ugh.

I wipe my palm over my clammy forehead and sit flat on my butt on the bathroom floor.

The thought pops into my head for the second time the past week.

Could I be pregnant?
So soon?

It's been two months since Armani and I first slept together. Doesn't it take longer before you have morning sickness?

Getting up off the floor, I walk to the kitchen and pick up my phone to Google 'morning sickness.'

My eyes widen when I read it can start at six weeks, and it's usually at its worst around week nine of pregnancy.

Oh my God.

My heart starts beating faster as the possibility sinks into my heart and takes root.

What if I'm pregnant?

Dear God, I'll be so happy!

I leave all the ingredients lying on the counter, and grabbing my purse, I rush out of the house.

Please.

I jog down the street, and one of the neighbors calls from the front door, "Why the hurry?"

I call back with a massive smile on my face. "I need something from the store,"

In record time, I hurry into the drug store and find the aisle with pregnancy tests. There are three kinds, and not knowing which one to take, I grab one of each and dart to the counter to pay.

The cashier glances between the tests and me. "I hope you get the news you want."

"I hope so too," I grin, anxious to get home so I can pee on a stick.

I tap the credit card Armani gave me to use, and taking the paper bag, I rush out of the store and run home. My heart beats faster and faster, and the anticipation becomes overwhelming.

Please.

Please.

Please.

I picture myself with a round belly. Holding a little bundle of joy. Giving Armani a son.

Dear God, please. I want to be a mother so badly.

I barrel into the house and head straight for the bathroom. Opening the paper bag, my fingers fumble with the boxes, and I quickly read the instructions.

When I've done everything, word for word, I stare at the three sticks.

They change one by one, giving me the answer I hoped to see.

I cover my mouth with my hands as I burst out in happy tears.

Pregnant.

Armani and I are having a child together.

We're going to be parents.

I'm going to be a mother.

I lower one of my hands to my flat abdomen and gently rub over the area.

I have a little human inside me. What a miracle this is.

My happiness comes in waves of emotions. I sob. I laugh. I coo at my stomach.

This is such a blessed day, and wanting to make it special for Armani, I gather the pregnancy tests and take them to the bedroom. I place them on his bedside table, and hurry to the kitchen to make cupcakes. I want to write on one that he's going to be a daddy and place it by the tests.

I can't wait to see his reaction.

Mamma will be over the moon with the news of her first grandchild.

I have the home I've always wanted, an amazing husband I love, and a baby on the way who I'll give the world to.

Thank you.

Chapter 34

Armani

When I return to my office after I checked a shipment of weapons, I notice a manila envelope on my desk.

Fuck, I'm tired of standing in the warehouse for hours. I can't wait for this day to be over so I can go home.

Dropping onto my chair, I pick up the envelope and tear it open. A digital voice recorder falls out with a note attached to it.

You should know the truth.

Maybe it's dirt on one of our drivers? Or a snitch.

Good, it's been a while since I've killed someone. It will help ease my stress.

I press play, and at first, there's just static, then I hear a man groaning, *'You take my cock so well, baby.'*

"What the fuck?" I mutter, frowning at the device in my hand.

I hear the slapping of skin, then Tiana's voice. *'Harder, moya lyubov'. Please. Oh, God, yes.'*

Everything in me stills, and violent anger creeps over my skin like a deadly virus. My eyes drift shut as I continue to listen to my wife fucking another man.

'Who do you belong to, my little whore?' the man asks, his Italian accent thick.

'I'm yours,' Tiana moans.

I listen as she orgasms, her cries of ecstasy destroying my heart in a single fucking blow.

Gesù Cristo.

Intense heartache rips through me with the destructive force of a nuclear bomb. As if hearing it once wasn't torturous enough, I fucking press play again and listen as Tiana throws everything we had away.

I fucking trusted her.

I gasp as raw pain tears through me, the viciousness of being betrayed by the person I loved most in the world, too much to cope with.

Pushing the chair back, I rest my forearms on my thighs and lower my head. I try to breathe through the unbearable agony.

"*Cazzo*," I grunt as I stand up. "No." I shake my head, my broken heart rattling in my chest as it tries to beat some life into my veins. "She didn't." A heart-wrenching sound leaves my lips before I roar and flip my desk over.

"FUCK!" I shout, my body shaking violently.

My door slams open, and Franco comes rushing in with his gun drawn. Wildly he glances around the office before he looks at me. "What the fuck, De Santis?"

I press a hand to my heart and stumble a step backward. My eyes land on the voice recorder, and the sounds of Tiana fucking another man echo through my very being.

I'm going to kill them.

"Armani?" Franco asks as he comes closer. "Are you okay? Did something happen to Tiana or your mother?"

I crouch down and pick up the device, and meeting my boss' eyes, my voice is devoid of emotion as I say, "I need a day off work to kill the fucker who's been fucking my wife."

Franco's eyes widen, then understanding washes over his face. "I'll cover for you. Let me know if there's any way I can help."

With a curt nod, I stalk out of the office, and in a haze of rage, I get into my car and drive home.

Home.

What fucking home?

I loved her, and she betrayed me.

I gave her everything, and she fucking played me for a fool.

Was it all an act? Her shyness? Her loving me?

My body shudders, and I grip the steering wheel tighter. I see nothing around me. I don't hear the other cars on the road.

There's only the rage.

Somehow I make it to the car park without causing an accident. Getting out, I open the trunk and grab my bag of weapons. I sling the strap over my shoulder and walk to where I get on a tram.

People give me a wide berth and wait for me to get off before they dare approach the door. There's no way to contain the rage emanating from me like a force field.

She fucked another man.

She begged another man.

She said the exact words to him that she's said to me while I was fucking her.

Turning up my street, I pull my gun out from where it's tucked into the waistband of my pants, and my fingers flex around the handle.

She said she's his.

My fucking wife, the woman I loved more than anything, betrayed me in the worst way possible.

She made a fool of me.

ME!

Armani De Santis.

The Reaper.

I'm going to fucking kill them both.

I slam the door open and take the steps up to the front door two at a time.

I loved her. She was mine.

The aroma of our dinner hangs in the air to welcome me home, but now it makes my stomach turn.

I drop the bag of weapons in the foyer.

"Armani? You're home early," I hear her say, her voice filled with happiness.

She comes out of the kitchen with a smile on her face, and I lift my arm, training the barrel of my gun on her.

Shock ripples over her face, and her eyes widen.

My voice is a blend of ice and the vast emptiness she's caused to form in my chest. "You fucking betrayed me."

Her face pales, and she shakes her head as she backtracks into the kitchen. "No, Armani! I didn't do anything."

Pulling the voice recorder from my pocket, I press play. When she hears the damming evidence, her hands fly up to cover her mouth as she continues to shake her head.

Once again, raw agony rips through me with a brutal force. The pieces of my heart are pulverized to dust as I look at the woman I love.

"You betrayed me," I whisper, my pain too much to bear.

My arm holding the gun falls to my side, and I struggle to remain on my feet. I try to inhale air into my lungs, but it feels like the walls are closing in on me as my entire world is ripped from beneath my feet.

I crouch down and breathe through the destruction.

"I didn't do that," Tiana sobs. "I don't know how they got the recording, but I've never been with anyone but you."

"Shut up," I hiss.

"Please, Armani. You have to believe me," she begs, and for the first time since I've met her, I hear her crying loudly. "I've been faithful to you."

If it weren't for the evidence, I might've believed her.

I move into a kneeling position and lift my eyes to her, the gun pressed against my thigh.

"I gave you everything." I shake my head. It's impossible to hide the pain she's caused me from her eyes. "I would've given you the world."

Tiana leans heavily against the doorjamb and slowly sinks to the floor. She wraps her arm around her middle, her eyes pleading with me. "I-it wasn't m-m-me."

I press play again, letting the sounds of her fucking another man fill the air between us with violence and destruction.

"Noooo," she cries. "It's not me!"

"Then who the fuck is it, Tiana? I've heard those same words and moans while I fucked you. I've heard you orgasm over a hundred times." I slam the gun against my thigh and shout, "How could you fucking do this to me?"

Her features tighten with anguish, "I didn't." Her body convulses from the sobs racking through her. "I promise."

"Your promises mean nothing to me," I say. Shaking my head, I stare at the woman I thought I'd spend my life with. "Who is he?"

"I-I d-d-on't k-know," she stutters. She sucks in desperate breaths and calms enough to say, "I've been faithful to you. I've never been with another man."

"Do you want me to play the recording again?"

She shakes her head wildly, then begs, "Just think rationally for a moment. Where would I meet this man? Where would I get the time? Venice is small. Someone would've seen us together."

I close my eyes and inhale deeply, then hiss, "None of that matters, Tiana." I press play again, letting her fucking moans fill the air.

"Stop that!" she cries. She scrambles forward on her hands and knees and grabs the device from me, throwing it to the side.

Anger pours into her eyes as she looks at me. She's so close I can smell the scent of cupcakes clinging to her.

She baked today.

It used to be my favorite smell.

Her voice trembles as she says, "I did NOT fuck another man."

I stare at her for a long moment, then shake my head in disbelief. "*Cazzo*, you're good. I have to give you credit where it's due. You really had me fooled." I let out a bitter chuckle as I gesture at her with the gun. "You're a fucking good actress."

She climbs to her feet and moves away from me. Her hands lift to her head, and she grips fistfuls of her hair, screaming, "It wasn't me!"

Pushing off the floor, I rise to my full height.

Merciless wrath ripples beneath my skin and seeps from my pores like a deadly fog.

Apprehension tightens her features as she stumbles farther away until her back presses against the wall, her eyes flicking between my face and the gun in my hand. Her voice trembles with desperation and fear. "Please. Don't do this."

I only want to know one thing. "What's his name?"

She shakes her head wildly. "I don't know."

Slowly, I tilt my head to the side. The expression on my face is one men see before I kill them. "Give me the name of the man you fucked."

"Armani!" she shouts, her panic and fear morphing into a rage that matches mine. She lifts her chin, a daring light igniting in her eyes. "His name is Armani De Santis."

I give her a look filled with warning. "Now is not the time to fuck with me, Tiana."

"It's the only name I have to give you," she snaps as she pushes away from the wall. Her body is practically vibrating with fear and anger. "What are you going to do, Armani? Shoot me? Beat me?"

She stops within reaching distance of me, which is a careless move on her part.

Her eyes bore into mine as she, once again, says, "I didn't fuck anyone but you." She slaps the flat of her hand against her chest. "I've been loyal. I've given you everything I have. I love only you." Her bravery falters, then she whispers with so much heartache, "I love you."

How can I believe anything she says?

Chapter 35

Tiana

I now understand how people feel when they know they're about to die.

The man before me is not my husband.

There's no sign of the Armani I fell in love with.

Even the mafioso is nowhere to be seen.

The man holding the gun is made of rage and pain, violence and revenge, loss and suffering.

There's no reasoning with him.

I'll admit, the recording sounds unbelievably real. Hearing another man's voice with mine in such an intimate setting is traumatizing.

I can't stop shaking my head as I look at Armani. The pain and agonizing expression of betrayal in his eyes feel like a million cuts to my soul.

My eyebrows pinch together as I say, "I'd never hurt you like that. I'd rather rip out my own heart than do that to you."

He keeps staring at me, the bond we shared broken, and the love he felt for me gone. In the blink of an eye, he's gone from the love of my life to a dangerous stranger.

It's madness.

Terrifying fear, unbearable heartache, and pure desperation fill my chest and coat my skin in a thin layer of sweat.

I can't believe this is happening.

As my eyes flit over Armani's face, I watch as all the emotions drain from his eyes.

Mother of God.

No.

His eyes become so dark they're almost black, and his voice is deceptively soft as he asks, "Did you fuck him on my bed?"

"No!"

I take a step back from him, feeling like a caged animal that's about to be hunted by the worst kind of predator.

"When did you meet him?" He takes a calculative step closer to me. "While I was working my ass off for us?"

I shake my head, and before I can answer, he asks, "Where did you even get the time?" He lets out an aggressive chuckle. "So, while I thought you were here at home, you've been sneaking around behind my back?"

Will anything I say matter?

"I didn't, Armani."

He lifts his arm and looks at the gun. Agonizing seconds pass before he tucks it back into the waistband of his pants.

Hopeful that he's calming down and we'll be able to talk rationally, I ask, "Can I make you some coffee? If we sit and talk–"

Armani's chillingly intense eyes flick to me. "You're going to pay for betraying me. I'm going to kill your lover in front of you and make you stand in a pool of his blood."

Dear God.

He lets out a harsh breath, and for a moment, it looks like he's going to be sick. "I need a fucking drink," he growls as he wipes his palm over his face. "*Cristo*, I can't even look at you."

The hatred in his voice is a destructive force, ripping every happy moment we've shared to shreds.

With crushing heartache, I watch Armani turn away from me and leave our home.

I wrap my arm around my stomach as I desperately gasp for air. My body convulses, and running, I make it to the toilet in the nick of time. I bring up everything in my stomach until bile burns my throat.

Slumping to the floor, a sob tears from me.

My perfect world continues to spiral into a black hole until all that's left is the grave worry and fear that Armani's going to kill me.

If I had received a recording like that, hearing Armani with another woman, I'd believe it too. The evidence is overwhelmingly stacked against me.

There's nothing I can say or do to defend myself.

I've seen what happens when Mr. Aslanhov has a drink to 'calm down.' It always had the opposite effect.

My baby.

Climbing to my feet, I rush to the bedroom. I yank a bag from the top shelf and haphazardly throw clothes and toiletries into it.

My panic grows with each passing minute I take to pack, and when I can't take the stress anymore, I shut the bag and hurry to the kitchen.

I grab the pretty shopping list that's stuck to the fridge with a magnet and write a quick note before grabbing my phone and shoving it into my purse.

It's all I have time to take with me.

Run, Tiana. Before he gets back and kills you and your unborn baby.

I rush down the stairs, and scared of running into Armani on the streets, I throw my luggage into the boat. For a terrifying minute, I struggle to start the engine, and when it finally roars to life, I sob with relief.

Steering it up the waterway, I head for the heart of Venice so I can catch a train.

Where will I go?

What will I do?

My chest implodes with unbearable pain when the reality of what I've lost hits.

I've lost the man I've built my entire existence around. The love of my life.

I can't find it in myself to place any blame at Armani's feet. I ache for the pain he's been forced to suffer.

I mourn the amazing man that's been stolen from me.

I weep for the happiness I had with him that's been cruelly ripped away from me.

I'll never feel his kisses again. I'll never have his arms wrapped around me again. I'll never make love to him again.

The severity of my loss threatens to strip me of my sanity, and it hurls me into a bottomless pit of despair.

I almost bump the boat against the side of the waterway and blink the tears away so I can see where I'm going.

Entering a busy canal, I have to slow the speed and maneuver between the other boats and gondolas.

My anxiety spikes sharply from the time I'm losing, knowing at any moment, Armani might realize I'm gone and come after me.

My breaths rush over my lips, and I try to keep an eye on the sidewalks for any sign of Armani.

I can't believe this is happening.

It hurts too much. More than anything, I've suffered through in my past.

Reaching a platform that leads to the train station, I haphazardly park the boat and climb out. I haul my luggage to the sidewalk and run with it bouncing behind me.

The need to get to safety, and to protect my unborn baby, drives me forward.

I keep glancing over my shoulder and plow into a woman who curses me in Italian. I don't even apologize but continue to race toward the train station.

When I reach a ticket machine, I dig out Armani's credit card and purchase a one-way seat to Milan. It's close to the border of Switzerland, where Misha is.

Grabbing my ticket, I rush to an ATM and slide the credit card into the slot. Frantically I keep checking my surroundings as I withdraw all the cash I can before the daily withdrawal limit is reached.

I shove it all into my purse and hurry to the train, climbing aboard. Out of breath and dangerously close to having a panic attack, I find my seat and slump down in it.

The luggage.

I get up and shove it into the compartment before taking my seat again.

Jesus.

My mind reels, my emotions a chaotic mess, as I try to catch my breath. Shock keeps shuddering through me with the force of a tsunami.

Armani believes I betrayed him. It's the one thing he hates most and won't forgive.

It's killed his love for me.

It turned him into a monster who will probably never stop hunting me.

I wrap my arms around my waist, and bending forward, a silent scream tears from me. In desperate need of comfort, I start to rock myself, trying to soothe the heartache.

I can't console myself and turn my attention to my unborn baby.

Shh...Mama won't let anything happen to you. We're going to be okay. I promise.

My heart squeezes painfully, my longing for Armani already setting in.

I want my life back to how it was.

I want my husband to come home and take me into his arms.

I want to share a meal with him. I want to feel his body on top of mine.

I want everything to return to the moment we were last happy.

I just want Armani to hold me and tell me everything will be okay.

But that's not going to happen.

I gave him everything, and he threw me away like I was nothing – all because of a recording.

Who's behind this?

Who's so cruel and hateful that they want to destroy us?

Chapter 36

Armani

Walking to the nearest bar, I order a tumbler of whiskey and tell the barman to keep them coming.

The burn of alcohol does nothing to douse the rage ravaging me.

The shock is still raw and potent, crashing over me in waves.

Tiana betrayed me.

She broke her vow.

I loved her so fucking much. She was a dream come true.

The image of her face as I made love to her fills my mind before it shatters.

Another man saw what was only meant for my eyes.

I toss my head back, draining the glass.

Fuck, she's a good actress. Not once did she waver while pretending to be the innocent victim.

She's probably calling Misha and crying to him.

Letting out a sigh, I pull my phone from my pocket and dial my best friend's number.

He's going to take her side.

I'm losing more than just my wife.

"Hey, it's been a while. Fuck, just one more week, and I'm done with training," he says.

He sounds happy to hear from me, which means Tiana hasn't called him yet.

"Brother?" he asks when I don't say anything.

Sitting at the bar, I rest my palm on my forehead. "Tiana cheated on me."

There's a long pause before Misha replies, "What the fuck did you just say?"

My tone is somber, danger flirting around the edges. "Tiana fucked another man."

"No." I hear the disbelief in the single word. "She wouldn't."

I pull the voice recorder out, and not giving a fuck that other people will hear, I press play and hold my phone to the speaker so Misha will hear.

"*Cristo,*" a man to my right mutters under his breath. He shakes his head, giving me a pitiful look.

When I bring the phone back to my ear, I mutter, "The proof is damming, Misha."

More silence follows my words before he says, "I don't care what I heard, Tiana wouldn't betray you."

Just like I thought, Misha will take her side no matter what.

"I'm going to find the fucker and kill him," I growl.

The man to my right nods his approval.

"And I'll help, but don't you dare lay a finger on my sister," Misha warns.

I let out an empty-sounding chuckle. "She got gifts and love notes from the bastard. They fucking rubbed it in my face, and I believed when she told me she didn't know who was sending her the packages. And then there's the recording of them fucking. What other proof do you need?"

"I'll have to see it with my own fucking eyes. I'll have to catch Tiana in another man's bed before I believe any of this."

Another chuckle escapes me. "I wish she was as loyal to me as you are to her."

"Armani," Misha says, his tone serious, "Don't do anything rash. Have you checked your apartment for bugs? Anyone could've recorded you and Tiana and altered it to make it sound like she's with another man."

True.

"But why? I've been searching high and fucking low to find out who sent the gifts. I'm hunting a fucking ghost."

"Send the recording to St. Monarch's. Let them take it apart and tell us if it's the real thing."

Because of the respect I have for Misha, I agree, "Okay."

"If it's the real thing and Tiana cheated on you, I'll help you kill the fucker."

"And Tiana?" I ask, hating that I'm placing Misha in such a difficult situation, but I need to hear him say he'll take my side.

"I can't turn my back on my sister, Armani. I'll support you any way I can, but I can't cut Tiana out of my life."

"Your support is all I want."

"Have a drink, calm down, and let's figure out what's going on."

I pick up the glass the bartender refilled and down the whiskey in one go.

Talking to Misha has cooled my anger, and I start to go over all the facts with him. "There are the two gifts and notes. I sent the last package to St. Monarch's, but it came back clean. I received the voice recorder at work."

"The package had no fingerprints?"

"None," I mutter.

"If Tiana were fucking a random guy, he wouldn't think to wipe the package clean."

True.

"You're the logical one between us," Misha says. "This looks like a setup to tear you and Tiana apart. Do you have any ex-girlfriends crazy enough to go to such lengths?"

I let out another chuckle. "No. I've been at St. Monarch's with you for three years. You know who's been in my bed."

"Yeah," he mutters. "What about enemies?"

"I have plenty of those after the job I did two months ago."

"It's a start."

Unable to wrap my mind around this shit show, I say, "It's such a stupid way to get revenge, though. That's not how we work. We torture, maim, and kill. We don't break up marriages."

"There's always a first time for everything. The fucker wants to hurt you, and honestly, this is worse than any torture I can think of. Nothing fucks you up like the woman you love betraying you."

"You're right," I sigh. "It fucking hurts like a bitch."

Doubt trickles into my heart.

What if this was all staged, and Tiana is innocent?

Jesus. Then I fucked up big time.

"Send the recording. I'll pass it on to Director Koslov and get him to check it. We'll get to the bottom of this."

I nod even though Misha can't see me.

"I'll be at your place first thing in the morning. Don't do anything until I get there. I'll talk to Tiana."

I nod again, feeling much calmer but fucking drained. "Thanks, brother."

"Have another drink and try to get some rest. I'll see you soon."

We end the call, and I drop the phone on the counter while picking up my tumbler of whiskey.

The man to my left gets up from his stool and places cash on the counter. "His drink is on me." He gives me a chin lift before he leaves.

He was probably fucked over by his wife.

As I sip on the amber fluid, I repeatedly go over everything that's happened, looking for some clue that will lead me to figure out what's going on.

What if Tiana is innocent?

She always answers when I call. She responds to text messages as soon as I send them. She spends a lot of time with Mamma and *Zia* Giada. The neighbors have seen nothing out of the ordinary. Tiana's always at home, waiting for me. Not once has she faked a headache to get out of having sex with me.

And it always felt real with her.

The emotions. The desire. The submissiveness.

Ice pours into my veins.

The recording could easily be put together with today's technology.

Rushing to my feet, I settle the bill for my drinks before running home. I burst through the front door and head straight for our bedroom to check for any listening devices.

I check the bed lamps, the bedside tables, our closet, and any fucking place I can think of. Finally, when I look inside the fire detector, I find a black device, so small it's the size of my pinky nail, stuck to the inside.

Staring at the proof that this has all been a set-up, intense relief pours through my body.

Tiana didn't cheat on me.

Cazzo.

My breaths speed up, and placing my hands on my knees, I gasp through the relief.

She hasn't been with anyone but me. She's still mine.

"Tiana!" I shout as I continue to search and find one in every room.

But I don't find Tiana anywhere.

"*Bella*," I call out, even though it's just me in the house.

She probably went to my mother's place. I'll check on her once I've sent the recording to Misha.

I put the bugs in a bag, and opening my laptop, I press play and record the audio. I send the email to Misha and organize for a courier to pick up the device so it can be delivered to St. Monarch's.

Closing the laptop, I take my phone out and dial Tiana's number. The call doesn't connect but instead goes to voicemail.

"Come home, *bella*. I believe you."

Exhausted from the hell I've been through, I walk to the bedroom again, and this time I notice the pair of leggings lying on the floor near the walk-in closet.

Moving closer, my stomach bottoms out for a second time today.

Her clothes are gone.

I swing around, and my eyes fall on the bedside table. I see the pregnancy tests and the cupcake.

Daddy.

"*Madre di Dio*," I breathe as the happy surprise registers. I walk closer and check the pregnancy tests.

She's pregnant.

Instead of enjoying the moment, my thoughts are bombarded with how I treated her tonight.

I fucking pointed a loaded gun at my pregnant wife.

Jesus, she was so upset.

She looked at me with no doubt in her mind that I would kill her.

Dio, what have I done?

Chapter 37

Tiana

It took me two and a half hours to get to Milan and another one and a half hours to reach Lovere, a small coastal town.

I got a bunk bed in The Lake Hostel because it's the cheapest place I could find.

The view of the lake is nice, though.

Exhausted, I let out a sigh as I switch on my phone. I ignore all the messages as they come through and dial Misha's number.

"Tiana! Are you okay?"

I shake my head and immediately burst into tears. Walking farther away from the hostel and toward the lake, I squeeze the words out, "Armani thinks I betrayed him."

"I know. I spoke with him. Is he back home yet?"

"I don't know." I wipe the tears from my cheeks. "I ran."

"Jesus Christ," my brother mutters. "Go home, Tiana. I'll be there first thing in the morning."

I shake my head again. "No. I'm just calling you to let you know I'm safe. I need time to process everything. Don't worry about me. I'll be in touch."

Not giving Misha a chance to talk me out of my decision, I end the call and turn off the phone. Walking closer to the lake, I throw the device in the water so I can't be tracked.

I've always put everyone else first, but now that I'm pregnant, it ends.

Only one life matters – my baby's.

Somehow I'll get through the heartache and loss I've suffered. I'll find a place to live and get a job.

But for the next ten days, I'll stay at the hostel while I try to deal with the blow I've been dealt and figure out where to go from here.

Another wave of unbearable pain hits, and I sit down flat on my butt. I bring my knees up and wrap my arms around my shins, and staring at the water from where I'm on a patch of lawn with darkness all around me, I cry.

I understand why Armani thought I betrayed him. I'd react the same if I heard a recording of him.

I understand why he's angry and hurt.

But he pointed a gun at me, and I knew in my heart of hearts he was going to kill me.

That's how it works in the bratva and mafia. Betrayal equals death.

My heart is completely and utterly shattered.

The man I love will probably hunt me down and kill me. When he finds out I'm pregnant, it won't matter because he'll think I'm carrying another man's baby.

I've been through hell before, but nothing like this.

I've watched Misha being beaten until he was unconscious.

I've been forced to vomit the food he stole for me. Then they made me eat it again.

I've been abused and degraded.

But nothing compares to the unbearable heartache of losing Armani.

He was my future, and now that it's been ripped away from me, I don't know what to do.

Suddenly a shiver creeps up my spine, and it feels like I'm being watched. Paranoid, I get up and glance around me as I rush back toward the hostel.

I'll have to get used to the feeling of being hunted because Armani is not the type of person to give up easily.

He gave up trusting and loving you.

I shake my head as I walk to the bedroom I'm sharing with three other people. I haven't seen any of them yet.

The irrefutable evidence crushed his trust in me.

Fully dressed, I climb into the foreign bed. I only kick off my shoes.

As I pull the covers over my body, I miss the smell of home – of Armani.

I turn my back to the rest of the room and squeeze my eyes shut as loneliness seeps deep into my bones.

It's the thing I feared most – being alone.

You have your baby.

I can't go to Misha, because he'll tell me to go home to my husband.

I can't go to Mamma, because she'll take her son's side, which is expected.

I can't go to the Aslanhovs. Not after I cost Mr. Aslanhov the deal with Karlin.

I can't go home because Armani hates me.

Armani hates me.

Suppressing a sob, I press my face into the pillow and weep for my marriage that's ended in such a brutal death.

I hear female voices approaching the room, but I don't understand what they're saying. It sounds like they're talking German.

The women come in, and the light is turned on. I keep still, hoping they'll think I'm asleep.

They laugh and talk some more, and even though I don't know them, I don't feel as alone as anymore.

I can't fall asleep, though, and lie awake, thinking about all that I've lost.

I remember our wedding day and the song that played when I walked down the aisle. *You're the reason* by *Callum Scott*. I've listened to it many times since then, wondering if that's how Armani felt about me, and that's why he chose it.

But he didn't climb every mountain. He didn't swim every ocean to be near me. He broke what we had.

The song feels like it was a premonition all along, only Armani isn't going to swoop in to save me again.

I never thought a man like him could love someone like me. But he did. He loved me more than I've ever been loved.

And I've lost it.

I miss the feel of his body sprawled over mine and his face pressed into the crook of my neck. I miss feeling his breaths on my skin.

I curl into a smaller bundle as the heartache shreds through me again.

God, what have I done that you're punishing me like this? You said you'd never give me more than I can bear, but I can't handle this. It's killing me.

Again I have to suppress a sob, so I don't disturb the other women in the room.

Time creeps by, and eventually, they switch off the light, quiet down, and fall asleep.

I place my hand on my abdomen and caress the spot.

I miss your daddy. I want you to know you were created out of love, little one. No matter what you hear in the future, your daddy's a good man. Things just…weren't meant to be between us.

Your daddy might not be around, but you'll have your Uncle Misha. I'll tell him about you as soon as I've found a place for us to live.

Devastating emotions crash over me, and my body shakes as I try to keep the sobs from escaping. I press my face into the pillow and gasp as my tears soak the fabric.

God, Armani. I wish you'd believe me.

Chapter 38

Armani

I'm losing my mind.

Where I'm known to be calm and collected, I'm nothing but a fucking mess since shit went down.

I've hired St. Monarch's to search for Tiana. They're scouring the fucking world for her.

Last night was the longest night of my life. I've never felt so powerless before. I kept trying Tiana's phone, but it kept going to voicemail.

I look at the note she left me.

> **I'm leaving to protect the baby and not because I'm guilty.**
>
> **I love you, Armani. So much.**

Misha called to say he heard from her, but she didn't tell him where she was.

I haven't even told my mother Tiana's gone.

She left because I threatened her. And our unborn baby.

I lost my shit entirely, and it terrified her. Even if I find her, will she be able to forgive me? Will she ever feel safe with me again?

Jesus, what have I done?

My phone vibrates in my hand, and my head snaps up. Not recognizing the number, I open the message.

God. No. Don't do this to me.

I stare at a photo of Tiana running toward a train, fear and heartache etched deep on her face. Her cheeks are wet with tears, and her eyes look frantic.

How easy it was to break your perfect little romance.

Let's see who can get to her first.

My breaths speed up, and my heart fucking shrivels.

Someone pounds on the door, and darting to my feet from where I was sitting in the courtyard because the house is too empty, I yank it open.

Misha barges inside, takes one look at my haggard face, then says, "We'll find her."

I hold my phone out to him. "We're not the only ones looking for her."

Frowning, he takes the device and reads the message. "*Blyad'!*" he curses in Russian. "We have to move. Jesus, where would she go?"

Walking out the door, I say, "Let's start at the train station."

I don't even bother locking the door behind me. Misha and I run to where we can get a gondola to take us to the other end of Venice.

When we reach the station, my phone vibrates again.

Target spotted in Milan, boarding another train to Lovere.

"St. Monarch's just notified me she was in Milan and headed toward Lovere."

"Thank fuck. At least we know in what direction we're going," Misha mutters.

We get two tickets, and boarding the train, I slump down in a seat. My knee immediately starts to bounce from the worry eating at my gut.

"Whoever is fucking with us has one hell of a head start," I grumble.

"Tiana is smart. She'll run at the first sign of danger."

I fucking hope so.

Just keep running until I find you, bella.

My phone vibrates again, and it's another photo of Tiana. She's sitting in the fucking dark, looking so hopeless, my heart cracks down the middle.

I can't make out much of her surroundings, so it doesn't give us any clues.

So pretty. So vulnerable.

I'll take from you what you took from me.

Jesus, the photo was taken close-up. He might already have her.

My breaths speed up, and I feel like a cornered animal.

"What's wrong?" Misha asks.

"Another photo," I say as I show the message to him. "We might get to her too late."

Misha clenches his jaw as anger tightens his features. "If he fucking hurts a hair on her head, I'll rip him apart with my bare hands."

He's already hurt her. So did I.

My woman's been through hell growing up, and now she's been thrown right back into the fiery pits.

It takes four fucking hours before we reach Lovere, and there's a burning need inside me to kill the fucker who's tortured us.

I will fucking find you, and you'll beg me to kill you.

When we get off the speed train, I glance around, wondering where the fuck to go.

Just as I open my phone to look at the photo again, another one comes through.

It shows Tiana sipping on a cup of coffee while looking at a lake.

We're waiting for you.

Intense relief washes through me. "She's alive." I show Misha the photo. "Let's go."

"Where?" he asks.

While tucking my phone into my pocket, I run toward the road where taxis are parked.

The partial sign in the background of the photo was all I needed.

"The Lake Hostel," I answer as I open the back door and climb inside. In Italian, I instruct the driver where to take us, then look at Misha, "The fucker is waiting for us."

"This has to be an enemy, you pissed off," Misha mutters.

"We'll find out which one soon enough." I pull my gun from behind my back and check the clip while keeping the weapon out of the driver's view.

Misha does the same, then whispers, "We'll have to make every bullet count."

"Trust me, I won't miss."

The taxi pulls up to the hostel, and I pay the fee. When we climb out, I scan our surroundings.

As the taxi drives off, I point to the left side of the property. "Go around that side. I'll take the right. If Tiana's not sitting by the lake, we can meet at the back entrance."

"Got it."

Splitting up, I jog toward the right side of the hostel while keeping my weapon ready by my thigh. As I come around the back, my eyes wildly search for my wife.

The moment I spot her walking back toward the entrance, I break out into a run.

She glances around her, and the second her eyes land on me, she throws the cup to the ground and runs into the building.

Fuck.

I hurry inside and see as she rushes straight through and out the front entrance.

"Tiana!" I shout, setting after her.

Cazzo, she's fast.

Tiana heads for the road, and not looking for oncoming traffic, she crosses and darts into the trees lining the side of a mountain.

"Tiana!" I shout again, following her into the forest. "Tiana. Stop!"

On the uneven terrain, I start to catch up to her when a bullet whistles past me, slamming into a tree trunk.

"*Cazzo!*"

Another bullet hits near Tiana's feet, and she shrieks before falling to her knees. She scrambles up and continues to run, screaming, "Please, Armani! Stop!"

She fucking thinks I'm shooting at her.

Stopping dead in my tracks, I search the area and see a man standing three hundred yards from us.

I return fire and catch sight of Misha as he runs toward the man. Knowing he'll take out the fucker, I set after Tiana again.

She's managed to put some distance between us as she darts like a hare over the rough terrain.

I put everything I have into the chase and start to close the distance between us.

"Tiana, wait!" I call out.

She glances over her shoulder, acute terror on her face. She stumbles again but keeps pushing forward.

When I'm close, I reach out to grab her, which has her shrieking and darting to the side. I reach for her again and manage to grab her shirt.

Tiana swings around, and my body plows into hers. I quickly wrap my arms around her and twist us, so I take the brunt of the fall.

The second my back slams against the ground, she tears free from my hold and pushes away from me.

"Stop!" I shout. "I'm not going to hurt you."

She scrambles to her feet, and I get a good look at the woman I've terrified. Her tears have formed tracks down her cheeks, and her breaths are coming way too fast.

"Please," she begs, taking a step back. Her hand covers her abdomen where our baby is. "You can do to me what you want once I've had the baby."

Slowly, I get up, holding an arm out to show her to wait. "I'm not going to hurt you, *bella*."

With extreme caution in her eyes, she takes another step away from me.

The way she looks at me flays my heart wide open.

"Tiana," Misha shouts as he comes toward us.

She whirls around, and seeing her brother, she runs for him. She throws herself into his arms and starts to sob her heart out.

And all I can do is stand and watch because I've lost the right to touch her when I threatened her life.

Chapter 39

Tiana

My chest is on fire as I cling to Misha.

I knew Armani would come after me, but I didn't expect him to find me so quickly. When I saw him run toward me, my heart almost gave out from fright.

All I could think was to protect my baby.

"I've got you," Misha says. "I've killed the fucker."

What fucker?

I pull a little back and glance over my shoulders, seeing Armani is still very much alive.

Thank God.

I might be terrified of him, but I still love him.

Feeling safe with Misha by my side, I ask, "Who did you kill?"

"The guy who's been causing all this shit between you and Armani," he explains.

They found him?

"Where is he?" I demand, wanting to see the face of the man who's ruined my life.

When Misha takes a step away from me, I grab hold of his left hand. He immediately wraps his arm around me and keeps me by his side as we head back in the direction of the road.

I'm overly conscious of Armani, who's right behind us.

When I glance over my shoulder again, he says, "I'm not going to hurt you."

Misha stops dead in his tracks and scowls at me. "Why did you run from Armani?" Then he directs the dark look at Armani. "Why do you need to reassure her that you won't hurt her?"

Shit.

I keep quiet, not knowing how Misha will react if I tell him why.

Armani steps forward. "I scared the shit out of her last night."

Misha's fingers flex around the handle of the gun. "What did you do?"

Keep quiet.

"I pointed a gun at her," he admits.

Dear God.

I dart in front of Armani, holding my hands up between Misha and me. "Stay calm."

His eyes are nothing but a violent storm as he hisses, "Don't fucking tell me to stay calm."

"Misha!" I shriek when he reaches over me to get to Armani. "I'm pregnant!"

My brother freezes, and his eyes snap to me. Instantly his face morphs from angry to surprised. "You're pregnant?"

I nod quickly. "So please don't kill the father of my child."

Misha yanks me to his chest, hugging the ever-loving crap out of me, then he pats Armani's shoulder as if he didn't want to kill him a second ago.

These men will be the end of me.

"Congrats," Misha says with a wide smile. "I'm going to be an uncle."

Wanting to get out of the forest, I remind him, "Where's the body?"

"This way."

We start to walk again, and when Armani falls in beside me, I move closer to Misha.

He might not want to kill me anymore, but it doesn't mean I'm okay with what happened.

We finally reach the body, but I don't recognize the man.

The three of us stare down at the dead man, then Misha mutters, "Who the fuck is he?"

"I have no fucking idea." Crouching down, Armani pats over the body and pulls a wallet out. He flips it open and checks all the cards. "Giovanni Sibilia?"

"Never heard of him," Misha says.

Just to be clear, I mumble, "Me too."

Armani rises to his feet, then locks eyes with me. The punch of his intense eyes makes me take a step back.

Yesterday they were filled with hatred.

"Are we going to stand here all day while the two of you stare at each other?" Misha asks. "Let's go home."

I look away. "Which home?"

There's a moment's silence before Armani murmurs, "Ours."

I shake my head. "No." Walking away from the men, I find my way through the trees until I reach the road. Checking for traffic, I cross over and head toward the hostel's entrance.

He didn't trust me.

Because of his actions, we could've lost our baby.

He hurt me.

"Tiana," Armani says when I walk out the back and toward the lake.

I stop when I reach the lake and sit down on the grass. Armani comes to crouch in front of me, so I turn my face away from him.

"I'm sorry, *bella*."

I shake my head, all the heartache and fear I felt because of him too raw in my chest.

"*Tesoro mia*," he whispers.

When he tries to reach for my face, I push his hand away from me and glare at him. "My words meant nothing last night. Yours mean nothing today."

Armani sits down and rests his arm on his knee. He leans forward. "Please look at me."

My eyes snap to his, and I let him see how much he hurt me.

I see my pain reflect on his face as he says, "I'm so fucking sorry."

I press my palm to my heart. "I understand why you were angry. I even understand why you didn't believe me. What I'm struggling with is that you pointed a loaded weapon at me."

He nods, guilt tightening his features. "What I did was unforgivable, but I never would've pulled the trigger."

"Is that supposed to make me feel better?"

He shakes his head, then glances around us before looking at me again. "It's not safe here. Can we please go home?"

I shouldn't, but I can't stop myself from asking, "How will I be any safer in *your* house?"

"*Our* house," he corrects me, then adds, "Misha will be there."

My shoulders slump, and I lower my gaze to my hands, where his ring is still on my finger. "What's going on?"

"Someone is targeting me." Armani climbs to his feet and holds his hand out to me.

I hesitate before laying my palm in his. He pulls me up, and before I find my balance, I'm yanked to his chest, and his arms wrap around me.

"Don't," I gasp as the heartache fills my chest.

He presses a kiss to my hair. "I'm sorry, *amore mia*. Please give me a chance to fix what I've broken."

I push against his chest, and I feel his reluctance when he lets me go.

"I need time," I mutter.

"I'll give you all the time you need. Just come home with me."

I might be angry with him, but it doesn't stop me from nodding.

We walk back to where Misha is watching us from the hostel. When we reach him, I say, "I have to get my luggage."

They follow me to the room, and I notice the pained expression on Armani's face when he sees where I slept last night.

He comes to take the bag from me, and then I'm ushered out of the hostel.

By the time we get home, it's already dark, and we're all exhausted. I slept a little on the train, but it didn't help much.

I quickly prepare the guest room for Misha, then go to the kitchen to make coffee.

Seeing the broken cup and mess on the floor, I grab paper towels and wet them beneath the tap.

"I'll clean up," Armani says as he comes into the kitchen.

He takes the towels from me, and crouching by my feet, he cleans the floor. I'm just about to take a step back, when he grabs hold of my hip. Moving onto his knees, he presses his forehead to my abdomen.

"I'm sorry, *bella*," he breathes before pressing a kiss to the area where our baby is growing.

I'm just about to place my hand on his head when Misha enters the kitchen, muttering, "Don't forgive him."

I turn away from Armani and take three cups from the cupboard.

Armani continues to clean the mess on the floor, discards the towels in the trash, then looks at Misha. "Let's talk in the living room."

My eyes dart to the men as they leave the kitchen, and I start to worry whether they're going to fight.

When their coffee is ready, I carry the cups to the living room and hear Armani say, "I know there's no excuse for what I did, but I lost my mind thinking she was with another man. What would you do if it were Aurora?"

I pause in the hallway and shamelessly eavesdrop.

"As your friend, I get where you're coming from. But as Tiana's brother, I'm fucking pissed."

"I understand," Armani replies.

I roll my eyes and walk into the living room. "Everybody understands everything. Here's your coffee." I set it on the table and walk right out of the room again.

Everybody understands, so things just have to be okay again.

I rush into the bathroom and shut the door behind me. Pressing my back to it, I sink down to my butt while trying to fight the tears.

It still hurts.

I can't just erase all the feelings.

I can't just forget the way Armani looked at me.

I can't just forget that for one night, he didn't love me.

It was so easy for him to go from loving to hating me. I could never do that to him.

Even when I thought he was chasing me to kill me, I still loved him.

I would've loved him even if he had shot me.

With my dying breath.

Chapter 40

Armani

It's almost midnight, and Tiana is still sitting in the living room, pretending to watch TV.

Misha went to bed a while ago, and I'm sitting way too far from my wife, who's not giving me the time of day.

I get why, though. She has all the right in the world to be angry with me.

I'll grovel for the rest of my life, if that's what it takes, but I'll win her back.

My eyes flick to Tiana, and I catch her looking at me before she quickly glances back at the TV.

"Aren't you tired?" I ask.

"You can go to bed if you want to sleep," she answers.

"You need your rest. You've had a crazy two days. All the stress can't be good for the baby."

She lets out a sigh, then switches off the TV and walks to our bedroom. Climbing beneath the covers, she turns her back to my side of the bed and pulls the covers so high they almost cover her head.

I leave the room to make sure all the doors are locked and switch off the lights before I return to climb into bed. Tiana still keeps her back to me, making it clear she doesn't want me to touch her.

I lie on my back and stare at the ceiling, the minutes ticking over into an hour. I listen to my wife drift off to sleep and relax now that she's getting some rest.

She just needs time.

Tiana turns onto her back, throwing her arm above her head like she always does. The corner of my mouth lifts, and I wait a bit longer before I move closer. Careful not to wake her, I spread my body over hers and press my face to her neck.

Inhaling her scent, I finally find some peace.

I wrap my arms around her and silently promise never to let go again.

I feel her hand on the back of my head, and closing my eyes, I whisper, "Thank you."

She curls into me, and I feel her jerk. Her breaths are warm on my shoulder before I feel the wetness of a teardrop.

I hold her tighter and begin to press kisses all over her hair and neck. "I'll never doubt you again. I promise I'll make up for the damage I've done."

She nods against me.

"We're having a baby," I murmur.

She nods again.

"I hate that I ruined the surprise."

She pulls a little back, and our eyes lock. "Did you see the tests?"

"Yes."

The heartache I've caused her still lives on her face as she whispers, "You scared me. How do I know whenever we fight, you won't fly off the handle again?"

"Because I'd rather die than hurt you like this ever again. Whoever's targeting us must know how I feel about infidelity. They used the perfect weapon against me."

"Who hates you so much that they'll try to tear us apart?"

"I have many enemies. It can be any of the bastards."

Her eyes shine in the meager moonlight falling through the windows. "Are we safe here?"

"I'm not leaving your side until I've killed the fucker. Misha will also stay for a while." I rest my head on my palm and stare down at her. "Do you think you can forgive me?"

"It's not the forgiving part I'm struggling with."

"Tell me what you're struggling with."

She turns on her side, facing me, and I feel her breath on my chest.

"It's that you hated me. It was so easy for you to stop loving me."

Jesus.

Before I can correct her, she continues, "When you were chasing me through the forest, and I thought you were going to kill me, I still loved you."

My heart stutters in my chest. "Loved?"

"Love."

Placing my finger beneath her chin, I tip her face up so she'll look at me. "I never hated you, *bella*. I was angry."

"I saw it in your eyes."

"I hated hearing the recording of you with another man. That's what was killing me. Even though I thought you betrayed me, I still loved you."

"It was traumatizing hearing my voice in such an intimate setting with a stranger."

I pull her against me and kiss her shoulder. "I'll find whoever's behind this and kill the fucker. I promise I will make him suffer a million times more than we've suffered."

Suddenly my phone starts to ring, and I reach for the bedside table. Not recognizing the number, I answer, "De Santis."

"Tell me, Mr. De Santis, how does it feel when someone fucks with you?" The thick Russian accent has me sitting upright in bed, and I try to place where I've heard it before.

"You and Misha made me look like a fool. It's not something I can forgive."

Madre di Dio.

"Makarova," I growl the fuckers name. "I considered you could be behind it but never actually thought you'd be such a bitch about losing a woman you didn't want in the first place."

Tiana darts upright, her eyes wide on me.

"It's not the woman I care about. It's my reputation."

"You started a war with the wrong man over such a trivial thing as your reputation."

Makarova lets out a chuckle. "You're a small fish in a sea for sharks, boy."

I'm going to enjoy killing you, fucker.

"A pirana can do more damage than a shark, fucker," I say before I end the call and quickly press dial on Luca's number.

"Armani?" he answers with concern already lacing his voice.

"Makarova fucked with my wife. I'm giving you a courtesy call to let you know I'm going to kill him."

"What did he do?"

"He made it look like she was having an affair, and he had a man watching her. The fucker shot at her." I don't even bother telling him the man also tried to take me out.

"*Cristo*," Luca curses. "Let me talk to Viktor. You can't take Makarova on your own."

A victorious smile curves my lips.

That's exactly what I wanted to hear.

"Thank you, sir."

We end the call, and I drop the device on the bedside table before lying down again.

Tiana shoves my shoulder, demanding, "What happened? Tell me."

Grabbing hold of her, I force her onto her back and cover her body with mine. "Makarova is butthurt because I got you, and now we're going to war."

"War?" she gasps. "Isn't there another way?"

I shake my head. "He fucked with you, *bella*. The only way is with him dying."

Her face fills with worry. "I don't want you, Misha, or Alek getting hurt."

"We won't. It sounds like Luca and Viktor will help out to take down Makarova."

Tiana stares into my eyes. "I barely survived losing you once, I won't survive a second time."

"You never lost me," I assure her. "I have a lot of groveling to do." I press a kiss to her jaw. "It will probably take me a lifetime." I kiss the corner of her mouth. "So don't forgive me too easily. Let me work for every day I get to spend with you."

Slowly a smile curves her lips, and it feels like the sun is shining again.

I watch her reaction closely as I lower my head, and when she allows me to kiss her, my heart feels whole again.

Chapter 41

Tiana

Even though we went to bed late and I didn't sleep the night before, I wake up at the crack of dawn.

I'm happy to be back at home, and the talk we had last night helped heal my heart a little, but I'm going to let Armani grovel.

I feel his cock harden against my thigh, and where I would usually push him onto his back and have my wicked way with him, I lie still.

Armani's arms tighten around me, and he presses a kiss to my neck. "Do you want me to beg, *bella*?"

A smile curves my lips. "Yes."

He chuckles as his hand moves down my side to settle on my abdomen. "Let me fuck you, *amore mia*. I need to be buried deep inside of you."

"Hmm," I tease him. "I'm going to need more begging."

His hand slips beneath my leggings and panties, and his middle finger circles my clit. "Please, *bella. Cazzo*, I need you. Without you, I'm half a man." His finger brushes through the wetness gathering between my legs, then he pushes inside me. "Let me show you how sorry I am."

"Okay," I give my permission.

Armani kisses my neck, and pulling his hand out, he starts to undress me while bathing my skin in more kisses.

When we're both naked, he covers my body with his, and stares deep into my eyes. "I would've died if I lost you."

My heart melts a little more.

"When I first saw you, I had no idea I'd fall so hard for you," he murmurs before pressing a tender kiss to my mouth. Lifting his head, he continues, "Please give me this morning and the rest of your life to love you. I'll never endanger our love again."

Emotion fills my chest, and just overwhelmingly happy to have my husband back, I nod. A mischievous smile forms on my face. "But you're still going to grovel."

"Yes, Mrs. De Santis." He gives me a hot grin. "Starting now."

He pulls me down the bed until my head is no longer on the pillow, and when he comes to kneel by my hair, I grin. I know what's coming, and I love it.

He leans forward, pressing kisses between my breasts before he sucks my nipples into his mouth, then he moves down to my abdomen.

As his hardness comes into my line of sight, I reach up and wrap my fingers around his thick girth, stroking him from base to tip.

"*Cazzo*," Armani hisses against my skin. "Suck me hard. I want to feel your teeth," he orders.

I spread my legs wide open while I swirl my tongue around the swollen head of his manhood.

I love how velvety his skin feels on my tongue, and I let my teeth scrape against him as I suck him deep into my mouth.

Letting out a groan, he praises me, "Yes, *bella*, just like that."

Armani plants his face between my thighs and sucks my clit so hard my hips buck off the bed. I return the favor by hollowing my cheeks and taking him to the back of my throat.

As his need grows, he shows no mercy, sucking and biting my sensitive flesh until I'm an aching mess beneath him.

Just as we're about to orgasm, he pulls away from me and comes to lie on top of me, so we're face to face. I let out a groan as he feathers kisses over my neck and jaw before locking eyes with me.

"You're killing me," I complain.

With a knowing smirk, Armani fills me slowly with his hardness, then he stills deep inside me. "I love how much you need my cock." His palm brushes up and down my side, the look in his eyes pure affection. "I love you, Tiana," he murmurs, his tone a little hoarse. "I love you so much I can't function in a world where I don't have you. I can't sleep without feeling you beneath me and being buried inside you. You've ruined me for anyone else. There will always be only you."

Lifting my hands to his face, I cup his jaw, and with my mouth an inch from his, I whisper, "I love you. You're my home. I couldn't sleep either. I missed feeling your breath on my neck and your weight covering me."

Our mouths fuse together, and slower than usual, Armani makes love to me. It's much more intense and loaded with emotions, and by the time we find our release, everything feels right in the world again.

Armani gives me one last kiss before pulling out of me and going to the bathroom.

I sit up and stretch out before getting out of bed. While I get ready for the day, Armani beats me to the kitchen.

I'm surprised when he hands me a cup of tea, then he explains, "I noticed you didn't drink coffee yesterday and figured it's not good for the baby. So tea it is."

I take a sit and give him a satisfied smile. "I can get used to this, Mr. De Santis."

He lets out a chuckle. "That's the plan, *bella*."

We enjoy our beverages in the courtyard, watching as the sun rises. When Misha finally wakes up, Armani prepares breakfast for us while my brother and I sit at the kitchen table.

Armani places a single flower beside my croissant, and kissing the top of my head, he murmurs, "Enjoy, *amore mia*."

"Hmm," Misha grumbles, "Someone's going to be spoiled rotten."

I grin at him before I take a bite of my pastry. "*Someone's* going to enjoy every second of it."

The men chuckle, but the happy atmosphere doesn't last long, because Armani says, "Makarova called in the middle of the night." His eyes lock with Misha's. "Turns out he's behind the fucking shit show."

"What the fuck?" Misha growls. "Seriously?"

With a thirst for vengeance darkening his eyes, Armani nods. "Luca is talking to Viktor. It sounds like the bratva and mafia will band together to take out the fucker."

"As long as I get a minute with him," Misha mutters.

"You can get your minute," Armani replies, his tone deep and dangerous, giving me goosebumps, "But I finish him off."

For a moment, I pity Karlin, but then I remember what he's done, and I hope he suffers severely at the hands of the men in my life.

Chapter 42

Armani

After leaving Tiana with my mother and aunt at St. Monarch's, where we met up with Alek, Viktor, and Luca, we traveled to Russia with an army of men.

Gathering in a bratva-owned warehouse before shit goes down, my muscles are wound tight, and I can't wait to get my hands on Makarov.

Today the fucker dies.

Viktor got his hands on plans for Makarova's property.

"We'll attack in two groups. Twenty men from the back of the property and twenty from the front," Viktor instructs while indicating on the map. "Luca and Armani will lead the mafia, of course." Viktor glances up to look at Misha and Alek. "The bratva follows me."

"Yes, sir," we all chorus.

"We need to move fast to keep the element of surprise on our side," Luca says. "That's if the fucker isn't expecting us."

"He'd be stupid not to," I mutter.

"Check your weapons before we head out," Viktor orders. "And for God's sake, don't fucking shoot me during all the action."

Some of us chuckle.

"Radio check," Luca says, and for the next minute, we all make sure we can communicate with each other.

Viktor nods, then orders, "Let's head out."

Under the cover of darkness, we all pile into SUVs and form a convoy as we drive to Makarova's house. We stop in a side street, and when we all get out, I notice a woman peaking through her curtains before yanking them shut.

Alek notices as well and says, "Don't worry, brother. Even if we blow up Makarova's house, no one will come out."

"Good," I mutter.

"Let's go kill some fuckers," he grins at me.

Misha pats Alek's back. "Leave some for us."

Alek shrugs and chuckles. "I'll leave Makarova for you. The rest are fair game."

I look at Alek and Misha before I join Luca and our men. The two groups split, and I sling my submachine gun over my shoulder while keeping my Glock in my hand.

Ducking low, we all run to the wall, and one by one, we scale it.

Landing in a crouching position, I wait until Luca says, "Forward."

The yard is mostly dark until you reach the immediate area around the house. Lights shine from the windows, and I count five men guarding the back.

This will be child's play unless the fucker has most of his guards inside the house.

"Everyone ready?" Luca asks into the earpiece.

"Yes," Viktor answers. "On your command."

Everything stills in my body, and my focus is one hundred percent on the mission.

Find and kill Makarova.

I was very clear that whoever gets to the fucker first has to keep him for me. I'll be pissed as fuck if someone else kills him.

"Breach!" Luca gives the order, and we all move forward.

With my arms raised and the barrel of my gun in line with my sight, I hurry toward the house.

The moment the guards become aware of us, gunfire breaks out.

We hear commotion from the front of the property while I take out the guard nearest to me with a shot to the head.

Luca takes out two guards who started shooting from a window on the first floor.

The consecutive popping of gunfire and shouts fill the air.

"The front is cleared," I hear Misha say, then Viktor follows with, "We're breaching the house."

"Entering from the back," I mutter. "No friendly fire, please."

We go in via the sliding doors and work our way to the stairway.

"*Blyad'*," Alek chuckles. "One of the guards fell over his own feet and shot himself. Funniest shit I've ever seen."

"Focus!" Viktor snaps.

Heading up the stairs, two guards open fire on us. I press my body to the banister and manage to take out one while a soldier kills the other one.

Reaching the first floor, we split into groups to search all the rooms. From the plans Viktor showed us, I know the main bedroom is at the end of the hallway. I don't waste time and head straight for it.

I kick the door open and cautiously step inside the dark room. Taking a flare from the belt around my waist, I ignite it and throw it in the middle of the room. I couldn't give two fucks whether it sets the house on fire and burns it to the ground.

From the light of the flare, my eyes take in everything around me, and seeing another door, I move toward it. Finding a hidden set of stairs, I grab my flashlight and hold it next to my weapon as I head down.

"Armani, check-in," Misha's voice sounds in my earpiece.

"Secret stairwell off the main bedroom," I murmur. "Approaching a door."

"I'm coming to you," Misha replies.

Because the door is hidden, I check it for traps before I kick it open. In a split second, I take in everything.

Counterfeit machines, stacks of cash that's ready to be shipped out, and Makarova, who's sitting behind a desk, smoking a cigar.

He grins at me, plumes of smoke wafting around him. "I expected you sooner, Mr. De Santis."

The hair on my neck rises, and my gut screams for me to run. Turning on my heel, I race up the stairs, and as I burst into the main bedroom, Misha comes in.

"Out! Get out!" I shout, and knowing we have no time, I shoot the window, shattering the glass, and hurl my body out of the room.

The air vibrates, and as I hit the grass, the house explodes, sending a shockwave of heat and debris over me.

My ears ring from the blast, and I shake my head as I push myself onto my hands and knees.

Jesus.

It takes a minute or so to catch my bearings before worry explodes in my chest, and I glance over the lawn. Seeing Misha a couple of yards from me, I crawl to him.

He lets out a groan. "Mother fucker."

"Up," I mumble as I climb to my feet. "We have to find Alek, Luca, and Viktor."

I turn around and look at the burning house while cradling my arm against my side. It took the brunt of my fall and feels broken.

"That fucking fucker," Misha growls as he stumbles toward me.

He has a massive gash across his chest, where glass probably cut him as he jumped out of the window.

He scowls at the flames and debris. "He knew his days were numbered, and he wanted the mafia and bratva in the same place to kill us all in one swoop."

I shake my head, unhappy as fuck that I didn't get to kill Makarova.

Men pour out of the burning house, some injured badly, while others seem to have survived unharmed.

"Alek," I say into the earpiece. "Check-in."

"I'm good, thanks for asking," Viktor replies. "Alek is with me at the back of the house. He's knocked out cold but looks okay. Any sign of Luca?"

He was on the top floor.

My eyes jump wildly over the survivors, and not seeing my boss, I don't hesitate and run into the burning house.

Instantly my lungs protest from all the smoke and heat, but I head toward the stairs. A beam falls from the ceiling sending sparks of embers into the air.

Coughing, I make my way up the stairs, where the banister is crumbling to pieces. My eyes are on fire and watering, the heat singeing my clothes.

"Luca!" I call out, immediately coughing again.

I see a body lying near a bedroom door, and hurrying toward it, I crouch. Intense relief shudders through me when I see it's my boss.

He's unconscious, and not wasting time, I haul his heavy body up off the floor. Wrapping his arm over my shoulders, I take his weight and drag him to the stairs.

"Where the fuck is Luca?" Viktor shouts over the earpiece.

Unable to let go of my boss, I can't answer that I have him and continue down the stairs. His dead weight throws me off balance, and we fall. Pain tears through my right arm, but I ignore it as I grab hold of Luca's wrists to pull him the rest of the way.

The moment I feel the cool air of the night against my back, Misha grabs Luca's arm and helps me drag him onto the lawn and away from danger.

"I have Luca," I finally answer. "He's unconscious."

When I check his breathing and find nothing, icy fear spreads through my veins. Not hesitating, I start CPR, and I don't fucking stop until he starts to cough and wheeze.

Thank fuck!

Sitting flat on my ass beside him, I slap his back while exhaustion creeps into my bones.

"We have to move," Misha says.

He grabs my right arm, and I let out a grunt of pain. "Not that arm. It's broken."

"Fuck, sorry."

I struggle to my feet and help Luca up. He's still dazed, so Misha helps me to drag him toward the SUVs where Viktor, Alek, and the survivors are waiting.

Viktor immediately takes Luca from us and guides him into the passenger seat of an SUV.

"Let's go," Alek shouts, taking the driver's side of another vehicle. Misha and I climb in, and as we drive away, I look at the house as it crumbles to the ground.

I might not have killed the fucker, but at least he's dead, even if it's by his own doing.

Like Misha said, Makarova knew his days were numbered, and he wanted to take as many of us as possible with him.

By the time we get back to St. Monarch's, I'm starting to get used to the pain of my broken arm.

During the flight from Russia to Geneva, we tried to take care of the wounded men, but I'm so fucking relieved when we hand them over to the care of the doctors at St. Monarch's.

I'm covered in soot as I walk into the castle, but before I can head to the suite where my family is, Luca grabs hold of my left shoulder.

"No. Get your ass to the infirmary and have them look at your arm," he orders.

When we enter the infirmary, the place is crowded. "I'll come back later when they're done tending to the wounded."

Luca shakes his head and calls a doctor closer. "Check his arm."

It takes a while because I have to get an X-ray, and when it's confirmed that my forearm is broken, it has to be set in a cast.

Just fucking great. Six weeks of walking around with this shit on my arm.

Luca stands with his arms crossed over his chest, an '*I told you so*' expression on his face.

"Yeah, you were right," I say, just to please my boss.

When I finally get to leave the infirmary, Luca drags my ass to the office and shuts the door behind us. "Thank you, Armani." He comes closer, and lifting a hand to my left shoulder, he gives me a squeeze. "You saved my life. I'll never forget it."

"I was just doing my job, sir. Without you, the mafia is fucked," I answer honestly.

His eyes lock with mine, and I see the gratitude in them. "I'm giving you the north of Italy. Franco will join me in America."

Jesus.

My lips part with shock. It's a huge fucking deal getting to control the northern territory. It takes a lifetime to work yourself up to such a high position.

He pats my shoulder. "You've proven your loyalty when you ran into a burning house for me. You deserve the promotion."

Feeling fucking elated, I grin at my boss. "Thank you, sir. I won't disappoint you."

He meets my smile with one of his own. "I know."

I finally get to head to the suite, and the moment I step inside, there's a chorus of shouts from my women.

"*Dio! Dio!* What happened to you?" Mamma worries.

"Jesus, Armani," Tiana gasps as she rushes to my side. "Come sit. Did you get medical attention? Where does it hurt? What can I do?"

I slump down on a couch and grin at my family, who's fussing over me.

"I'm fine," I say to set them all at ease. "I only have a broken arm."

When Mamma is sure I'm not going to die, she says, "You need to eat." She and *Zia* Giada check the menu and order half the dishes on it.

Tiana keeps inspecting every inch of my body, her fingers gently brushing over the fresh cast on my forearm.

"I'm fine, *bella*," I reassure her.

"Misha and Alek?" she asks, worry still dancing in her eyes.

"They're fine, too."

She lets out a sigh of relief. "I was so worried."

I press a kiss to her mouth and pull her closer until she's nestled against my side. "Makarova is dead."

Mr. Aslanhov went to Makarova's property and notified us just before we landed in Geneva. There was enough of his body left to identify him but not enough to fill a coffin. Viktor demanded a photo as proof, and I got a glimpse of the charred body.

Needless to say, I was fucking happy to see Makarova's dead body.

I hope the fucker suffered.

Once again, relief washes over her beautiful features. "Finally, we're rid of him."

I press a kiss to her hair before resting my cheek against the silky strands. "Now we can go on with our lives."

She nods. "And live happily ever after."

I place my hand against her abdomen. "With our baby."

"And us," Mamma mutters, then surprise flutters over her features. "Baby? We're having a baby?"

When I nod, *Zia* Giada and Mamma let out shouts of happiness and come to pull us up from the couch so they can hug us.

When they calm down, I say, "Let's go home. I want to sleep in my own bed tonight."

"But I ordered food," Mamma protests.

"I'll cancel the order," I say before calling the kitchen to tell them not to worry.

Ushering my family out of the suite, we pass Misha in the hallway.

"We're heading home," I tell him.

He quickly hugs Tiana and meets my eyes over the top of her head. "Let me know when you're safely home. I'll bring Aurora for a long weekend visit once I finish the training."

"Which means we'll see you in a week."

Alek comes out of a room, and I ask, "Are you coming to visit as well once you're done here?"

He shakes his head. "Sorry, I won't be able to. I'm leaving with Viktor and joining him in LA."

Closing the distance between us, I give my friend a brotherly hug. "Don't be a stranger. Come visit when you get the chance."

"Same goes for you," he mutters.

When I pull back, I can see he's happy about joining Viktor in America. I think the change of scenery will do him a world of good. And he'll get away from his father.

Happy for Alek, I ask Misha, "Do you know what you'll do when you're done with training?"

Nodding, he says, "I'll supervise Czechia, Slovakia, and Hungary."

My eyebrows fly up. "That's a huge area, brother. I'm happy for you."

Alek and Misha walk us to the front entrance of the castle, and we pause to say our goodbyes. Promising to stay in touch, I bundle my family into an SUV, and as we drive away, I hope to all that's holy, I don't have to come back to St. Monarch's ever again. I've had my fill of the place the past three years.

Chapter 43

Tiana

Seven months later…

The moment the nurse placed our son in Armani's arms, I watched him fall irrevocably in love.

It was a sight to see and left me wiping tears from my cheeks.

Diego De Santis.

I let Armani choose the name because Diego is our firstborn, who will carry on his father's legacy.

I had to spend three days in the hospital, but we're finally on our way home.

With our baby.

I stare at the sleeping bundle in my arms, vowing once again to give him the world.

Mama loves you so much, my little boy. I'll give you everything I never had.

Armani glances at us, and a stupidly happy grin spreads over his face. "I can't stop looking at you holding our son. It's the most beautiful thing I've ever seen."

Diego makes cute little sounds, making Armani and I melt in our seats.

"He's so cute," I coo. "Look at his tiny fingers."

When we get home, we walk to the nursery, and I check Diego's diaper before laying him in his brand-new crib.

We stare at our sleeping son, then Armani says, "He's sleeping in our room, right?"

"Definitely." I pick him up again and carry him to our room.

We climb on the bed and lay Diego down between us. Obsessed with our newborn, we stare at him for an hour before he wakes up.

The moment he lets out a cry, Armani darts upright. "What's wrong?"

I let out a chuckle. "He's probably hungry."

I move into a comfortable position, propping the pillows behind me, and lift Diego to my chest. The moment I pull my shirt and bra out of the way, he makes fussing sounds, his lips parting. I get him to latch onto me, and he begins to suck.

"Can I get you anything?" Armani asks.

"Water, please."

He darts out of the room and is only gone a couple of seconds before he returns with a bottle of water. He sits down on the bed and watches as I feed our son.

Slowly, he shakes his head. *"Dio, bella.* You've never been more beautiful than you are right now."

My lips curve up. "You look scorching hot when you hold our son."

Armani chuckles, "Seems that having a baby acts as an aphrodisiac."

I let out a happy sigh, and look down at Diego, who's starting to grow sleepy again.

I find myself unable to tear my eyes away from his face. Armani gets comfortable next to us, and pressing his face into the crook of my neck, he drapes his arm over my stomach. Gently he caresses his fingers over Diego's tiny leg.

It doesn't take long for Armani to join his son in dreamland, and with my husband's breath on my neck, and our son fast asleep in my arms, my chest fills with so much happiness, I'm unable to contain it.

A tear spirals down my cheek, and I don't bother brushing it away.

Thank you for answering my prayers and giving me everything I've ever wanted.

I have a beautiful home, a husband I love more than life itself, and a son I'll die for.

I finally have a family of my own.

Epilogue

Tiana

Three years later...

After we land in Russia, Armani drives us to our destination.

I've begged him to tell me where we're going, but he refused to give me any hints.

The area looks vaguely familiar, and when the SUV turns up a specific street, my heart starts to beat fast.

My head snaps to Armani. "Why are we here?"

The corner of his mouth lifts. "You'll see soon enough. Patience, *bella*."

Diego is playing with his cars on the back seat, blissfully unaware that his mother's about to have a panic attack.

"Armani," I complain. "I don't want to go back there."

He reaches across and grips my hand tightly. "I know it's hard, but the surprise will be worth it."

I shake my head as he turns up the driveway, and when he stops in front of the orphanage, I feel like crying.

He gets out and grabs Diego from the back seat before coming to open my door.

I shake my head again.

Armani takes my hand again and pulls me out. "Trust me."

Following my husband to the front door of the one place on earth, I never wanted to see again, I can't think of a good reason for him to bring me here.

A friendly-looking lady meets us at the door. "Mr. and Mrs. De Santis. It's so good to finally meet you in person." Her eyes lock on Armani, "I just want to thank you for all the donations you and Mr. Petrov have made to the orphanage. It helps so much."

I look at Armani with shock as he murmurs, "You're welcome."

Wow. I wasn't aware Armani and Misha are taking care of the orphanage.

It fills my heart with warmth as we walk through the familiar hallways.

Stepping out the back, children are running around and playing.

We were never allowed to play outside. We had to keep quiet and do our chores.

Glad to see the place has changed, I take the steps down, my eyes on all the children.

Armani points to the left of the lawn, where a little girl is playing in a sandpit. "We're here for her." A shockwave hits me square in the heart, and my eyes fly to Armani's face. "You said you wished we could have a little girl, so I called the orphanage and made the arrangements."

Oh my God.

My hands cover my mouth as I start to walk toward her.

After I had Diego, I couldn't fall pregnant again. I was devastated when the doctor told me I wouldn't be able to have more children.

When I reach the girl, she looks up at me and smiles. "Hi."

I crouch in front of her, drinking in the sight of her pretty face. She has black hair and blue eyes.

God, she reminds me so much of myself when I was here.

I sit down flat on my butt and look at the patterns she's drawing in the sand.

"Hi, precious," I whisper. "What are you doing?"

She shrugs. "Nothing."

Unable to resist, I lift my hand and brush my palm over her hair. "Why aren't you playing with the other kids?"

She shakes her head, ducking her face away from my view. "They say I stink."

"Oh no." My heart shrinks for her. I lean closer and take a deep breath, then say, "Nope, you don't stink. You smell pretty."

Her eyes dart to my face again. "Really?"

With an affectionate smile, I nod.

We stare at each other for a moment, then I open my arms and ask, "Can I hug you?"

She hesitates before she crawls into my lap. I hug her tightly and press a kiss on her hair.

Armani comes closer, and crouching, he places Diego in the sandpit. He ruffles the little girl's hair, then says, "Hi, Karina." He gestures to our son. "This is Diego."

She gives Armani and Diego a shy look, then whispers, "Hi."

"Diego wishes he could have a sister," Armani says. "Do you think that's something you'd like?"

Her little face furrows. "A brother?"

I nod. "And a mama and papa."

Her eyes widen as she looks at us, then her face crumbles, and she hides her tears against my shirt.

I hold her tight and pepper her hair with kisses. "Would you like to come home with us?"

She nods and mumbles, "I thought no one would want me because I wet the bed."

Brushing my hand up and down her back, I say the words every child in an orphanage wants to hear, "I want you."

We sit for over an hour outside, and Karina doesn't move from my lap. I learn she likes milk, monkeys, and just about anything that starts with an M.

Her eyes are glued to my face as she admits, "Mostly, I'd like a mama."

"And I'd like a daughter," I admit.

A smile curves her mouth, and pushing up against me, she wraps her arms around my neck. With the innocence of a child, she whispers, "I'll be yours if you'll be mine."

"I like the sound of that." My eyes meet Armani's, and I swallow hard on the tears of happiness.

Not once has this man stopped doing everything in his power to make me happy.

With Karina in my arms, I climb to my feet. Armani picks up Diego, and as a family, we walk to the office to sign all the documents so we can take our little girl home.

The End.

Published Books

CORRUPTED ROYALS
Mafia / Organized Crime / Suspense Romance
(Can be read in this order or as standalones)

Destroy Me
Control Me
Brutalize Me
Restrain Me
Possess Me

THE SINNERS SERIES
Mafia / Organized Crime / Suspense Romance
(Can be read in this order or as standalones)

Taken By A Sinner
Owned By A Sinner
Stolen By A Sinner
Chosen By A Sinner
Captured By A Sinner

THE SAINTS SERIES
Mafia / Organized Crime / Suspense Romance
(Can be read in this order or as standalones)

Merciless Saints
Cruel Saints
Ruthless Saints

Tears of Betrayal
Tears of Salvation

BEAUTIFULLY BROKEN SERIES

Organized Crime / Suspense Romance
(Can be read in this order or as standalones)

Beautifully Broken
Beautifully Hurt
Beautifully Destroyed

ENEMIES TO LOVERS

College Romance / New Adult / Billionaire Romance

Heartless
Reckless
Careless
Ruthless
Shameless

TRINITY ACADEMY

College Romance / New Adult / Billionaire Romance

Falcon
Mason
Lake
Julian
The Epilogue

THE HEIRS

College Romance / New Adult / Billionaire Romance

Coldhearted Heir
Arrogant Heir
Defiant Heir
Loyal Heir
Callous Heir
Sinful Heir
Tempted Heir
Forbidden Heir

Stand Alone Spin-off
Not My Hero
Young Adult / High School Romance

THE SOUTHERN HEROES SERIES

*Suspense Romance / Contemporary Romance /
Police Officers & Detectives*

The Ocean Between Us
The Girl In The Closet
The Lies We Tell Ourselves
All The Wasted Time
We Were Lost

Connect with me

Newsletter

FaceBook

Amazon

GoodReads

BookBub

Instagram

Acknowledgments

I needed a break from Enemies To Lovers, and Armani & Tiana gave me the opportunity. Their story feels different from what I usually write, but I hope you enjoy it. (Don't worry. We're back to Enemies To Lovers with Maxim & Cami's book.)

My editor, Sheena, has nerves of steel with all the deadlines whooshing past us. Thank you for putting up with me.

To my alpha and beta readers – Leeann, Brittney, Sherrie, Kelly, and Sarah thank you for being the godparents of my paper-baby.

Candi Kane PR - Thank you for being patient with me and my bad habit of missing deadlines.

Yoly, Cormar Covers – Thank you for giving my paper-babies the perfect look.

My street team, thank you for promoting my books. It means the world to me!

A special thank you to every blogger and reader who took the time to participate in the cover reveal and release day.

Love ya all tons ;)

Made in the USA
Las Vegas, NV
31 March 2023

69985373R00219